Fading Echoes

Ivy Hale

Published by Ivy Hale, 2024.

This is a work of fiction. Similarities to real people, places, or events are entirely coincidental.

FADING ECHOES

First edition. October 30, 2024.

Copyright © 2024 Ivy Hale.

ISBN: 979-8227081834

Written by Ivy Hale.

Chapter 1: A Glimpse of Shadows

As I stood on the balcony of my apartment in vibrant downtown Charleston, the salty breeze wrapped around me, but I couldn't shake the chill that ran down my spine. I had just moved back to my hometown after years in the city, hoping for a fresh start and to escape the suffocating grip of my past. Little did I know that my neighbor, Nathan Hale, was the most infuriating man I'd ever met. With his brooding looks and icy demeanor, he made my skin prickle with a mix of annoyance and something else I couldn't quite name. When our paths crossed in the narrow hallway, tension crackled like static electricity, igniting my temper and stirring feelings I desperately wanted to ignore.

The apartment complex was a historic gem, its red-brick facade glowing warmly in the afternoon sun, each window framed by white shutters that added a touch of charm. Yet, the charm faded whenever Nathan was around. He often appeared in the most inconvenient moments—like now, when I was trying to enjoy the view of the bustling street below, a canvas of colorful umbrellas and happy chatter. I had just settled in with a book, eager to lose myself in the pages, when I heard the unmistakable sound of his heavy footsteps approaching. It was as if the universe conspired to ruin my tranquility.

"Careful with that book, or you might actually learn something," Nathan said, his voice a deep rumble that somehow managed to be both teasing and infuriating. He leaned against the doorframe of his own apartment, arms crossed, an amused smirk playing on his lips.

"Funny, coming from the guy who looks like he crawled out of a brooding novel," I shot back, unable to resist the urge to defend my sanctuary. "What are you doing? Lurking? Or just waiting for the perfect moment to ruin my day?"

His laughter, rich and unexpectedly warm, cut through my irritation like a knife. "I was hoping to catch you when you weren't hiding behind those curtains like a startled raccoon. But it seems you've gotten too good at it."

I rolled my eyes, fighting the smile that threatened to break through. There was something disarming about his confidence, but I refused to let it affect me. "I was enjoying the view until you showed up," I declared, attempting to maintain my composure. "Do you always make it a habit to invade people's personal space?"

"Only when they make it so delightfully easy," he replied, stepping out onto his own balcony, the sun casting a shadow across his sharp features. "Besides, you should learn to embrace the unexpected. It makes life more interesting."

"Interesting? Is that what you call a man who can't stop being an insufferable jerk?"

"Insufferable? Now that's a compliment I haven't received before." His playful tone threw me off guard, but I refused to let him see the effect he had on me.

Shaking my head, I turned back to my book, though the words danced on the page, refusing to settle into anything coherent. My mind was a whirlwind of thoughts, each one crashing against the other. Nathan had a way of intruding not just into my space but into my mind as well, stirring emotions that lay dormant for far too long. I could feel the prickling awareness that this wouldn't be just another mundane encounter. There was something beneath the surface—a current of connection that terrified and thrilled me in equal measure.

As the evening descended, I decided to take a walk along the cobblestone streets, hoping the gentle rhythm of my footsteps would quiet the thoughts that whirled in my head. The soft glow of the streetlamps cast a warm light over the historic buildings, illuminating the rich, dark wood of the shutters and the vibrant flowers spilling over window boxes. The air was thick with the scent of blooming magnolias, a nostalgic reminder of summers spent in this very town.

I passed by the local bakery, its windows fogged up with the warmth of freshly baked pastries, the aroma wafting out and wrapping around me like a comforting blanket. I couldn't resist the temptation. A moment later, I found myself inside, the bell above the door chiming softly as I stepped in. The warmth enveloped me, and the sight of the glass display case filled with goodies made my mouth water.

"Can I help you?" The cheerful voice of the baker, an older woman with flour-dusted hands and a welcoming smile, broke me from my reverie.

"I'll take a chocolate croissant, please," I said, my voice barely above a whisper as I fished out my wallet.

"Ah, a classic choice! You have good taste," she replied, her eyes twinkling with warmth.

Just as I was about to pay, the door swung open, and in walked none other than Nathan. My heart sank and then raced at the same time. "You have got to be kidding me," I muttered under my breath.

"Fancy seeing you here," he said, his smirk reappearing as he sauntered toward the counter. "I see your taste in pastries is as poor as your taste in company."

I shot him a glare that could have melted steel. "I was here first, so don't think you can claim this place as your territory, Hale."

"Territory? I simply appreciate fine pastries," he retorted, a playful challenge in his eyes. "But if you want to play territorial games, I'd be more than happy to engage."

"Why do you have to make everything into a competition?" I huffed, unable to ignore the thrill that his banter ignited in me.

"Because it makes you more interesting," he said with a wink. "And I have a feeling you need a little more interesting in your life."

I rolled my eyes again, but inside, my heart raced at the thought. He was infuriating yet charming in a way that left me wanting to know more about the man behind the smirk. I took my croissant and stepped aside, not willing to let him see how much he had gotten under my skin.

As I walked out, the croissant warm in my hands, I could feel his gaze on me. The night felt electric, and as I took a bite of the flaky pastry, I couldn't help but think that maybe this unexpected turn of events was precisely what I had needed—a taste of life beyond my carefully constructed walls, no matter how frustrating Nathan Hale was.

As the sun dipped below the horizon, casting a warm golden hue over the cobblestone streets, I found myself more aware of Nathan's presence than I cared to admit. He had moved in just before I returned, a fact I had learned through whispered rumors among the neighbors. They described him as a man of mystery, someone with a past cloaked in shadows. But they didn't mention his capacity for aggravation. The first time I encountered him in the hallway, it felt like stepping into a thunderstorm—sudden, electrifying, and entirely unsettling.

"Watch where you're going," I snapped, barely avoiding a collision as I hurried to my apartment. My heart raced, not just from the near miss but from the unexpected flutter that accompanied his piercing gaze. He merely arched an eyebrow, a slight smirk tugging at the corners of his mouth, which only fueled my irritation.

"I could say the same," he replied coolly, his voice deep and smooth like aged whiskey, both intoxicating and infuriating.

For days, our encounters became a dance of barbed exchanges. It was as if we were two opposing forces drawn together by an unseen magnetism. He'd linger just outside his door, casually leaning against the frame, and every time our eyes met, I felt the air shift—charged and heavy, like the calm before a storm. I hated how easily he invaded my thoughts, disrupting my carefully constructed walls with his mere presence.

Yet, I couldn't escape the pull of curiosity. Despite his aloofness, I noticed the little things: the way he meticulously tended to his plants, an array of vibrant greens that seemed to thrive under his touch, or how he often sat on his balcony with a book, engrossed in a world that seemed far removed from the chaos of ours. It was as if I were watching a silent film, each gesture eloquent in its simplicity. But those moments only deepened my frustration, for they stirred something within me that I was desperate to ignore.

One balmy evening, as I stood on my own balcony nursing a glass of wine, I caught a glimpse of him, silhouetted against the twilight sky. He was engrossed in whatever story had captured his attention, and for a moment, I allowed myself to wonder what thoughts lay behind his enigmatic expression. I could imagine the lives he read about—bold adventures and daring romances that were a world apart from my own. The ache of my own stagnation flared painfully, reminding me that my past was a weight I carried heavily.

Suddenly, the glass slipped from my hand, shattering against the tiles below. The noise shattered the serene evening, and I flinched, embarrassment washing over me as Nathan glanced up, concern flickering across his features before he swiftly masked it with indifference.

"Careful, there," he called, his tone teasing yet underpinned with a sincerity that made my heart skip. "Wine stains are harder to clean than you'd think."

I rolled my eyes, half amused, half annoyed. "I'll remember that when I'm looking for new decor tips."

He chuckled softly, the sound unexpectedly warm. "I could offer you some tips if you want. I have a knack for interior design."

"Is that what you do in your spare time, Nathan? Arrange throw pillows and pretend to care about color palettes?" I shot back, leaning against the balcony railing, my confidence surging.

"Touché," he replied, his expression shifting from playful to contemplative. "But if you ever need a hand with your plants, I'm just a few feet away."

The offer hung between us, heavier than the summer air. There was something about the way he said it, a subtle shift in tone that hinted at a deeper connection, an understanding of the loneliness that clung to us both. I hesitated, my pride warring with a strange desire for companionship. Finally, I took a sip of my wine, letting the moment linger.

"Fine," I replied, forcing nonchalance into my voice. "But don't expect me to turn my living room into a jungle."

"Deal." He smirked, and for a fleeting second, it felt like we were on the precipice of something more than mere banter.

Days turned into weeks, and Nathan and I continued our verbal sparring, each interaction a delicate balance of teasing and challenge. He had a way of digging under my skin, peeling back layers I thought were well hidden. Despite my best efforts to keep him at arm's length, I found myself drawn to him in ways that confounded me.

Then came the night of the summer solstice celebration, a local tradition that filled the streets with laughter, music, and the sweet scent of festival treats. As I wandered among the crowds, the vibrant colors and cheerful atmosphere seemed to pull me from my melancholy. I laughed with familiar faces and danced to the infectious rhythms, feeling the weight of my past gradually lift.

As the night deepened, I spotted Nathan across the square, his tall frame leaning against a food stall, a curious expression on his face as he observed the festivities. An impulse surged within me, and before I could second-guess myself, I made my way toward him, determined to engage in one of our spirited exchanges.

"Enjoying the spectacle, or just trying to figure out how to escape?" I called out, a playful smile dancing on my lips.

He looked down at me, a spark of surprise in his eyes, and then a grin broke through his stoic facade. "Why not both? Though escaping sounds tempting. Crowds aren't really my thing."

"Not a fan of fun?" I shot back, my heart racing, aware of the way our chemistry crackled in the air.

"Fun has its limits. But it's not all bad," he replied, his gaze lingering on me longer than necessary.

As the evening wore on, we found ourselves engrossed in conversation, laughter punctuating the air between us like fireworks. The walls I had carefully constructed began to crumble under the weight of our shared words, revealing glimpses of vulnerability that surprised me both. Beneath his aloof demeanor lay layers of complexity, each revelation drawing me closer, enticing me to peel back more.

Just as I began to believe that perhaps we could forge a connection beyond our usual banter, an unexpected figure stepped into our moment, shattering the fragile spell we had woven. A woman, elegantly dressed with a smile that seemed both genuine and predatory, approached Nathan, her eyes gleaming with an unsettling familiarity. The air around us grew thick with unspoken tension, and my heart sank at the sight.

"Nathan! I didn't expect to find you here," she exclaimed, her voice dripping with feigned sweetness. "I thought you preferred your solitude."

I watched as Nathan's expression shifted, the warmth evaporating in an instant, replaced by a coldness that sent a chill through me.

"Just enjoying the festivities," he replied, his tone clipped, betraying none of the openness he had shown to me moments earlier.

The woman leaned in closer, her laughter ringing like silver bells. "You know you could always join me for a drink at The Velvet Lounge. They have the best cocktails in town. Or are you too busy with your new friend?" She cast a glance in my direction, a thinly veiled challenge in her eyes.

I felt a wave of irritation wash over me, battling with an unexpected surge of jealousy. The carefree atmosphere that had enveloped us moments ago had been stripped away, leaving a hollow ache in its place. Nathan's posture stiffened, and I could see the flicker of discomfort in his gaze as he turned away from her.

"I'm good here, thanks," he said, his voice lacking conviction, but the tension had already seeped into our conversation, leaving it strained and uncertain.

As she sauntered off, I could feel the remnants of our connection unraveling. Nathan's eyes darted to mine, filled with a mix of regret and something I couldn't quite grasp. "I'm sorry about that," he said, his voice barely a whisper.

"Why do you let her get to you?" I challenged, crossing my arms defensively. "You don't owe her anything."

He sighed, running a hand through his tousled hair, frustration etched across his features. "It's complicated. She and I... we share a history I'm not proud of."

"Is that why you hide behind that icy exterior?" I retorted, emboldened by my irritation. "You think pushing people away will protect you?"

He stepped closer, the tension palpable between us. "And what do you know about it?" His voice was low, a challenge sparking in his dark eyes.

"I know that people can surprise you," I shot back, not backing down. "Sometimes you just have to let them in."

In that moment, as the sounds of laughter and music faded into the background, I felt a shift—a promise of something deeper than the playful banter we had exchanged for weeks. But just as quickly as the connection ignited, it flickered, threatened by the shadows of our pasts.

And as the last remnants of the celebration faded into the night, I realized that our journey had only just begun, fraught with unexpected turns and the specters of our histories lurking just out of sight.

The vibrant pulse of Charleston thrummed in the background as I retreated inside, the remnants of the evening fading behind me. With each step I took toward my living room, the nagging tension between Nathan and me played on loop in my mind, reminding me of our unexpected encounters. The air was thick with unsaid words, and the questions that danced just beneath the surface haunted my thoughts. What exactly was this magnetic pull that drew me to him, yet simultaneously irritated me to my core? The answer eluded me like a shadow slipping through my fingers.

Determined to distract myself, I sank into my well-worn couch, a refuge amidst the whirl of my new life. I flipped through a stack of books I had brought from the city, but the words swirled together in a haze of frustration. No novel could absorb my focus, not when my thoughts kept straying to the man next door. Instead, I found myself pacing the room, my fingers brushing against the cool walls as if they could ground me.

Just then, a soft knock echoed through the apartment, startling me from my reverie. Heart racing, I approached the door cautiously, a mix of curiosity and dread coursing through me. I swung it open, half-expecting to find Nathan with that infuriating smirk plastered on his face. Instead, I was met by the wide-eyed, innocent gaze of Lily, my childhood friend, who had been a beacon of joy during my youth.

"Hey there, stranger!" she exclaimed, her enthusiasm instantly contagious. "I was in the neighborhood and thought I'd drop by. Can I come in?"

"Of course! Come in!" I replied, relief flooding through me at the sight of her familiar face. It felt like a welcome splash of warmth in the cool, confusing waters of my new life.

As we settled onto the couch, Lily's presence transformed the atmosphere of the room. We shared laughter and stories, the air filled with nostalgia. "I can't believe you're back! You really needed a break from the big city, huh?" she teased, her eyes sparkling with mischief.

"You have no idea," I sighed dramatically. "And to think I thought I could escape my problems by coming back to this sleepy little town."

"Sleepy? This place is alive with drama!" she countered, leaning in closer, a conspiratorial whisper escaping her lips. "I heard about the new neighbor. Nathan Hale? What's he like? I mean, he's a bit of a heartthrob, don't you think?"

A rush of heat flooded my cheeks at the mere mention of Nathan's name. "Heartthrob? More like a headache. He's infuriating, and I can't quite figure him out."

"Infuriating or intriguing?" Lily raised an eyebrow, a smirk playing on her lips. "Come on, I know that look. You're not fooling me."

"Okay, maybe a little intriguing," I admitted reluctantly, tapping my fingers against my knee. "But it's more annoying than anything. We can't seem to have a conversation without it turning into a duel of wits."

"Or a game of attraction?" she quipped, waggling her eyebrows, and I couldn't help but laugh. The thought struck me as absurd yet tantalizing, and I quickly pushed it aside.

"More like a battle of egos. Besides, he's probably used to getting under people's skin. I refuse to be another notch on his belt."

Lily nodded knowingly, her expression shifting to one of understanding. "Well, if anyone can hold their own, it's you. But maybe you should give him a chance? It could be entertaining."

"Entertaining, sure. But do I really want to get involved in that drama?" I pondered aloud, biting my lip. Just then, I heard a sound outside—a low rumble that seemed out of place.

"What was that?" Lily asked, her head tilting toward the window.

I stood up, instinctively moving toward the glass. The view outside was obscured by shadows, but the thrum of unease settled in my stomach. "I don't know, but it doesn't sound good."

Before I could process the situation, I saw Nathan standing on his balcony, his gaze fixed intently on something across the street. He seemed tense, a contrast to his usual aloof demeanor. As our eyes met, he gestured urgently for me to come outside. A wave of confusion washed over me—what could possibly warrant this level of urgency?

"I'll be right back," I whispered to Lily, my heart racing with a blend of curiosity and concern. I stepped outside, the warm night air wrapping around me like a comforting shawl, but the weight of Nathan's expression heightened my anxiety.

"Did you hear that?" he asked, his voice low and urgent.

"What's going on?" I demanded, glancing around as if the answer would emerge from the shadows. The street seemed eerily still, the festive sounds from earlier replaced by a tense quiet.

"I think something's wrong. There's been talk of strange occurrences in the neighborhood—people vanishing, odd noises. I'm not sure what we're dealing with, but we need to stay alert," Nathan explained, his brow furrowed with concern.

"Vanishing? You can't be serious," I replied, incredulity coloring my tone.

He leaned closer, lowering his voice. "It's real, I promise you. My friend from the old neighborhood called me earlier. Something isn't right. We need to look out for each other."

I swallowed hard, the seriousness of his words hitting home. "But what can we do?"

"I have a few ideas, but we need to be careful. I can't explain everything right now, but you have to trust me," he said, his eyes locking onto mine, filled with a fierce intensity that sent a shiver down my spine.

"Trust you? After our charming interactions? That's a tall order," I shot back, but the resolve in his gaze made me hesitate.

"Just for tonight. Please," he insisted, an urgency creeping into his voice.

With the weight of the unknown pressing in on me, I finally nodded, though trepidation coiled in my gut.

As we stood side by side, staring into the depths of the shadowy street, a low growl echoed from somewhere nearby, chilling the air around us. My heart raced, and I turned to Nathan, but before I could utter a word, the growl morphed into a series of frantic shouts.

Suddenly, a figure burst from the darkness, sprinting toward us with wild eyes. "Help! They're coming!" The words were barely discernible through panic, and as he drew closer, I could see the terror etched into his features.

Nathan's protective instinct kicked in, and he stepped forward, a fierce determination radiating from him. "What's happening?" he demanded, but the figure only stumbled forward, collapsing at our feet, gasping for breath.

Just then, the growls intensified, echoing through the air, and I felt an icy grip of dread tighten around my heart. Nathan and I exchanged a glance, the unspoken realization settling between us—whatever was lurking in the shadows was no longer just a rumor.

As the sounds grew louder, the urgency of our situation crashed down on us like a tidal wave, and I couldn't shake the feeling that our lives were about to change forever. With the figure still trembling on the ground, the night around us shifted, the air thick with the promise of danger.

Chapter 2: The Uninvited Guest

The door swung open with a flourish, the sudden gust of wind announcing Lila's arrival before she even stepped inside. Her laughter cascaded into the room, buoyant and unfiltered, as if she had just left a world of sunshine and had no intention of dimming her light for anyone, least of all me. I blinked, caught off guard by her boundless energy, a stark contrast to the heavy clouds of irritation still swirling in my mind from my last encounter with Nathan.

"Guess who's here!" she exclaimed, throwing her arms wide as if to embrace the whole room. Lila's auburn hair danced around her shoulders, tousled and wild, much like her. I couldn't help but smile at her enthusiasm, even if it felt like an unwanted intrusion. I had been relishing my solitude, my quiet rebellion against the world outside. "I brought snacks! You know, the chocolate kind that make everything better."

I leaned back against my lumpy couch, raising an eyebrow. "I'm not sure if chocolate can fix a broken spirit, but I'm willing to test the theory."

"Ha! You're such a drama queen," she laughed, plopping down beside me. The couch groaned in protest, a sound that had become all too familiar. "Besides, it's not just any chocolate. It's dark chocolate with sea salt! A perfect blend of sweet and savory."

"Isn't that what they call you? A perfect blend?" I quipped, taking a piece from the crinkly bag she brandished as if it were the Holy Grail. The rich aroma wafted through the air, tempting my senses. I took a bite, and a small part of my irritation dissolved into the luscious flavor.

We chatted about mundane things—what she had been up to, her latest escapades at the art gallery where she worked, and her newest crush, a painter with a penchant for abstract art and a jawline that could cut glass. But amidst our playful banter, the topic shifted to the recent string of break-ins that had rattled our quiet neighborhood.

"Have you heard about the Whitakers?" Lila asked, her expression turning serious as she nibbled on a piece of chocolate. "They had their front door kicked in last week. Can you believe it?"

I felt a chill creep down my spine. The notion of someone violating the sanctity of our homes felt abhorrent. "What do you mean? Were they home?" I tried to sound casual, but the concern threaded through my voice was undeniable. The idea of lurking shadows and shattered glass echoed in my mind, conjuring images I desperately wished to banish.

"Fortunately, no. They were visiting their daughter in the city," she replied, her voice dropping to a conspiratorial whisper. "But still, it's alarming! They've never had any trouble before. And now this... it's like something out of a horror movie. I can't shake the feeling that it's going to happen again."

My heart raced. The thought of being cooped up at home, only to have some stranger burst in, sent a shiver through me. "What's the neighborhood coming to? First Nathan, and now this?" I grimaced, conjuring Nathan's annoyingly handsome face, with his dark hair that always seemed to fall perfectly into place and that infuriating smirk. He had been the bane of my existence for as long as I could remember, his unyielding arrogance a sharp contrast to my quiet resolve.

"Maybe you need to get out more," Lila suggested, her teasing tone returning. "You know, find a little adventure. Like the time we tried to sneak into that abandoned amusement park."

"Adventure? Or a one-way ticket to the ER?" I shot back, but my lips curled into a smile despite myself. Memories of our daring escapade—a whirlwind of laughter, fear, and the sweetness of sibling camaraderie—filled my mind. That night had been a whirlwind, a perfect blend of reckless and innocent.

But the joy faded as I thought of Nathan again. His disdain for my presence in our little corner of the world felt suffocating. "Seriously though, Lila, I think it's better to stay inside. There's something unsettling about all of this."

Her gaze turned probing, and for a moment, the room felt smaller, as if the walls were closing in. "Are you still mad at him? About the way he treated you at the party?"

A twinge of annoyance bubbled up inside me. "It's not just about that. It's everything. He thinks he can just strut around like he owns the place, while I'm over here trying to survive high school like it's a post-apocalyptic world."

Lila chuckled, shaking her head. "You're being dramatic again. He's just a guy, and a ridiculously attractive one at that. But trust me, he's not worth the energy. You know that, right?"

I huffed, crossing my arms in defiance. "It's easy for you to say! You're not the one he scoffs at every time you enter a room."

"Look, if he scoffs, it's his loss. Besides, there are plenty of other fish in the sea. You just need to find one that doesn't come with a side of ego."

Her words hung in the air, but they felt like empty platitudes against the weight of my emotions. As if reading my thoughts, Lila changed the subject, pulling a face. "Let's not focus on Mr. Smug and his irresistible cheekbones. What about a little mystery-solving? We could investigate the break-ins ourselves."

I groaned, imagining us lurking in the shadows, only to end up being the next headline news. "I think I'd rather leave that to the professionals, thank you very much."

"Come on! It'll be fun! We'll grab flashlights, maybe some of those chocolate bars, and be like detectives. Just think of the stories we could tell!"

Her enthusiasm was infectious, but a flicker of hesitation danced in the back of my mind. The thought of venturing out into the night, armed only with sugary snacks and determination, felt reckless. But then again, perhaps I needed a little chaos in my orderly world—a distraction from my simmering frustrations with Nathan, the break-ins, and everything else that felt too heavy to carry alone.

"Fine," I relented, a reluctant smile breaking through my resolve. "But if we get caught, you're taking the blame."

"Deal!" Lila beamed, and in that moment, the tension in my chest eased, even if just a little.

The sun dipped low in the sky, casting a golden hue that seeped through the thin curtains of my living room, illuminating the chaos of scattered books and half-finished art projects that adorned every surface. As I turned to Lila, who was now rifling through her bag for more chocolate, I couldn't help but admire the way her vibrant energy filled the room. She was like a firecracker, full of life, while I felt more like a slowly fading candle, barely flickering in the shadows.

"Okay, detective partner," she said, pulling out a flashlight that gleamed brightly against the clutter. "What's our first move? We need a game plan before we dive into the world of mystery-solving."

I couldn't suppress a grin at her enthusiasm. "What makes you think we'll be solving any mysteries? I'm more likely to trip over my own feet and set off an alarm than uncover the next great neighborhood secret."

Lila rolled her eyes dramatically, a playful smirk tugging at her lips. "Come on! We'll be like Nancy Drew and her trusty sidekick, except, you know, cooler. And with better snacks."

"Right. Because snacks are the ultimate crime-fighting tool," I retorted, taking another piece of chocolate and letting its rich sweetness melt away my worries for a brief moment. "We could just set up a stakeout right here. I can see it now: two bored sisters waiting for excitement to come to them like it's an invitation."

"Who says it has to be boring?" she challenged, her eyes sparkling with mischief. "We can make it exciting! You could pretend to be a secret agent. I can be the tech genius feeding you intel through an earpiece. Imagine it! The criminals won't know what hit them."

I snorted, the image of myself in a trench coat, attempting to blend in while holding a bag of chocolate, making me chuckle. "Yes, because nothing screams 'undercover' like a bag of sweets and a wardrobe that screams 'I just rolled out of bed.'"

"Exactly! That's the beauty of it," Lila replied, her grin widening. "Nobody would suspect a thing. It's the perfect disguise."

As we plotted our grand adventure, a sudden noise outside jolted me upright. It was just a branch brushing against the window, but the momentary panic that coursed through me sent my heart racing. I forced a laugh, trying to play off the tension. "See? Even the trees are in on the mystery!"

"Or they're just trying to freak you out," Lila said, leaning closer, her voice dropping to a conspiratorial whisper. "Maybe they're in cahoots with the burglars! We should investigate the shadows, uncover their secrets."

I groaned playfully. "Do we have to investigate the shadows? How about we stick to the broad daylight? My nerves can only take so much."

"Wimp," she teased, nudging me. "Come on, let's at least go for a walk. We can keep an eye out for anything suspicious. It'll be fun!"

After a moment of hesitation, I nodded, my curiosity piqued despite my reluctance. "Fine, but if we end up in some sort of horror movie scenario, I'm blaming you. You and your chocolate-fueled whims."

"Deal!" Lila jumped to her feet, her exuberance palpable as she flung the door open wide, revealing the soft evening light. The cool breeze washed over us, a gentle reminder that the world outside was both inviting and unpredictable.

As we stepped onto the quiet street, the neighborhood looked deceptively serene, with its neatly trimmed lawns and friendly porch lights flickering on one by one. Yet, an underlying tension clung to the air, a feeling of unease that hung around like a bad smell. The distant sound of a dog barking punctuated the silence, but everything else felt eerily still, as if the world was holding its breath.

"So, where do we start?" I asked, glancing at Lila, who was already scanning the area with a detective's focus.

"We could head over to the Whitakers' place," she suggested, pointing down the street where a "For Sale" sign swayed gently in the breeze, a testament to their recent misfortune. "If they've been broken into, their house might hold some clues."

"You mean the clues you're so determined to find, despite our complete lack of training?" I teased, but part of me was intrigued. The Whitakers had been a cornerstone of our neighborhood for as long as I could remember. Their sudden departure felt like a bad omen, as if the very fabric of our tight-knit community was unraveling.

We made our way to their house, the grass crunching beneath our feet, the evening air thick with the scent of freshly cut lawns and blooming jasmine. As we approached, the house loomed larger, its once-vibrant facade now dulled by neglect. We exchanged cautious glances before inching closer, half expecting a ghost to pop out at any moment.

"Do you think we'll find anything?" I whispered, an uneasy feeling gnawing at my stomach.

"Only one way to find out!" Lila declared, her adventurous spirit igniting a spark of courage in me. "Let's check the back. That's where the burglars would've come in, right?"

"Right, because that's the most logical place to go—into the house of a potential criminal," I muttered under my breath, but I followed her nonetheless, drawn by a mixture of curiosity and concern.

We crept around to the back of the property, where the sun began its descent, painting the sky in hues of orange and pink. The backyard felt abandoned, a relic of happier times. Toys lay strewn about, and a swing swayed gently in the breeze, reminding me of carefree childhood days spent running amok.

Lila knelt beside the back door, her eyes gleaming with mischief. "I'm going to see if it's unlocked," she whispered, glancing over her shoulder like a cat burglar about to commit the ultimate crime.

I held my breath, half-expecting alarms to sound, or worse, a shadowy figure to appear from the darkened corners of the porch. To my surprise, the door clicked open, and Lila shot me a triumphant grin.

"Victory is ours!" she whispered dramatically, pushing the door ajar just enough for us to slip inside. The moment we crossed the threshold, the air changed—thick with dust and memories. A wave of nostalgia washed over me, a bittersweet reminder of the warmth that once filled these rooms.

"Let's be quick," I urged, my voice barely above a whisper. "If anyone sees us..."

"Oh, come on! We're just looking for clues!" Lila replied, her eyes darting around the dimly lit kitchen, still brimming with a sense of normalcy despite its disarray. "We're practically public service volunteers."

Just then, a sudden noise from the living room sent my heart into a frantic beat. It sounded like something—or someone—shifting amid the shadows. I glanced at Lila, whose excitement instantly morphed into concern. Our eyes locked, the unspoken tension crackling between us like static electricity.

The soft glow of the kitchen light barely pierced the heavy air as Lila and I stood frozen in the doorway, the unsettling noise echoing from the living room. It was a shuffling sound, like someone—or something—was shifting just out of sight. My heart pounded in my chest, each beat like a drum announcing our intrusion into this silent home.

"Did you hear that?" I whispered, my voice trembling slightly despite my best efforts to sound calm.

"Yeah, and I wish I hadn't," Lila replied, her bravado slipping. She glanced around, her adventurous spirit dimmed momentarily by a dose of reality. "We should definitely not be here."

"Ya think?" I shot back, rolling my eyes even as adrenaline surged through my veins. "But here we are, ready to be the neighborhood's worst detectives."

Another noise—a soft thump—came from deeper inside the house. This one was more distinct, more ominous, as if something heavy had just been dropped. I swallowed hard, glancing back at the door, weighing my options. The thrill of adventure had been intoxicating until now, and my earlier bravado felt dangerously misplaced.

Lila took a step forward, compelled by curiosity despite the rising dread. "Maybe it's just a cat? Or a raccoon? I mean, they do like to make themselves at home."

"Right, a raccoon could definitely be causing a ruckus in the living room of the Whitakers' home," I replied, my sarcasm a poor cover for the rising panic within me. "How about we just leave?"

"Leave? And miss our big break?" Lila looked at me incredulously, her excitement battling against my caution. "We're already in here. We can't just turn back now!"

Before I could protest, she slipped into the living room, her flashlight cutting through the dimness like a beacon. I hesitated, glancing over my shoulder as if expecting someone to come barreling down the hallway. Still, I knew Lila wouldn't back down easily. With a resigned sigh, I followed her, my heart racing as we stepped cautiously into the darkened room.

The air felt thick and stale, heavy with an unsettling silence that wrapped around us like a shroud. I shined my flashlight across the furniture, the beam flickering over overturned chairs and scattered belongings. It looked like the house had been ransacked, a vivid testament to the recent chaos that had unfolded here.

"Is it just me, or does this place feel...alive?" Lila murmured, her voice barely above a whisper. The shadows seemed to shift and flicker, as if they had their own pulse.

"Alive?" I repeated, a nervous laugh escaping me. "More like haunted. This isn't a ghost tour, Lila. We're probably trespassing on someone's private nightmare."

Suddenly, a distinct clatter echoed from the back of the house, slicing through the tension like a knife. My breath hitched as I turned toward the sound. "What was that?"

"Maybe it's just the wind?" Lila suggested, though her eyes were wide, betraying her own fear.

"Yeah, right. The wind that apparently knows how to knock things over?" I retorted, my nerves fraying as I gripped my flashlight like a weapon.

Before I could form a coherent thought, a shadow darted across the hall. My heart lurched, instinct urging me to run, but Lila's hand gripped my arm. "Did you see that?" she breathed, her voice quaking with a mix of fear and thrill.

"See what? You mean the ghost of burglars past?" I hissed, my sarcasm serving as a thin veil over my dread.

The shadow flickered again, darting into a side room, and before I could protest, Lila was off, her determination carrying her forward. "Wait! We shouldn't—" I began, but it was too late. She had already vanished into the dark.

"Lila!" I called out, my voice echoing in the silence, panic prickling my skin. I had a decision to make: follow her into the abyss or remain standing like a fool. With a reluctant sigh, I took a step into the hallway, the beam of my flashlight trembling in my grip as I ventured into the unknown.

The air grew colder as I entered the room where Lila had disappeared, the shadows deepening like a living entity. The beam of my flashlight illuminated remnants of what used to be a cozy sitting area—an overturned coffee table, a shattered vase, and a blanket thrown haphazardly across the floor.

"Lila!" I called again, my voice more desperate now. I stepped deeper into the room, my heart racing as I searched for any sign of her. The oppressive quiet seemed to press down on me, and I was acutely aware of how vulnerable we were.

"Over here!" came Lila's voice, slightly muffled but unmistakable. Relief flooded through me, cutting through my fear as I hurried toward the sound.

I found her crouched next to an old, battered trunk in the corner, her flashlight illuminating her excited expression. "Look what I found!" she exclaimed, practically bouncing on her heels. "This must have belonged to the Whitakers! What do you think is inside?"

"Probably their hopes and dreams," I replied, attempting a lighthearted tone to mask my lingering fear. "Or maybe just more junk. Can we please not open anything right now? I'm having enough of a heart attack as it is."

"Oh, come on!" Lila pouted, her eyes sparkling with mischief. "This could be our ticket to the mystery of the century! What if there's something valuable in there? Or a diary detailing their lives? We could find out why they left!"

"Or we could find a rabid raccoon. Let's not pretend this is a fairy tale," I countered, crossing my arms.

But Lila's curiosity was relentless. She reached for the trunk's rusted latch, her fingers dancing with anticipation. "Just a peek? Please?"

With a resigned sigh, I watched her fumble with the latch, my nerves tingling in protest. As it clicked open, the trunk creaked ominously, revealing a jumble of old clothes and books, layered with dust that swirled into the air like forgotten memories. "See? I told you it would be junk," I muttered, my disappointment palpable.

But Lila didn't seem deterred. She began rifling through the contents, tossing items aside until a small, leather-bound journal caught her eye. "Wait! Look at this!"

I leaned closer, my curiosity piqued despite myself. The journal's cover was worn, its edges frayed with age. "What does it say?" I asked, inching forward, my heart fluttering with both trepidation and excitement.

Lila opened it carefully, her brows furrowing as she scanned the pages. "It's filled with notes... about the break-ins!"

The blood drained from my face as she read aloud. "There's a list of names and dates. They wrote down every incident, and look—there's a pattern! This goes back months!"

"Months?" I echoed, a chill creeping up my spine. "Why would they keep track of that?"

"It's like they were expecting it," Lila said, her voice shaking slightly. "Like they knew something would happen. What if the Whitakers weren't just victims?"

Before I could respond, a loud bang echoed through the house, reverberating through the very walls as if a thunderstorm had erupted inside. We both jumped, the journal slipping from Lila's hands and tumbling to the floor.

"Did you hear that?" I gasped, wide-eyed, my heart racing as I glanced at the open door.

"Yeah, and I think we should get out of here!" Lila grabbed my arm, tugging me toward the exit.

But just as we turned to flee, the shadow we had seen earlier darted across the hallway once more, more pronounced this time, blocking our only escape. A figure emerged, tall and cloaked in darkness, their features obscured but their intentions crystal clear.

"Not so fast," a voice commanded, smooth and chilling, sending an icy shiver down my spine. I froze, my instincts screaming at me to run, but the weight of fear held me in place.

Lila's grip tightened on my arm, her breath hitching in her throat as the figure stepped closer, the darkness wrapping around them like a living cloak. In that moment, the truth settled in like a heavy fog: we were not alone, and whatever had been lurking in the shadows had just revealed itself.

Chapter 3: Crossing Paths

The neighborhood meeting felt like a gathering of disgruntled bees, buzzing with anxiety and anger. The dimly lit community center echoed with murmurs, a mixture of apprehension and hope swirling in the stale air. I took a seat at the front, a determined fire igniting my resolve. Tonight, we were supposed to address the rising crime in our quiet corner of the world, but as I glanced around, it became clear that our little utopia had taken a hit.

The room was a collage of faces—some familiar, others barely recognizable. But it was Nathan who commanded my attention. He sat across the long, battered table, his sharp jawline shadowed by the overhead fluorescent lights, framing a visage that was both infuriating and strikingly handsome. I caught the glint of his dark eyes scanning the room, dissecting every worried expression as if he were a judge at a beauty pageant for disgruntled citizens. There was a certain disdain etched into his features, and it grated on me like a fingernail against chalk.

When I began to speak, my voice rose above the murmurs, steady and passionate. "We can't just sit here and let fear dictate our lives. We need to unite as a community and watch out for one another. We can organize neighborhood patrols, create an emergency contact network, or even set up a community watch. We cannot be victims in our own homes."

As the words left my mouth, I felt a wave of energy ripple through the room. A few heads nodded in agreement, but then there was Nathan, arms crossed, brow furrowed. His eyes narrowed slightly as he leaned back in his chair, a picture of skeptical relaxation. I could practically hear his internal monologue—a dismissive commentary on idealism that was meant to be constructive. I took a deep breath, and the determined fire inside me flared.

"Don't you think it's a bit naïve to think we can change anything?" he shot back, his tone dripping with that blend of mockery and curiosity that left me half-amused, half-annoyed.

"Naïve?" I echoed, feeling my cheeks flush. "If we don't try to do something, we're surrendering to the very fear that's strangling our community. Is that what you want?"

"Hardly," he replied, his voice smooth and unyielding. "But actions need to be grounded in reality, and rallying the troops might just be a feel-good strategy that changes nothing."

"Or it could change everything," I retorted, my pulse quickening. The air between us crackled with an intensity that felt electric, like the moments before a storm breaks.

His lips quirked into a sly grin, the kind that made me want to both laugh and smack him upside the head. "You really believe that, don't you? That a few posters and a couple of neighborhood meetings will actually make a difference?"

"Why do you keep dismissing everything I say?" I challenged, leaning forward, a mix of anger and intrigue propelling my words. "Why is it so hard for you to see that people want to feel safe again? They need a reason to trust one another."

The room buzzed around us, but in that moment, it felt as though we existed in our own little world, the lines of our argument blurring with something deeper—a magnetic pull that made my heart race faster than my words. I could see the amusement flickering in his eyes, and it irritated me how much I liked the challenge he presented.

Nathan shrugged, the tension in his shoulders easing as he gave me a look that was both playful and sincere. "Maybe it's because I see a lot of idealism and not enough pragmatism. You know what happens when you ignore the reality of a situation? You end up with a lot of disappointed people and very little change."

I scoffed, but inside, my mind churned. He was infuriatingly right in some ways. Disappointment was a beast lurking at the edges of every grand plan, waiting to pounce when expectations soared too high. "So, what's your grand solution then?" I shot back, my eyes narrowing.

His expression shifted for just a second—like a curtain lifting to reveal an unexpected vulnerability. "I'm not saying we shouldn't try. I just think we need to be realistic about what we can actually accomplish."

"Realistic?" I countered, frustration coursing through me. "How do you expect to inspire action with pessimism? People need hope, Nathan. Without hope, we're just waiting for the next crisis to hit."

"Hope is nice and all, but I prefer to build things that last," he replied, his gaze steady, and something unyielding in his demeanor made my heart flutter against my ribcage. "What happens when your hope gets shattered?"

"Then we rebuild," I said, softer now, feeling the tension shift as I glanced around the room, suddenly aware of the rapt attention we had drawn. "We stand together, we support each other, and we find a way to make it work. Isn't that the whole point of being a community?"

The moment hung between us, both charged and fragile. I watched as he contemplated my words, his features softening, albeit imperceptibly. For a fleeting instant, I wondered if this dance of banter was something more—an unexpected connection beneath the layers of skepticism and pride. But just as quickly as it flickered to life, the moment evaporated, replaced by the buzz of frustrated neighbors and the dull thud of reality crashing back in.

"Well, then," Nathan said, his tone shifting back to that wry edge, "I guess it's time to see if your hope can spark a fire."

As the meeting continued, I couldn't shake the feeling that this was just the beginning. The interplay between us—a rivalry tinged with a spark of something deeper—set the stage for a story that was only just unfolding, layers of tension and attraction interwoven in ways I couldn't yet fully comprehend.

The meeting room buzzed with a mix of chatter and tension, the atmosphere thick like the humidity of a summer afternoon. After a vigorous exchange, I felt both exhilarated and drained, my mind racing with the implications of what we'd discussed. The reality of our community's situation had become painfully clear: we were at a crossroads, teetering between hope and despair. Nathan remained an ever-present thorn in my side, his piercing gaze still haunting me as he leaned back, arms crossed, his expression inscrutable.

As people began to filter out, I lingered, grappling with my thoughts. The fluorescent lights flickered overhead, casting an unnatural glow that mirrored the awkwardness still lingering in the air. I was caught between wanting to confront Nathan about his relentless skepticism and the inexplicable desire to understand him better. The way he challenged my ideals both frustrated and fascinated me. It was a puzzle, and I was more than willing to play detective.

Finally, as the crowd thinned, I found my resolve. I approached him, hands tucked nervously into the pockets of my jacket. "You know," I said, keeping my voice steady despite the flutters in my stomach, "you might consider taking the stick out of your—"

"'A stick out of my what?'" he interrupted, feigning shock as he leaned in closer, his dark hair falling across his forehead. "I'm just trying to save you from your own optimism."

"Optimism isn't a bad thing, Nathan. You could use a little yourself," I shot back, my heart racing as his proximity amplified the tension.

"Oh really? And how do you suggest I embrace this optimism? By throwing a neighborhood block party? Maybe invite the local criminals to join us?" His smirk was infuriatingly charming, and for a moment, I lost my train of thought.

"Or perhaps by engaging in constructive discussions instead of dismissing them outright," I replied, crossing my arms defiantly. "You know, people actually respond well to encouragement."

"Encouragement is nice, but it doesn't fix broken windows or stolen bikes," he countered, leaning back and tilting his head as if trying to see the world through my eyes.

"Is that really how you view this? Just a series of broken things?" I asked, a hint of disbelief creeping into my voice.

He paused, the teasing glint in his eye dimming slightly. "Sometimes it feels that way. We can pretend that community meetings and posters will change everything, but the truth is, they won't. People are still going to make bad choices."

"What if we change the narrative?" I insisted, unable to hide the passion in my tone. "What if we can inspire people to come together rather than retreat into fear?"

He raised an eyebrow, clearly amused. "And you think that's going to work because you've seen a few uplifting videos on social media?"

"It's more than that. It's about showing people that they're not alone," I shot back, a fire igniting within me. "When you feel isolated, that's when fear takes root. But when you know your neighbors are there for you, it makes all the difference."

"You really believe that, don't you?" he said, his voice softer now, tinged with genuine curiosity.

"Of course I do," I replied, surprised by the earnestness in my own words. "I've seen it work. Communities can rally together to create change."

For a moment, silence enveloped us, and I could sense the shift in our dynamic. There was a flicker of something deeper in his gaze, a shared understanding, or perhaps a challenge waiting to be acknowledged. The chemistry between us felt charged, a silent dance of possibilities weaving in and out of our banter.

"Alright, Miss Optimism," he said, breaking the silence, "let's say I'm intrigued. How would you propose we do this? Gather everyone for a drum circle and sing 'Kumbaya'?"

"Why not?" I shot back, unable to keep the laughter from bubbling up. "Just imagine: a community drum circle right in the middle of Main Street, our lovely town full of rhythm and unity."

"Or a total cacophony that scares off anyone within a mile," he replied, chuckling despite himself. "I can see it now—a bunch of disgruntled residents banging on drums, wondering where they went wrong."

"Hey, every revolution starts somewhere, right? Maybe it'll just take a few bad drummers to get people on board," I said with a grin, enjoying this unexpected back-and-forth.

He tilted his head, an amused smile tugging at the corners of his lips. "Alright, how about we brainstorm a plan that involves a little less banging and a little more... actionable strategies?"

"Now you're speaking my language," I said, excitement bubbling up again. "What if we create a neighborhood watch, but make it more appealing? Like a friendly 'community vigilance' initiative? We could host events that promote connection—potlucks, game nights, and activities that help people know each other. It'll break down barriers."

"Potlucks, huh?" he said, stroking his chin theatrically. "I can already hear the complaints about Aunt Betty's infamous three-bean salad. But... it could work."

"See?" I replied, my heart racing. "You're starting to think like a hopeful citizen."

"You might just convince me yet," he said, his tone shifting from playful to something more serious. "But it's going to take more than a couple of potlucks and drum circles to change hearts and minds."

"Maybe. But we have to start somewhere," I said, meeting his gaze, the air thick with unspoken possibilities. "What if we set up an initial meeting to discuss ideas? Gauge interest?"

"Consider me intrigued," he replied, leaning closer, the air between us charged with a new energy, as if the friction of our earlier banter had sparked something more profound. "You have my attention, and I can't wait to see where this goes."

The connection between us felt electric, the sharpness of our previous arguments giving way to a shared purpose. For the first time, I found myself contemplating the idea of partnership—not just in the community efforts but in something that could linger beyond the confines of our verbal sparring.

As we discussed potential dates and times, the tension that had once felt antagonistic shifted into something rich with promise. With each suggestion and playful jab, the room faded away until it was just the two of us, standing on the precipice of an unexpected alliance that neither of us had seen coming. The night was far from over, and as I stepped into the cool evening air, I couldn't shake the feeling that this was the beginning of something significant—a new chapter that intertwined our paths in ways we had yet to fully understand.

Days passed after the meeting, each moment tinged with an excitement that felt both thrilling and disconcerting. The sun hung high in the sky, casting golden rays over our quaint neighborhood, where the blooming flowers seemed to mock my internal struggle. I couldn't shake the image of Nathan's dark eyes, sharp wit, and that infuriating yet charming smirk. Every time I ventured outside, whether it was to pick up groceries or walk my dog, I half-expected to see him, ready to challenge my optimism with his relentless pragmatism.

As I walked through the local park one afternoon, my mind replayed our banter like a favorite song. The air was sweet with the scent of blooming lilacs, and the laughter of children echoed nearby. I spotted a small group gathered around a picnic table, a couple of parents overseeing a game of tag. The image felt comforting, a stark contrast to the unease that had settled over our community. Just as I began to relax into the moment, a figure emerged from behind a tree—Nathan, leaning casually against the trunk, arms crossed and a knowing smile playing on his lips.

"Caught you daydreaming again," he said, his voice low and teasing.

"Don't you have more important things to do?" I shot back, crossing my arms defiantly but unable to mask the thrill that raced through me at the sight of him.

"Maybe I'm just here to ensure you don't float away on a cloud of idealism," he replied, stepping closer, the sunlight filtering through the leaves, creating a halo around him. It was infuriating how much I enjoyed this back-and-forth.

"Who says I want to float away?" I challenged, trying to maintain my composure. "Sometimes, it's the clouds that provide the most beautiful view."

"Or they could rain on your parade," he countered, that infuriating grin making a return. "What if instead of staring at clouds, we focused on solid ground?"

"Is that your way of saying you want to plan something?" I asked, tilting my head, intrigued.

"I might be open to it," he admitted, the lightness in his tone suggesting he was half-joking. "But only if you promise not to suggest any more drum circles."

"Deal. Let's leave the percussion to the professionals," I laughed, surprising myself with the ease of our exchange.

We ended up walking together, the park's winding paths taking us deeper into a world filled with laughter and blooming trees. The air was sweet, and for the first time in days, I felt hopeful, not just for our neighborhood but for this unexpected camaraderie blossoming between us.

As we strolled, I decided to broach the subject that had been swirling in my mind since our last encounter. "What do you think about forming a community committee? We could rally a few more people to join us—make a real effort to engage the neighborhood."

"Sounds ambitious," Nathan replied, his tone shifting slightly. "And also somewhat risky. What if it flops?"

"Then we'll learn from it and try something else," I countered, my passion igniting. "But if we don't try, we'll never know what we could achieve."

He paused, looking out at the children playing nearby, their carefree laughter contrasting sharply with the worry that had settled over the adults. "You really believe in this, don't you?"

"I do," I insisted, my voice firm. "But I also need your support. You have the ability to influence people more than I do, especially those who seem to gravitate toward your cynicism."

He chuckled softly, shaking his head as if he were trying to shake off the weight of my words. "You might be surprised by how much I'm willing to help. But only if we keep it grounded. No fairy-tale expectations."

"Fairy-tale expectations are precisely what I'm hoping to avoid," I said, grinning. "Just good old-fashioned community spirit."

"I can get on board with that," he replied, a glimmer of respect creeping into his voice.

As our conversation continued, I found myself drawn to his more serious side, the layers beneath his bravado revealing a depth I hadn't anticipated. The moments between us felt rich, as if we were slowly weaving a tapestry of connection with each shared thought and lingering glance. Yet, with every exchange, the tension simmered just beneath the surface, a magnetic pull that left me wondering where we stood.

We decided to meet at the local café the next day to flesh out our ideas, a cozy spot where the aroma of freshly brewed coffee mingled with the scent of pastries. As we discussed our plans over steaming cups, the café buzzed with life. The sound of clinking cups, muffled laughter, and the barista's cheerful greetings created a comforting backdrop.

"Okay, so let's say we gather a few volunteers," Nathan said, leaning in closer, his voice low as if we were sharing a secret. "What's the first step? Posters? Flyers?"

"How about we start by sharing our vision?" I suggested. "Invite people to brainstorm with us, so they feel invested from the beginning. It's about fostering a sense of ownership in the project."

He nodded slowly, considering my words. "That's actually not a terrible idea. But let's not get too carried away. I don't want a hundred people showing up expecting fireworks."

"Then we'll set reasonable expectations," I said, my pulse quickening at the thought of rallying our neighbors. "How about a casual gathering in the park? We can keep it low-pressure. Snacks, some casual games—an icebreaker for everyone to get to know each other."

"Games, huh?" he said, smirking again. "What do you suggest? A neighborhood tug-of-war? Because I'm pretty sure I could win that one."

"I'd love to see you try," I shot back, laughter bubbling between us. "I'd have to make sure I had my team of enthusiastic cheerleaders ready to support me."

As the conversation flowed, I felt an undeniable shift—a camaraderie that transcended the playful banter, but the weight of unspoken words still lingered between us, thickening the air.

Just as we finished outlining our plan, a loud crash erupted outside, startling us both. The café's patrons turned their heads toward the sound, whispers and murmurs spreading like wildfire. My heart raced as Nathan's expression shifted to one of concern.

"Stay here," he said, urgency threading through his voice.

"What? Where are you going?" I asked, the sense of foreboding growing.

Before I could grasp his intention, Nathan rushed outside, pushing through the café door. I followed, heart pounding as I stepped into the late afternoon sun, a harsh glare reflecting off the pavement.

Chaos greeted me—shouts echoed through the air, and I saw a group of people gathering around a toppled bike, the owner frantically searching for something among the wreckage. Nathan was already in the mix, trying to assess the situation, his brows furrowed in concentration.

Then, a distant sound pierced the cacophony—a siren wailing in the distance, drawing closer, an ominous harbinger of trouble.

And in that instant, everything shifted. A dark figure appeared at the edge of the crowd, just out of focus, watching intently. The atmosphere crackled with tension, a palpable shift that sent chills down my spine. My instincts kicked in, and I could feel that whatever had been brewing beneath the surface of our community was about to boil over.

I stepped forward, drawn to Nathan's side, the weight of the moment settling over us like a heavy fog. "What's happening?" I whispered, my voice barely audible above the chaos.

He turned, his expression shifting from concern to something darker as he met my gaze. "I don't know yet, but I have a feeling this isn't just an accident."

And as the sirens drew nearer, I couldn't shake the sense that the real trouble was just beginning.

Chapter 4: The Storm Breaks

The storm crashed into Charleston with all the subtlety of a cannonball, sending sheets of rain that pelted the pavement like a thousand furious drummers. I had been cruising down the street, music blaring and windows down, oblivious to the brewing tempest until my car coughed and sputtered, the engine protesting with a final, gasping wheeze before dying altogether. Stranded, I peered out at the looming clouds, their dark underbellies roiling and heavy with promise—none of which was good.

With a resigned sigh, I leaned against my steering wheel, knowing my options were limited. The nearest payphone felt like a relic of the past, and my phone had opted for a lengthy nap, refusing to even flicker to life. So, with a combination of dread and a strange thrill that often accompanied desperate situations, I reluctantly trudged toward Nathan's apartment complex, my shoes squelching against the waterlogged ground. The rain poured down in sheets, a chaotic symphony that matched the turbulence in my heart.

Nathan had always been a bit of a mystery to me. Our friendship had blossomed out of necessity rather than choice; I was thrust into his orbit when I moved to Charleston for a fresh start, hoping to outrun the ghosts of my past. Nathan, with his brooding looks and sharp wit, had the kind of presence that could clear a room or fill it with electricity in equal measure. When I knocked on his door, the sound echoed against the hall's damp walls, a lonely plea for refuge.

When he opened the door, his expression shifted from surprise to irritation, as if he had been caught off guard by my very existence. "What do you want?" he grumbled, his voice grating against my ears, yet I couldn't help but notice the way his hair clung to his forehead, damp from his own run-in with the storm.

"I need to borrow your phone," I stated, folding my arms defiantly, though I felt a shiver creep down my spine—not just from the cold, but from the intensity of his gaze, which seemed to slice through the tension hanging between us.

"Why didn't you think ahead?" he snapped, though I could see the way his annoyance wavered beneath the surface. We danced this dance often—two stubborn people circling each other, both equally too proud to back down. "You could've planned better."

"Ah yes, because I can totally control when my car decides to explode," I shot back, rolling my eyes dramatically, even as the sincerity in my tone revealed how much I craved a break from the storm—both outside and in the depths of my mind.

"Fine. Come in," he relented, stepping aside. I crossed the threshold into his small apartment, the familiar scent of coffee and something spicy wrapping around me like a warm blanket. But there was no comfort in this moment; rather, it was a battlefield of wills.

The room was a cluttered mix of old furniture and eclectic décor—posters of bands I couldn't identify plastered on the walls, a mismatched sofa that had seen better days, and a kitchen counter filled with the remnants of his last cooking adventure. My gaze landed on a half-empty bottle of whiskey sitting beside a stack of unopened mail. I suppressed a smile at the chaos—classic Nathan, living in organized disarray.

I watched him pick up his phone, the atmosphere thickening as he tried to dial my roadside assistance number. Rain hammered the windows, creating a rhythmic backdrop that intensified the tension. With every rumble of thunder, it felt like the world outside mirrored the storm brewing between us. "You should really take better care of that hunk of junk," he muttered, handing me the phone with a frown that deepened as he caught my eye.

"Funny, I could say the same about you," I countered, tossing my hair over my shoulder with a flick of defiance. The corners of his lips twitched, almost as if I'd struck a nerve, but he quickly masked it with irritation.

"Real mature," he replied, crossing his arms, yet I could see the way his shoulders relaxed slightly, as if my jab had released some of the pent-up energy in the room.

As I spoke to the operator, arranging for a tow truck that felt like an eternity away, I could sense Nathan watching me, his gaze a steady burn that made my cheeks flush. I finished the call, turning to face him, expecting more bickering, more sarcasm. Instead, the sight of him, his brow furrowed with concern, took me by surprise. It was a vulnerability I had rarely glimpsed, a crack in the façade that kept him hidden.

"Are you okay?" he asked, his tone softer now, the challenge fading from his voice like the storm clouds outside. There was something genuine in his eyes, a flicker of concern that made my heart beat just a little faster.

"I will be, once I get out of here," I replied, my bravado slipping as I felt the weight of my own fears creep in. "It's just...everything's a mess right now."

He nodded slowly, as if weighing his words. "Yeah, I get that. Life throws curveballs when you least expect it." The moment hung between us, charged with an intimacy I hadn't anticipated. I was acutely aware of the warmth radiating from him, a sharp contrast to the chill of the storm.

"Funny, coming from you," I quipped, trying to recapture our earlier banter, but the softness lingered like a ghost, refusing to be chased away.

"I might be a mess, but at least I know how to fix a car," he shot back, a teasing glint in his eye, and I couldn't help but laugh. The tension that had threatened to spiral out of control morphed into something palpable, something that hinted at the unspoken connection we both felt.

"Maybe you should start charging for your services," I replied, feeling the warmth spread through me, illuminating the shadows of doubt that had clouded my mind.

"Maybe I should," he said, his smile lingering just long enough for me to catch a glimpse of the man beneath the bravado—a man who hid behind layers of sarcasm but was ultimately just as vulnerable as I was.

Outside, the storm raged on, but within the confines of his apartment, a different kind of storm was brewing, one that held the promise of understanding and perhaps even something more.

The storm raged on, an incessant percussion of rain and wind that danced against the windows like a frantic orchestra. Inside Nathan's apartment, the air was thick with an electricity that had nothing to do with the weather outside. As we exchanged barbs, I could feel the playful rhythm of our banter shifting, weaving through a labyrinth of uncharted emotions. The heat of the moment wrapped around us, and it felt like we were caught in a bubble, the chaos outside fading into a dull roar.

"Do you always make a habit of breaking down at the most inconvenient times?" he teased, leaning back against the counter, arms crossed over his chest. There was a smirk on his lips, but his eyes betrayed a deeper concern, one that pulled at me like an anchor.

"Only when I have a destination worth reaching," I shot back, raising an eyebrow. The warmth of our exchange made me wonder if the air was growing thicker or if I was merely becoming more aware of the subtle tension threading through our conversation.

He tilted his head slightly, a flicker of curiosity sparking in his gaze. "And what makes this destination so special? Is it the company?"

"Maybe it is," I replied, the truth slipping out before I could reel it back. The admission hung between us, a fragile thread that could unravel with the slightest breath. For a heartbeat, we both froze, caught in the web of our own making.

Before either of us could respond, the storm chose that moment to roar its approval, a clap of thunder shaking the walls and sending shivers racing down my spine. I jumped slightly, my heart racing as the sudden crash echoed through the apartment, and Nathan took a step closer, concern etched on his features.

"Are you scared of storms?" he asked, a genuine softness bleeding through the sarcasm.

I hesitated, the truth of my answer bubbling beneath the surface. "More like they remind me of how small we are," I finally admitted, feeling a twinge of vulnerability seep into my tone. "Especially when you're stuck out in one."

"Good thing you're not out there now," he replied, a hint of amusement creeping back into his voice. "You're safe here with me, at least until the tow truck arrives. And who knows? Maybe I can find you a towel or something, though I doubt it would match your—"

"Don't even think about making a comment on my fashion choices right now," I interrupted, holding up a finger in warning. The drenched remnants of my outfit—a once-chic sundress now plastered to my skin—were hardly worthy of praise.

His eyes twinkled with mischief. "I wasn't going to say a word. But I'm just saying, you might want to rethink that ensemble if you plan on sticking around for more storms."

"Gee, thanks, Nathan. Fashion advice from the king of chaos himself," I shot back, the banter flowing effortlessly between us once more. But even as I laughed, there was an undeniable warmth spreading in my chest, an odd mixture of safety and something more complicated that I couldn't quite grasp.

We settled into a comfortable rhythm, sharing stories and laughter that danced like the shadows on the walls. He told me about the ridiculous roommate antics that had made his living situation a soap opera, and I shared my own mishaps in the culinary department that had left my kitchen looking like a war zone. With each anecdote, the walls we had built around ourselves crumbled a little more, revealing the fragile humanity beneath our masks.

Then, as the rain began to lighten, the air shifted again, the weight of unspoken words heavy between us. I felt it first—an awareness that threatened to spiral into something I wasn't prepared to name. My heart raced, not from fear of the storm but from the sudden urge to lean in closer, to bridge the gap that seemed to beckon between us.

"Why do you keep pretending to be this tough guy?" I asked, half teasing, half serious. "It's exhausting just watching you."

He opened his mouth, then closed it again, his expression shifting from playfulness to something more serious. "Maybe it's easier this way," he replied finally, his voice barely above a whisper.

"What do you mean?" I pressed, sensing that this was the moment where we could either backtrack into playful banter or leap into deeper waters.

He took a breath, as if bracing himself against the weight of his own revelation. "I've had my share of storms, you know. Not just the weather ones." His gaze flickered to the window, where the rain had turned to a soft drizzle, mirroring the uncertainty in the air. "It's easier to push people away than to let them in and risk getting hurt."

I felt a pang in my chest, the honesty of his words wrapping around me like a warm blanket on a cold night. "You don't have to do that with me," I said softly, surprised at how sincere my own voice had become. "I'm not going anywhere. Not right now, anyway."

The moment stretched, pregnant with possibilities, and I saw the flicker of doubt in his eyes, mingling with something deeper—a yearning that echoed my own. Just as it seemed we might cross the invisible line that separated us, his phone buzzed loudly against the counter, shattering the moment like glass hitting the floor.

"Great timing," he muttered, irritation flashing across his features as he picked up the device. "Just a second."

I stood there, feeling the remnants of our conversation swirl around me like the storm that still lingered outside, a cacophony of emotions that made my heart race and my mind whirl. His words had stirred something deep within, a longing for connection that I couldn't shake.

As he stepped away to answer the call, I forced myself to breathe, reminding myself that this was Nathan—a man who wore his heart behind a wall of sarcasm and strength. Yet, somehow, I had glimpsed the cracks, and it left me reeling with possibilities.

"Hey, I'm in the middle of something," he said, his tone clipped as he glanced at me, concern now evident in his expression. "Can I call you back?"

The exchange faded into background noise as I pondered what this moment meant for us. The storm might have subsided outside, but within the confines of Nathan's apartment, a tempest raged on—one that promised to reveal truths, shatter facades, and perhaps, if we dared to lean into it, forge an unexpected bond between two storm-tossed souls.

He ended the call and looked back at me, a flash of frustration crossing his features, but it quickly softened as he saw the concern etched on my face. "Sorry about that," he said, running a hand through his damp hair, causing it to fall across his forehead in a charming, boyish way that made my heart skip just a little. "Business stuff."

"Right," I replied, my tone light, though I could feel the tension of the moment still hanging in the air like humidity before a storm. "I figured a guy like you would be too busy saving the world to worry about little ol' me."

"Saving the world?" he scoffed, but there was an underlying warmth to his voice, the playful tone creeping back in. "I'm more like the guy who's usually buried under a pile of paperwork while trying not to burn his toast."

I laughed, the sound breaking the lingering tension. "Well, at least you've got your priorities straight." I paused, studying him for a moment. "But I have to say, if saving the world means dealing with more stormy nights like this one, I'd call in sick."

Nathan chuckled, shaking his head. "Believe me, I'd take a raincheck on that job any day."

As the rain began to lighten, I felt a strange sense of camaraderie forming between us, a bond born from shared laughter and the shelter of this makeshift refuge. The world outside continued to murmur, the wind weaving stories through the trees, but in here, it was just us—two unlikely allies navigating the chaos.

"Can I get you anything?" Nathan asked, moving toward the small kitchenette that was barely bigger than a closet. He rummaged through the cupboards, the light glinting off his strong arms, revealing the intricate tattoos that decorated his skin. "Coffee? Tea? I might even have some instant ramen somewhere if you're feeling adventurous."

"Instant ramen sounds great, actually," I replied, settling onto the worn sofa, which sagged slightly under my weight. The fabric felt cozy against my damp skin, and for a moment, I let my guard down, allowing the warmth of the space to envelop me. "But just to clarify, I'm not holding you to your 'world-saving' promise. Ramen will do just fine."

"Noted," he said with a mock-seriousness that made me smile. "Ramen it is. But if the world starts to end while we're enjoying this gourmet meal, I expect you to help me save it."

"I'm a natural-born hero, you know," I quipped, crossing my arms in mock bravado. "Right after I finish my noodles."

As Nathan prepared the ramen, I couldn't help but admire the way he moved—confidently, yet with an undercurrent of something more fragile. It was an intriguing contrast that made me want to dig deeper, to understand the layers of complexity hidden beneath his tough exterior. "So, what's your grand plan for this evening?" I asked, leaning forward, genuinely curious. "A movie marathon? An impromptu karaoke session?"

He turned, a teasing glimmer in his eyes. "I think you'd be a terrible karaoke partner. Too much judgment in your laughter. I'd need a more forgiving audience."

"Hey! I only laugh at the truly awful performances—yours would be top-tier, trust me," I replied, waving a hand dismissively, but my heart raced at the thought of us sharing a more intimate moment, filled with laughter and warmth. "But honestly, what do you do when you're not saving the world or enduring epic thunderstorms?"

"I write," he said simply, setting down a steaming bowl in front of me. "Mostly freelance stuff—articles, opinion pieces, the occasional rant on social media." He shrugged, a hint of embarrassment coloring his cheeks. "Nothing too glamorous."

"Really? That's pretty cool," I said, genuinely impressed. "What do you write about?"

"Anything and everything," he replied, leaning against the counter. "But lately, I've been focused on social justice issues, the kind of stuff that makes people uncomfortable." He paused, his expression growing serious. "It's a way to channel some of my frustrations. Writing helps me make sense of things. I can spill my thoughts onto the page instead of letting them fester."

"Sounds like you've got a lot to say," I said softly, touched by his openness. "I get that. Sometimes, it's easier to put pen to paper than to face the chaos of life head-on."

He nodded, the atmosphere shifting once more. "Exactly. And you? What's your story?"

The question hung between us like a whisper in the night, and I felt my chest tighten. I'd spent so long running from my past, building walls to protect myself from the hurt. But something in Nathan's gaze urged me to let down my guard, to share more than just a playful quip.

"I moved to Charleston for a fresh start," I began, the words spilling out before I could second-guess myself. "I was in a rough place after...well, let's just say my last chapter wasn't exactly a happy one. I thought a change of scenery would help, but sometimes it feels like I'm just carrying my baggage with me."

Nathan's eyes softened, and he leaned in closer, his curiosity palpable. "What kind of baggage?"

"Just the kind that comes from heartbreak and bad decisions," I admitted, feeling exposed yet strangely free. "But I'm working on it. One day at a time."

"Good for you," he said, his tone sincere. "We all have our storms to weather, don't we? It's how we handle them that defines us."

I met his gaze, the weight of our shared understanding anchoring us in this moment. "You make it sound easy," I replied, my voice barely above a whisper. "But it feels anything but."

Before he could respond, a loud crack of thunder interrupted us, louder than before, rattling the windows and sending my heart racing again. The lights flickered ominously, then dimmed to a ghostly glow, throwing our reflections into shadowy outlines.

"Great," Nathan muttered, moving to the window and peering out into the darkness. "I think the storm's just getting started. I'll check the circuit breakers."

I watched as he moved to the back of the apartment, his silhouette framed by the dim light. The air buzzed with tension, each moment charged as if the universe was holding its breath. Suddenly, a deafening crash echoed outside, and I sprang up, heart pounding in my chest.

"What was that?" I called, panic seeping into my voice.

Nathan turned, worry etched across his features. "I don't know, but it didn't sound good."

Before I could respond, there was another noise—this one sharp and unsettling—like the sound of shattering glass. It echoed from the direction of the front door.

"Nathan?" I whispered, unease creeping into my bones. "What is happening?"

He took a cautious step toward me, the atmosphere thickening with uncertainty. "Stay here. I'll check it out."

"Are you kidding?" I shot back, my pulse racing. "Like I'm going to sit back while you play hero?"

He hesitated, glancing between me and the door, torn between protecting me and facing whatever danger lay outside. "Fine. But stay close."

Together, we approached the door, the sounds of the storm amplifying the trepidation that filled the space. I could feel Nathan's muscles tense beside me, a silent agreement that whatever was about to happen would change everything.

He opened the door just a crack, and the howling wind rushed in, slapping us with a damp chill. The scene outside was surreal—debris littered the ground, and the sky flickered ominously, casting eerie shadows on the sidewalk. But that wasn't what drew my attention; it was the figure standing just beyond the threshold.

"Who—" I began, but the words caught in my throat as I recognized the silhouette, heart hammering in disbelief.

The figure stepped closer, and the world around me faded into a hush, leaving only the pounding of my heart echoing in my ears. It was someone I thought I'd never see again, someone from my past, and the storm that had felt so contained moments before now loomed large with the weight of impending chaos.

Chapter 5: Secrets in the Shadows

The sun hung low in the sky, casting long, jagged shadows that danced ominously across the cobbled streets of Silverbrook. The air was thick with tension, crackling like the static before a storm. I had no particular destination in mind as I meandered through the town, my senses heightened, attuned to the whispers of the wind and the muted conversations of locals sharing their fears about the recent break-ins. Each doorway I passed felt like a potential hiding place for the anxiety that had gripped the community, and I was determined to uncover its source.

I wandered through the town square, where the scent of roasted coffee mingled with the sweet fragrance of pastries from the nearby bakery. The bustling chatter of neighbors only deepened my sense of isolation; I was an outsider, desperately searching for clues that might lead me to answers. The barista, an elderly woman with eyes like storm clouds, served me a steaming cup of herbal tea. "It's not just the break-ins," she murmured, her voice low as if afraid to be overheard. "People are disappearing, too. Last week, young Henry from the north side vanished. Just poof, like that. You keep your wits about you, dear."

Her words clung to me, heavy and foreboding. I offered a grateful nod, but my heart raced as I left the warmth of the café, the chill of uncertainty creeping back in. I could feel the weight of her warning pressing down on me, a reminder that danger wasn't just lurking; it had woven itself into the very fabric of Silverbrook.

Drawn by an inexplicable force, I veered down a narrow side street, where the architecture grew older, the buildings leaning toward one another as if sharing secrets. The light began to fade, swallowed by the encroaching shadows. As I took another step, I caught sight of a dark alley tucked away from prying eyes. It beckoned to me, a siren call laced with intrigue and peril. Against my better judgment, I stepped inside, curiosity outweighing caution.

The alley was littered with remnants of the town's forgotten stories—discarded newspapers, rusted bicycles, and crumbling bricks. The air felt heavier here, thick with the scent of dampness and something more sinister, something that whispered of danger. My heart thudded in my chest as I pressed further into the gloom, each footfall echoing against the brick walls like a heartbeat. I was hyperaware of the stillness that enveloped me, every instinct screaming that I was not alone.

Suddenly, a low rustle shattered the silence. I froze, the adrenaline coursing through my veins like wildfire. Shadows shifted, and panic clawed at my throat as I strained to see the source of the sound. My mind raced with scenarios—an assailant? A thief? I felt trapped, the walls closing in around me, a predator's den. Just as I was about to turn on my heel and flee, a figure emerged from the darkness.

"Nathan," I breathed, a mix of relief and irritation flooding my senses. There he stood, his frame outlined by the dim light, an enigmatic presence that both reassured and annoyed me. I felt like a moth drawn to a flame, knowing I shouldn't get too close but unable to resist the pull. He approached with a calm intensity that belied the chaos around us. "What are you doing here, Amelia?" His voice was a low rumble, steadying my racing heart but igniting something else entirely.

"I was trying to—" I began, but before I could finish, I was pulled into the safety of his side as a sudden noise echoed through the alley. A dumpster rattled violently, sending a cascade of sound that felt like the breaking of glass against the eerie quiet. We ducked instinctively, the brush of our bodies igniting an electric tension that made my skin prickle. I hated that I needed him, that his presence calmed the storm brewing within me, yet the thrill of our shared danger made me breathless.

"We need to get out of here," he urged, his eyes scanning the shadows with the precision of a predator. I couldn't help but marvel at how effortlessly he slid into protective mode, each move deliberate and instinctive. "Stick close to me."

Together, we moved deeper into the alley, my heart pounding not just from fear but from the undeniable awareness of him beside me. The world outside faded, leaving only the adrenaline coursing through my veins. With every step, I felt a tug-of-war between my annoyance at his sudden appearance and the undeniable chemistry crackling between us.

Just as we neared the mouth of the alley, a figure loomed ahead. I halted, pressing against Nathan's side, the unexpected contact sending shockwaves through me. The figure stepped forward, emerging from the shadows—an older man, his face lined with age and hardship, eyes glinting with a mixture of curiosity and something more sinister.

"Look what we have here," he said, his voice gravelly and layered with menace. "A couple of lost souls, are we?" His gaze flicked between us, lingering on our closeness with a mix of amusement and disdain. I could feel Nathan tense beside me, a wall of solid resolve ready to shield me from whatever danger lurked in the man's gaze.

"We're just leaving," Nathan replied coolly, positioning himself slightly in front of me. I could sense the protective instinct radiating off him, and it both thrilled and irritated me.

"Not so fast," the man drawled, stepping closer. "You've stumbled into something far beyond your understanding."

The words hung in the air, a promise laced with danger, sending a shiver down my spine. The thrill of the chase was morphing into something darker, something that threatened to pull us deeper into the heart of Silverbrook's secrets. I glanced at Nathan, his jaw set in determination, and realized then that I was right in the thick of it—tangled in a web of intrigue and danger that I hadn't asked for but was unable to escape. As our eyes met, a silent agreement passed between us: together, we would confront whatever lay ahead, even if it meant unearthing the secrets lurking in the shadows of our town.

The man's presence hung heavy in the air, tension wrapping around us like a thick fog. His words felt like tendrils of smoke, curling around the remnants of my earlier bravado. I shot a glance at Nathan, who stood resolute, the way a lion would, prepared to protect its territory. "What do you mean by that?" I found myself asking, my voice steadier than I felt. There was something unnerving about the stranger, an aura of familiarity laced with menace that set my instincts on high alert.

"Silverbrook has a history, you see. A history that shouldn't be disturbed," he replied, his smile twisting into something grotesque. "And you two are stirring the pot quite a bit." He took another step closer, eyes narrowing, and I could feel Nathan's body tense beside me, ready to spring into action.

"What do you know about us?" I shot back, my bravado almost masking the tremor in my voice.

The man chuckled, a sound that echoed in the narrow alley, unsettling in its familiarity. "I know enough. This town keeps its secrets hidden, but you've already begun unearthing them, haven't you? You shouldn't be poking around places you don't belong."

"What are you, the town's self-appointed guardian?" Nathan quipped, his tone laced with sarcasm, though I could sense the underlying seriousness in his posture.

"More like a warning," the man countered, not missing a beat. "There are forces at play here that are far beyond your understanding. You tread on dangerous ground."

With a sharp movement, Nathan stepped forward, effectively closing the distance between us and the looming threat. "We're not afraid of you," he said, his voice low but resolute, the protective instinct oozing from every pore.

For a moment, the air crackled with tension, and I held my breath, waiting for the next move in this unexpected standoff. The man's smirk faltered slightly, revealing a glimpse of his own unease before he laughed again, a mirthless sound. "Fear isn't what you need to worry about. It's the consequences of curiosity that will haunt you." With that, he turned, blending back into the shadows like smoke dissipating into the night.

I released a breath I didn't realize I'd been holding, my heart racing. "What the hell was that about?" I asked Nathan, who was still scanning the darkness as if expecting the man to return at any moment.

"I don't know, but we need to get out of here," he replied, the urgency in his tone pulling me from the lingering unease. He reached for my hand, the contact sending an electric thrill up my arm, and we hurried out of the alley, the light of the street illuminating our escape.

As we emerged into the bustling street, the noise enveloped us, a stark contrast to the heavy silence of the alley. People moved about, blissfully unaware of the peril we had just escaped, laughing and chatting, the sounds mingling into a symphony of normalcy. But beneath that veneer, I could still feel the weight of the man's warning pressing down on my shoulders.

"Do you think he was serious?" I asked, glancing at Nathan, who seemed lost in thought.

"About as serious as he looked," he replied, his eyes still scanning the crowd. "Silverbrook has its secrets, but I don't know what they are. What I do know is that we need to be careful."

"Careful," I echoed, mulling over his words. "I thought that was what we were doing." The irony didn't escape me. "How do we even start to figure out what's going on?"

He looked at me then, a flicker of something—was it admiration?—crossing his features. "We keep digging. But we have to be smarter about it. No more wandering into dark alleys alone."

"Fine, no more dark alleys," I conceded, though a part of me was already plotting my next move. "But we can't let this drop, Nathan. Something is happening, and we need to find out what it is."

A small smile crept onto his lips, and for a moment, the tension that had enveloped us lifted. "You're stubborn, you know that?"

"Stubbornness is a virtue in times like these," I shot back, crossing my arms playfully, enjoying the banter that broke through the earlier anxiety.

"Is that what we're calling it now?" He laughed, a warm sound that made the chaos of the day feel momentarily distant. But beneath that laughter lay the current of unease, a reminder that our town was harboring dark secrets we were only beginning to touch.

"Okay, so what's next?" I asked, a renewed sense of purpose surging through me.

"Let's start with the townspeople," Nathan suggested. "You have a knack for talking to people, and if anyone knows what's happening, it's them. Plus, we can figure out who might have seen anything unusual lately."

The idea ignited my spirit. I was ready to dive into the depths of Silverbrook's secrets. "You mean like our own little investigation? I love it! A mystery-solving duo—like a modern-day Sherlock and Watson."

"More like the unprepared and the reluctant," he countered with a smirk, but the light in his eyes told me he was all in.

Chapter 6: Intentions are Everything

We set off, weaving through the streets, the setting sun painting the sky in hues of orange and purple, casting long shadows that seemed to stretch into the unknown. The local diner beckoned, its neon sign flickering like a lighthouse guiding us through the growing darkness. The place was a hub of gossip, and I knew if there were whispers to be heard, they would be here.

Inside, the diner buzzed with life, the scent of fries and milkshakes thick in the air. As we settled into a booth, I scanned the room, my senses attuned to the rhythm of conversation. The laughter of a group of teenagers spilled over from a nearby table, punctuated by the clink of silverware and the sizzle of the kitchen.

"Let's eavesdrop," I whispered, my heart racing with excitement.

Nathan raised an eyebrow but grinned. "You really want to take that route?"

"Desperate times call for desperate measures," I declared, leaning closer to the adjacent table where two older women gossiped animatedly.

"Did you hear about the break-ins?" one of them exclaimed, her voice just loud enough for us to catch snippets of the conversation.

"Oh, and that poor boy, gone without a trace. I just don't understand how this could happen in our town," the other replied, her brow furrowed with concern.

The words sent a shiver down my spine. I exchanged a quick glance with Nathan, the unspoken understanding flashing between us. This was just the beginning, and whatever lay ahead, we would face it together.

As the women's conversation continued, their voices a soothing backdrop to the chaos swirling in my mind, I leaned in closer, my curiosity piqued. The air in the diner buzzed with energy, laughter bouncing off the walls, but all I could focus on were the fragments of gossip floating just within reach.

"Honestly, it's like something out of a horror movie. They say he just disappeared after his shift at the mill," the first woman said, her brow knitted in concern. "I saw him just the day before, right outside the diner. A bright kid, so full of life."

The second woman nodded, her expression darkening. "And it's not just him. They say there are others, too—kids vanishing, no signs, no nothing. It's like they've just... faded away."

A chill crept up my spine, and I instinctively glanced at Nathan, who was studying the women with an intensity that suggested he was also taking mental notes. "What do you think?" I whispered, barely able to contain the excitement bubbling in my chest. "This could be our lead."

"We should find out who they're talking about," he replied quietly, leaning back in the booth and crossing his arms. "But let's not get too hasty. We don't want to raise any alarms."

I nodded, though my mind was already racing ahead. "Maybe if we keep listening, we can learn more about the missing kids. Who knows? We might even discover a connection to the break-ins."

The women's chatter swirled around us like a fog, and I felt as if we were perched on the edge of an unraveling mystery, a secret society of lost stories just waiting to be discovered. I leaned back, feigning disinterest, and sipped my tea, my eyes trained on the women as they continued their discussion, weaving in and out of topics like skilled storytellers.

"But what about that strange man?" the second woman interjected, her voice low. "The one who's been lurking around the mill? I saw him last week, right before Henry disappeared. He looked like he didn't belong."

"Another mystery," the first woman replied, her voice dipping conspiratorially. "You don't think he's connected, do you? They say he's been seen near the old cemetery as well."

A cemetery? My heart raced. There it was, the faintest flicker of a connection, a path to follow. "Did you catch that?" I murmured to Nathan, a sense of urgency igniting my words. "The mill and the cemetery. We need to check them out."

He shot me a glance, a mixture of excitement and caution flickering across his face. "Let's finish up here first. We can't afford to be too obvious."

Just then, a raucous laugh erupted from the group of teenagers nearby, shattering the tension. One of the boys, his hair a riot of curls, leaned back in his chair, animatedly recounting some ridiculous stunt he'd pulled. The girl beside him, wide-eyed and laughing, made a playful jab at his expense. It was a stark reminder of normalcy, of carefree days that felt so distant from the shadows we were navigating.

"Can you believe they'd actually try to scare us with ghost stories?" the girl giggled. "I mean, come on! This is Silverbrook, not a haunted theme park."

"I don't know, maybe we should start believing in ghosts," the boy replied with a smirk. "After all, kids have been disappearing, and nobody seems to know why."

My breath hitched at his words, the casualness of it striking me like a slap. Nathan's eyes darted to mine, and I could see the realization dawning on him too. "We need to leave," he said, urgency creeping back into his voice. "This isn't just idle gossip anymore."

I nodded, adrenaline coursing through me as we slipped out of the booth and made our way toward the exit. As we stepped into the cool evening air, the sounds of the diner faded behind us, leaving only the low hum of streetlights and the distant murmur of the town settling into night.

"What's our next move?" I asked, my heart racing, the thrill of the chase tingling in my fingertips.

"The mill first," Nathan said, glancing around to ensure we weren't being followed. "Then we'll check out the cemetery."

As we walked briskly down the streets of Silverbrook, I couldn't shake the feeling that we were being watched. Shadows clung to the corners of my vision, and the comforting glow of streetlamps suddenly felt inadequate against the encroaching darkness. "Do you ever get the feeling someone's following us?" I said, lowering my voice as we neared the mill.

"Yeah," he replied, his gaze sharp. "Keep your eyes open. We'll be in and out. No lingering."

The mill loomed ahead, its silhouette stark against the darkening sky, the windows dark and vacant, like soulless eyes watching our approach. The rusted machinery outside creaked in the breeze, adding to the sense of foreboding. My stomach twisted in knots, half-excited and half-terrified. What secrets lay hidden within those walls?

Nathan pushed open the heavy door, and we stepped inside, the air thick with dust and memories of labor long past. Shadows danced along the walls, and the faint sound of water trickling somewhere in the distance echoed like a heartbeat.

"Stay close," he murmured, scanning the interior for any signs of life—or the absence of it. The beam of my phone's flashlight flickered as I pointed it toward a series of old crates stacked against the wall. They looked untouched, but something about them seemed off, like they were hiding more than just the passage of time.

"What do you think they were hiding?" I asked, the curiosity in my voice tinged with a hint of dread.

"Maybe clues," he suggested, moving closer to examine them. "Or evidence that connects the disappearances to the break-ins."

I stepped forward, running my fingers over the rough surface of one crate. "Whatever it is, we need to find it before someone else does."

Just then, a noise echoed from the back of the mill—a low, shuffling sound that sent a jolt of adrenaline racing through me. Nathan froze, his posture shifting from curious to defensive. "Did you hear that?" he whispered, his voice barely above a breath.

"Yes," I replied, my heart pounding against my ribs. The sound grew louder, accompanied by a faint scraping, as if something—or someone—was moving closer.

Before I could react, a shadow darted across the back of the room, slipping into a darker corner. Nathan and I exchanged a panicked glance, the tension crackling in the air between us.

"Stay here," he ordered, his voice steady, but I could see the tension in his jaw.

"No way," I shot back, stepping closer to him. "I'm not letting you go alone."

He opened his mouth to protest, but before he could speak, a figure emerged from the darkness, and my breath caught in my throat. It was the man from the alley—the one who had warned us to stay away. His expression was unreadable, his eyes gleaming with something unrecognizable.

"Interesting place you've chosen for your little investigation," he drawled, his tone almost mocking, sending chills racing down my spine.

"Who are you?" I demanded, trying to project confidence I didn't feel.

He smiled, but it didn't reach his eyes. "Just a concerned citizen. But you'd do well to heed my warning."

Before I could retort, Nathan took a protective step forward, positioning himself between me and the man. "What do you want?" he asked, his voice low and menacing.

"More than you can imagine," the man replied, his gaze flicking between us with a predatory gleam. "And time is running out."

The weight of his words hung in the air, thick with unspoken threats and ominous implications. Just as I opened my mouth to respond, a loud crash echoed from deeper within the mill, shaking the very ground beneath us.

The man's smile widened, revealing teeth that glinted in the dim light. "Looks like your little adventure just got a lot more interesting."

Before I could react, he slipped back into the shadows, leaving Nathan and me standing on the precipice of a new and terrifying reality. As the sounds of chaos erupted behind us, I realized we were no longer mere investigators; we were players in a game that could end in tragedy—or something far worse.

Chapter 7: A Night of Revelations

The neon lights of the diner flickered in the chilly air, casting vibrant patterns across the rain-slicked pavement outside. I had come here hoping for a quiet cup of coffee, but instead, I found myself ensnared in a spontaneous stakeout with Nathan, whose very presence stirred a whirlwind of emotions in me. The aroma of sizzling bacon mingled with the scent of freshly brewed coffee, wrapping around us like a warm blanket on this otherwise bleak night.

Our booth was tucked away in a corner, partially obscured by a plastic potted plant that was far too artificial for its own good. I watched him as he leaned back, his elbows resting on the vinyl upholstery, his casual demeanor contrasting sharply with the tension crackling in the air between us. There was something about the way he ran a hand through his tousled hair, a mix of mischief and sincerity that made my heart race in a way I had almost forgotten it could.

"So, tell me again why we're hiding out in a diner?" I asked, my voice teasing, though a thread of seriousness wove through my tone.

Nathan grinned, his blue eyes sparkling with the reflection of the diner's garish lights. "Because," he said, mimicking the tone of a game show host, "the best stakeouts require copious amounts of coffee and an extraordinary amount of patience. Plus, it's all part of my master plan."

"Master plan?" I quirked an eyebrow, crossing my arms as I leaned back in my seat, feigning indifference even as my curiosity piqued.

"Yes, the master plan to catch a glimpse of the elusive Mr. Dawson," he said, leaning in closer, his voice dropping to a conspiratorial whisper. "You know, the one rumored to be involved in—how do they say it?—nefarious activities."

"Right, because hanging out in a diner, drinking coffee, is the best way to catch a criminal," I shot back, rolling my eyes, but unable to suppress the laughter bubbling up inside me. "What's next? A stakeout at the library?"

"Hey, don't knock the library. That's where all the best spies gather," he replied, an easy smirk playing on his lips.

I felt a flutter of something—was it affection or annoyance? Maybe both, tangled together like the strands of our conversation. The bickering felt strangely familiar, comforting even, and I couldn't help but lean closer, my knee brushing against his as I savored the moment. The diner was beginning to feel less like a trap and more like a refuge, a hidden world where we could indulge in witty repartee.

As the hours ticked by, the din of clattering dishes and the soft chatter of other patrons faded into the background. Instead, it was just us, caught in this bubble of shared stories and laughter. I told him about the time my brother attempted to barbecue and almost burned down our backyard, while he regaled me with tales of his overly dramatic cat, who clearly believed she was royalty.

The warmth between us began to grow, thawing the frosty barriers we had erected, the vulnerability in our stories wrapping around us like a gentle embrace. But as I looked into Nathan's eyes, I realized there was more lurking beneath the surface, something unspoken that made my heart race.

Just as the atmosphere shifted, thickening with unacknowledged tension, a sudden commotion erupted outside. The door swung open with a bang, slapping against the wall as a group of teenagers tumbled in, shrieking with laughter and exuberance. The air was instantly filled with their chaotic energy, a whirlwind of youthful exuberance that shattered the intimate moment we had been sharing.

"Is this a diner or a circus?" I muttered, watching the scene unfold with a mixture of amusement and annoyance.

"Looks like our stakeout is compromised," Nathan said, rolling his eyes but unable to hide his smile. "So much for subtlety."

"Maybe they're just trying to liven up the place," I quipped, my eyes darting back to him. "You know, breathe some life into this dimly lit paradise."

"Or they're plotting to start a flash mob," he replied, a glimmer of mischief in his eyes. "I can see it now: 'Dance Like No One's Watching' night at the Good Eats Diner."

We both burst into laughter, the sound mingling with the ruckus around us, and for a moment, it felt like we were the only two people in the world. The laughter came easier now, the weight of our earlier animosity dissipating like smoke on the wind.

But as the laughter faded, I couldn't shake the feeling that beneath the light banter and shared jokes lay something deeper, something unresolved. I wanted to ask him about the things he kept hidden behind that charming façade, the layers that made him more than just the witty guy I had initially dismissed.

I hesitated, my heart pounding in my chest. "Hey, Nathan—"

Before I could finish, the diner's bell jingled again, and a familiar figure walked in, his face shadowed by a hood. My heart dropped as recognition surged through me. The man who had been the subject of our stakeout stood just inside the door, glancing around with a calculating gaze.

"Stay low," Nathan whispered, his voice a hushed urgency that sent a thrill down my spine.

The atmosphere shifted once more, the lightheartedness vanishing, replaced by a sense of purpose and danger. I ducked instinctively, pressing myself against the booth, my heart racing as Nathan's shoulder brushed against mine. I could feel the heat radiating from him, an electric connection that pulsed in the air around us.

"What do we do now?" I breathed, my pulse quickening as the man scanned the room.

"Wait," Nathan said, his eyes locked on the intruder, determination etched on his features. "Just wait."

In that moment, I felt the fragile truce we had built begin to crack under the weight of reality. This was more than just a night of shared stories and laughter. This was a night of revelations, and I wasn't sure if I was ready for the truths that lay ahead.

I barely had time to catch my breath before the man inside the diner made his move. With a casualness that belied the tension in the air, he strolled toward the counter, glancing over his shoulder as if he could sense our eyes tracking him. I shifted, pressing my back against the wall of the booth as if it could provide some sort of invisible shield. My heart raced not just from the adrenaline of the moment but from the realization of what was unfolding.

Nathan's grip tightened on the edge of the table, and I could feel the heat radiating from him, a silent promise that we were in this together. "He's definitely not just here for the pancakes," he murmured, his gaze flicking between me and the stranger.

"What do you think he's doing?" I whispered, straining to keep my voice steady. The man's demeanor suggested he was no ordinary diner-goer; he surveyed the room with a predator's precision, his eyes glinting with purpose.

"Looks like he's waiting for someone," Nathan replied, his voice low, every word laced with intent. "We can't let him see us. If this is about what I think it is, we're in deep."

"Deep?" I echoed, trying to suppress the flutter of fear mingling with excitement. "As in 'possible criminal conspiracy' deep or 'I-need-a-cup-of-coffee-to-deal-with-this' deep?"

"More like 'why-did-I-ever-think-this-was-a-good-idea' deep," he said, his smirk breaking through the tension. I couldn't help but roll my eyes at his attempt to lighten the mood.

Just then, the man's head turned sharply in our direction, and I ducked instinctively, heart pounding against my ribcage like a frantic drum. I glanced at Nathan, whose expression had shifted from playful to intensely focused. "I think he saw us," I breathed, barely keeping my voice from shaking.

"Not yet. Just stay calm," he whispered, shifting slightly to block my view as we both sank lower into the booth. The world outside faded, and it was just us in our little pocket of reality, the atmosphere thickening with unspoken words.

The stranger approached the counter and leaned in to speak with the waitress, a friendly woman with a ready smile that didn't seem to reach her eyes. I caught snippets of their conversation, the undertones of urgency threading through her responses. She glanced around, her gaze flicking nervously toward us before she returned to him. Whatever this was about, it had escalated beyond simple diner chit-chat.

"Are you always this calm under pressure?" I quipped, desperately trying to hold on to that semblance of levity, even as the fear tinged my voice.

"Only when my life is in danger," Nathan replied, an eyebrow raised. His playful tone was a thin veneer over the tension that had us both on edge.

As the stranger stepped away from the counter, I could see something metallic glinting in his hand—a cell phone, perhaps? The thought sent a chill down my spine. What kind of call would he be making in a place like this?

"Do you think we should—" I began, but the words hung in the air, heavy with the weight of our precarious situation.

"I think we should just sit tight and observe," Nathan interjected, his eyes never leaving the stranger. "If he's dangerous, we don't want to draw attention."

I nodded, my pulse quickening as the man settled into a booth not far from us, but still too far to overhear anything. I felt a rush of frustration at the world's timing. Just as we had been slipping into a comfortable rhythm, this chaos erupted, shattering the fragile connection we had forged.

The diner felt like a stage, the fluorescent lights casting harsh shadows on our little drama. The clinking of forks and knives blended with hushed whispers and the sizzle of the grill. Outside, the rain fell steadily, a soft drumming that seemed to mock our predicament.

"Do you think he's waiting for someone important?" I whispered, trying to keep my voice low as I risked a glance at Nathan.

"Or someone who owes him money," he replied, his brow furrowing. "I don't like this. We need to figure out what he's up to."

With that, Nathan stood up slightly, pretending to stretch as he casually turned to get a better view. I held my breath, heart hammering as he edged closer to the edge of our booth, careful not to attract the stranger's attention. The tension crackled around us, and I felt a rush of exhilaration mixed with the palpable danger lurking just out of sight.

"Tell me if you see anything," I urged, gripping the edge of the booth as if it could anchor me to sanity.

Nathan nodded, his focus unwavering. "I will. Just stay close."

The seconds felt like hours as we observed the man, his phone glued to his ear, speaking in a hushed tone. The flicker of his eyes darting around the diner made me uneasy. He was waiting for someone—someone who might change everything.

Then, as if the universe had decided to up the ante, the bell above the diner door jingled again, and another figure stepped inside. My breath hitched in my throat. The newcomer was cloaked in a long trench coat, the collar turned up against the drizzle outside. There was something familiar about the way they moved, a confidence that turned heads as they walked toward the stranger's booth.

"Do you know them?" I whispered urgently, my eyes wide as I focused on the scene unfolding before us.

Nathan shook his head, his expression grave. "I can't tell. But this doesn't look good."

As the trench-coated figure slid into the booth opposite the man, they exchanged terse words, their body language tense and loaded. I leaned closer to Nathan, instincts kicking in, wanting to catch every whispered syllable that might spill secrets in this diner cloaked in shadow.

"Should we intervene?" I whispered, adrenaline coursing through my veins.

"Not yet," he replied, his gaze sharp. "Let's see what they're discussing. We might be able to gather some intel."

As I watched, the atmosphere thickened, the stakes rising as the two figures leaned closer, sharing words that could change the course of our night. The world outside faded further, the diner becoming a microcosm of intrigue, danger, and perhaps unexpected alliances. I felt the gravity of the moment settle in the pit of my stomach, an electric thrill of possibility.

The tension, the mystery, and the unexpected entanglement of our lives had turned this stakeout into something far more than I had bargained for, igniting a spark that threatened to set the entire night ablaze.

The trench-coated figure leaned in closer, their voice dropping to a conspiratorial whisper as the two exchanged furtive glances. My heart pounded against my ribs, each beat resonating like a drum heralding some impending revelation. Nathan's grip tightened on the edge of the booth, the intensity of his focus palpable as he scrutinized every movement, every flicker of expression that passed between the strangers.

"What do you think they're talking about?" I asked, my voice barely above a whisper, my curiosity battling the unease coiling in my stomach.

"Whatever it is, it's serious," Nathan replied, his voice low and steady. "If they're meeting here, it's not just casual chit-chat."

The air crackled with tension, the atmosphere around us thickening like the syrup on the diner's pancakes. The world outside faded into a dull hum, reduced to mere background noise as we became engrossed in this clandestine exchange. I could feel the heat radiating from Nathan, a comforting presence amid the uncertainty.

Suddenly, the trench-coated figure leaned back, their demeanor shifting from conspiratorial to confrontational. "You told me this would be safe," they hissed, their voice sharp enough to cut through the thick air. "I don't like being exposed like this."

The man in the booth shrugged, his expression unreadable. "The diner's the last place anyone would look for us. Just keep your voice down."

A bead of sweat trickled down my spine. The urgency in their words hinted at something more than just casual banter, something layered with risk and danger. I leaned in closer, straining to catch every word. "What are you involved in?" I murmured to Nathan, trying to keep my panic in check.

"I'm not sure, but it's definitely not good," he replied, his eyes narrowing as he focused on the scene unfolding before us.

Before I could respond, the waitress approached, her cheerful smile in stark contrast to the charged atmosphere. "Can I get you two anything else? More coffee? A slice of pie?"

"Uh, we're good!" I blurted, flashing a grin that felt more like a grimace. I didn't want to draw attention, not now, not when we were teetering on the edge of something potentially explosive.

"Right. Just let me know," she said, her gaze lingering for a moment too long before she moved on to another table.

As soon as she walked away, the tension snapped back into place. The trench-coated figure continued to glower at the man, their frustration palpable. "You promised me anonymity. If anyone sees me here..." They trailed off, their eyes darting nervously to the windows as if the shadows themselves might betray them.

"Relax," the man replied, a sly grin spreading across his face. "No one's going to recognize you. Just stick to the plan, and we'll be out of this mess before you know it."

The promise of a plan sent my mind racing. If they had a plan, it meant they were up to something—a plot swirling in the air like the steam from the coffee cups on our table. I glanced at Nathan, who looked equally apprehensive. "What do we do?" I whispered, feeling the weight of the situation pressing down on us.

"We wait and listen. We need more information," he said, determination lighting his eyes. "We can't just walk away from this. It might lead us to something big."

"Like what? A criminal organization?" I asked, the incredulity creeping into my tone. "What are we, amateur detectives now?"

"Maybe it's time we embrace our inner sleuth," he teased, but the seriousness in his gaze was unmistakable.

As the strangers continued their hushed conversation, the trench-coated figure leaned closer, their voice lowering to an urgent murmur. "We don't have much time. If this goes south, it's not just my neck on the line."

At that moment, I felt a shiver run through me, a visceral understanding that we were teetering on the brink of something monumental. The stakes had never felt higher, the atmosphere laden with possibilities and dangers that were just out of reach.

Then, as if the universe had decided to throw another wrench into our already chaotic night, the door swung open once more. The clatter of heavy boots echoed through the diner, and my heart sank as a group of men stepped inside, their presence a jarring contrast to the warm, cozy atmosphere. They were dressed in dark jackets, their expressions stern and unyielding, the kind of look that made the hairs on the back of my neck stand on end.

"Great," Nathan muttered under his breath. "Just what we need—more trouble."

I barely had time to process his words before one of the men locked eyes with me, a flash of recognition igniting in his gaze. I felt my breath hitch, an instinctive urge to shrink back, to disappear into the booth as if I could become one with the vinyl seat. Nathan's body shifted, instinctively positioning himself in front of me, a protective barrier against whatever was coming.

"What are they doing here?" I whispered, my voice a thread of panic. "Do you think they're with him?"

"Only one way to find out," he replied, his voice steady, but I could see the tension radiating from him, a taut string ready to snap.

The men moved through the diner with purpose, their eyes scanning the room like hunters on the prowl. I could feel the air shift, the dynamic morphing into something darker and more dangerous. The trench-coated figure's demeanor changed instantaneously, their confident facade crumbling into something more vulnerable as they glanced at the newcomers with a mixture of fear and trepidation.

The man in the booth, however, seemed unfazed, his smirk widening as if he had expected this confrontation all along. "Well, well," he said, his voice dripping with sarcasm. "Look who decided to join the party."

The tension escalated as the new arrivals stopped near their booth, their leader crossing his arms and leaning in, a predatory gleam in his eye. "You thought you could pull this off without us noticing?" he hissed, the threat lacing his words palpable. "You've put us all at risk."

"Relax, it's all under control," the man replied, though his bravado was quickly crumbling under the weight of their collective scrutiny.

I exchanged a frantic glance with Nathan, the weight of uncertainty pressing down on us like a heavy fog. The stakes were rising, and every instinct screamed at me that we were caught in a web of deception and danger, our lives hanging in the balance.

"Should we—" I began, but Nathan cut me off with a sharp glance, his expression a mix of determination and caution.

Suddenly, the trench-coated figure reached for something hidden beneath their coat, their movements swift and sudden. "You don't understand," they said, their voice a frantic whisper. "I have what you're looking for."

And just like that, the atmosphere shifted once more, the air thick with anticipation as the diner fell into a tense silence, all eyes drawn to the impending confrontation. I held my breath, the world around me fading into the background as I realized that whatever happened next would change everything.

In that moment, I knew we were at the precipice of discovery, a cliffhanger poised to plunge us into the unknown.

Chapter 8: Shadows Deepen

The night was thick with tension as I stood in the flickering light of my living room, the shadows creeping along the walls like whispers of secrets yet to be revealed. The faint aroma of freshly brewed coffee mingled with the metallic tang of anxiety that hung in the air, a cocktail of comfort and dread. I turned the small, well-worn mug in my hands, the heat radiating against my palms, grounding me even as my mind raced with questions.

Nathan was due to arrive any minute. The last few days had felt like a whirlwind of chaos and connection, an intoxicating blend that both exhilarated and terrified me. It had begun with a simple break-in at my neighbor's house—one that had spiraled into a series of baffling incidents, each more perplexing than the last. Cryptic notes had been left behind, scrawled in uneven handwriting, like the frantic thoughts of a mind teetering on the edge of sanity. They were taunts, really, snippets of riddles that hinted at something darker lurking in the shadows, playing with us like a cat with a mouse.

As the clock ticked steadily toward the hour of his arrival, I found my thoughts drifting back to Nathan. He was a paradox wrapped in mystery—brimming with confidence yet haunted by something I couldn't quite decipher. The way he spoke made my heart race, his voice a warm baritone that felt like a soothing balm against my frayed nerves. But there was an intensity in his gaze that often sent a shiver down my spine, as if he were trying to peel away the layers of my guarded exterior.

The sound of gravel crunching underfoot drew me from my reverie. I peered out the window and caught sight of him striding up the path, the moonlight illuminating his tousled hair and the determined set of his jaw. My pulse quickened. I couldn't decide if I was more eager or anxious; perhaps both were blending into an irresistible cocktail of emotions. I hurriedly set the mug down, half-expecting it to spill, and opened the door before he could knock.

"Hey," he said, flashing that disarming smile that made my insides flutter. "Ready to crack this case wide open?"

"Ready as I'll ever be," I replied, forcing a playful grin even as my heart thudded like a drum in my chest. I stepped aside to let him in, trying to ignore the way his presence filled the room with an energy I couldn't quite name.

He scanned the space, his brow furrowing slightly. "You should really get some curtains," he remarked, his tone teasing. "You know, for when the shadows start to creep in."

"Isn't that part of the charm?" I shot back, unable to hide my amusement. "A little drama keeps things interesting."

"Interesting is one word for it," he said, raising an eyebrow, the corners of his mouth tugging upward in a way that made my heart skip. "How about we get to work?"

I led him to my small kitchen table, which had become our makeshift headquarters. Scattered across its surface were our notes, the remnants of our late-night brainstorming sessions. The dim light cast an almost theatrical glow on the scattered papers, each one holding fragments of the puzzle we were desperate to solve. Nathan leaned over the table, the tension palpable as he scrutinized the notes, his brow furrowed in concentration.

"Okay, let's review what we've got," he said, tapping a finger against one of the notes. "This one—'The past always returns, like an unwelcome guest.' What do you think it means?"

"Something personal, maybe?" I offered, my mind racing back to the shadows lurking in our lives. "Something that connects to whoever is behind this?"

He nodded, his eyes narrowing thoughtfully. "Could be. And this one, 'Look beyond the light to find the truth.' It's almost poetic, but it feels like a threat. Like they want us to dig deeper."

"Or to scare us away," I countered, crossing my arms as unease crept into my gut. "What if they know we're onto them?"

"Then we can't back down," he said, his voice firm, igniting a flicker of determination in me. "We have to find out who this is before they escalate things."

My heart raced at the prospect. It felt reckless and dangerous, but the thrill of the chase tugged at something deep within me. I didn't want to admit it, but the idea of diving into this mystery with Nathan felt more intoxicating than terrifying. The danger sparked something wild in me, a desire for adventure that I hadn't realized had been dormant for so long.

Before I could respond, the phone rang, slicing through the charged atmosphere like a bolt of lightning. I hesitated, glancing at the caller ID. It was my neighbor, the one whose home had been broken into. Anxiety coiled in my stomach as I answered, "Hello?"

Her voice trembled on the other end, panic threading through her words. "You have to help me. I think they're back."

My heart sank. Shadows were deepening, and as I exchanged glances with Nathan, I could see the flicker of fear reflected in his eyes. We were in this together, bound by the perilous path ahead. Whatever game was being played, it was no longer just a puzzle—it was a dangerous dance, and I was determined to lead.

"Are you sure?" I asked, the phone pressed tightly against my ear as a chill slithered down my spine. My neighbor's voice quivered like a fragile note played on a worn-out violin. "I thought they were gone, but I heard something outside. It felt... wrong."

Nathan shot me a questioning look, the kind that begged for clarity, and I nodded, trying to maintain my composure despite the urgency thrumming in the air. "Just stay inside and lock the door," I instructed, my tone firm as if that could somehow shield her from the unknown. "We'll be right over."

As I hung up, I felt the weight of dread settle in my chest, heavy and oppressive. "We need to go," I said, glancing at Nathan, whose expression was a mix of determination and concern.

"Do you think it's safe?" he asked, his eyes scanning the room, taking in every shadow as if it might spring to life at any moment.

I wanted to tell him that we had to be brave, that we had already plunged into this murky world together, but the reality of the situation weighed heavily on my heart. "We can't just sit here and wait," I replied, steeling myself against the fear that threatened to seep into my bones. "She needs us."

We grabbed our jackets and slipped out into the night, the air crisp and charged with the electricity of impending rain. The streetlights flickered, casting ghostly shadows on the pavement, as if they, too, were wary of the darkness encroaching upon us. As we walked, the rhythmic crunch of gravel beneath our feet echoed in the silence, amplifying the tension that had settled between us.

"Do you really think it's connected to the break-ins?" Nathan asked, breaking the silence, his breath visible in the cool air.

"It has to be," I replied, my voice steady despite the unease swirling within me. "These notes, the break-ins, now this—there's a thread connecting all of it, and I'm not sure if it's a lifeline or a noose."

"Either way, it's something we need to unravel," he said, his tone resolute. "Just remember to stick together, okay? No heroic acts without backup."

I chuckled lightly, grateful for the brief reprieve from the tension. "What, you think I'd charge in like a knight in shining armor? Please, I prefer my armor a bit more... comfortable."

He laughed, a sound that felt like warmth in the encroaching cold, but it quickly faded as we approached my neighbor's house. The porch light flickered sporadically, casting eerie shadows that danced along the walls. I felt an unsettling sensation in the pit of my stomach, a premonition that we were stepping into something far darker than we'd anticipated.

We crept closer, our footsteps muffled by the thick carpet of fallen leaves that crunched underfoot. I glanced at Nathan, who nodded as if sensing my unease. Together, we made our way to the front door, which hung slightly ajar, a gaping mouth that whispered of secrets waiting to be uncovered.

"On three," Nathan murmured, his voice barely above a whisper. "One, two—"

We pushed the door open and stepped inside. The living room was dimly lit, casting an otherworldly glow on the furniture, and for a moment, I felt like we had stepped into a painting, frozen in time. My neighbor's silhouette appeared in the doorway, trembling and wide-eyed.

"There's something in the back," she breathed, pointing towards the darkened hallway that seemed to stretch endlessly. "I saw something move..."

"Stay here," I instructed, my voice steady despite the storm of anxiety swirling inside me. I couldn't let her fear infect me; I had to be strong. I gestured for Nathan to follow, and together we ventured deeper into the house, the air thick with anticipation and dread.

Each step echoed like a drumbeat in my ears as we approached the kitchen. Shadows flickered at the edges of our vision, dancing in and out of the light, teasing us with their elusive forms. I caught Nathan's gaze; it was filled with a mixture of determination and unspoken questions.

We entered the kitchen cautiously, the faint smell of something acrid lingering in the air. The back door was slightly ajar, swinging gently with the wind, revealing the dark backyard beyond. "Did you leave that open?" Nathan asked, his voice barely above a whisper.

"No," I replied, my heart racing. "I always lock it."

The hairs on the back of my neck stood on end as I felt an invisible presence creeping up behind me, a shadow lurking just out of sight. "Let's check outside," I suggested, even though every instinct screamed for me to turn back. The thrill of danger tinged with dread made my blood rush; it was both terrifying and intoxicating.

We stepped onto the porch, the chill of the night air hitting us like a wave. The backyard was shrouded in darkness, the trees standing like sentinels, their branches swaying gently in the breeze. I squinted, trying to make out any movement, but the world felt still, as if holding its breath in anticipation.

"I don't like this," Nathan murmured, his eyes scanning the shadows. "It feels too quiet."

"Yeah, but quiet can be good, right?" I attempted to joke, forcing a lightness that felt brittle.

Just then, a rustling noise broke the silence, echoing from the far corner of the yard. My heart raced as I turned toward the sound, adrenaline flooding my veins. "Did you hear that?"

"Of course," he replied, his voice low and steady. "Let's check it out, but stay close."

We moved cautiously toward the sound, tension coiling between us like a taut string ready to snap. Each step felt like a gamble, the ground beneath our feet unstable. The rustling grew louder, a mix of leaves and branches, and I could feel my pulse quickening, a crescendo of fear and anticipation.

As we approached the edge of the yard, the darkness shifted, and in a sudden flash, a figure darted into view, only to vanish behind the old oak tree. My breath hitched in my throat. "Did you see that?"

"Yeah," Nathan said, his voice barely a whisper. "Let's go."

We moved together, my heart hammering in my chest, the stakes soaring higher with each passing moment. The night had become a canvas of uncertainty, and whatever we were about to uncover felt like it would change everything.

The figure darted behind the oak, its movements too quick for my eyes to catch. My breath caught in my throat, a mixture of fear and curiosity igniting a primal instinct to chase after it. "Did you see that?" I whispered, half-expecting Nathan to reassure me that it was just a trick of the night. Instead, his gaze was sharp, assessing.

"Yeah, I saw it," he said, his voice steady. "Let's be smart about this. We don't know who—or what—we're dealing with."

"Right, because I'd hate to end up as an episode of a crime documentary," I replied, trying to infuse humor into my jittery nerves, though my heart hammered against my ribcage like a frantic bird trying to escape its cage.

We crept closer to the tree, every rustle of leaves and crack of twigs beneath our feet sounding like thunder. The yard seemed to stretch into a vast abyss, where shadows twisted into phantom shapes that threatened to swallow us whole. I stole a glance at Nathan, whose jaw was set, determination etched into every line of his face. The man had a way of making danger feel like an adventure, even as my instincts screamed at me to retreat.

"On the count of three," he said, glancing at me with a serious expression. "One, two—"

Before we could reach three, a sudden, low growl erupted from behind the tree, making me freeze. My heart plummeted into my stomach. "Did you hear that?"

"Yeah," Nathan said, the bravado in his voice replaced with palpable tension. "And it doesn't sound like a friendly dog."

Without waiting for another second, I whispered, "Maybe we should go back inside." The thought of whatever was lurking in the shadows filled me with dread, but my feet felt glued to the ground.

Just then, a shape emerged, and I gasped as a feral cat leaped into view, its eyes gleaming like emeralds in the moonlight. Nathan let out a breath of relief, and I couldn't help but laugh at the absurdity of it all. "You're telling me I nearly wet my pants over a cat?"

"Hey, it's not just any cat. That thing could take on a bear," he joked, his eyes sparkling with mischief.

My laughter faded, replaced by the awareness that we still had a job to do. "Let's not get distracted. We're here for a reason," I said, squaring my shoulders as I stepped further into the yard.

We approached the oak tree, careful not to make sudden movements. Nathan glanced around, his instincts finely tuned to the environment. "Stay close to me," he said, his voice a low rumble that sent a shiver down my spine.

I couldn't help but admire his courage. There was something magnetic about him—a pull that made me want to be closer, even when the danger felt palpable. Together, we rounded the tree, our eyes scanning the darkness, searching for anything out of the ordinary.

A rustling noise came from the bushes nearby, and I stiffened. "What was that?"

"Probably just the wind," Nathan replied, though his eyes narrowed as he peered into the underbrush. The tension in the air thickened, wrapping around us like a tightly drawn noose. "Or maybe it's our friend again."

Before I could reply, a flash of movement caught my attention—a figure slipping through the shadows like a ghost. "There!" I exclaimed, pointing toward the movement, my heart racing again.

"Let's go!" Nathan urged, darting toward the shadow. It was an instinct born from adrenaline and the thrill of the chase, a reckless abandon that seemed to bind us together in this moment. We sprinted, the wind whipping past us, drowning out the sound of our footsteps.

As we reached the edge of the yard, I spotted the figure once more, a silhouette flitting through the trees, its movements graceful yet hurried. I had a fleeting impression of dark clothing and a flash of something metallic before it disappeared deeper into the woods.

"Nathan!" I shouted, but he was already a step ahead, vaulting over a fallen log in a single bound. I followed, my heart pounding in my chest as we plunged into the thicket, the underbrush clawing at my legs.

"Where are you?" I called into the thickening shadows, my voice echoing back like a haunting reminder of our pursuit.

"Keep moving!" he yelled back, his urgency slicing through the dark as he led the charge. We pushed forward, branches snapping beneath our feet, the forest coming alive around us. The cool air was rich with the scent of damp earth and pine, grounding me amidst the chaos.

Suddenly, Nathan halted, raising a hand. I skidded to a stop beside him, breathless and confused. "What's wrong?" I whispered.

"Listen," he said, straining to hear. The silence was thick, an almost palpable thing that draped over us like a heavy blanket. My pulse raced as I focused, hearing only the distant call of an owl and the rustling of leaves.

Then, a voice pierced the stillness—low and menacing, like gravel scraping against metal. "You shouldn't have come here."

My stomach dropped as the words washed over me, chilling my blood. We were being watched.

Nathan's grip tightened on my arm as he pulled me behind a thick tree trunk, our bodies pressing against the rough bark. "Who is that?" I barely managed to whisper, my voice quaking with fear.

"I don't know, but we can't stick around to find out," he replied, urgency lacing his words.

Just as we turned to escape, the voice called out again, this time louder, sharper. "You're playing a dangerous game, and you don't even know the rules."

The weight of those words hung heavy in the air, an ominous warning that sent a shiver down my spine. I could feel the heat radiating off Nathan as he shifted, his protective nature flaring to life.

"Run," he commanded, and we took off, sprinting through the underbrush, branches whipping against our skin as we tore through the darkness. The weight of unseen eyes bore down on us, the tension electrifying the air.

With every stride, I could feel the stakes rising higher, the danger palpable in the atmosphere. Whatever was lurking in the shadows was relentless, and I knew that we were far from safe. Just as we reached the edge of the woods, the world around us erupted into chaos—a figure lunged from the darkness, colliding with Nathan and sending us both sprawling to the ground.

The last thing I saw was Nathan's face, a mix of determination and fear, as the shadow closed in, darkness swallowing us whole.

Chapter 9: Tangled in the Web

The musty scent of old paper hung in the air, a potent mix of history and neglect that sent shivers down my spine. Sunlight streamed through the tall windows of the library, illuminating motes of dust that danced like spirits in the warm glow. I glanced at Nathan, his brow furrowed in concentration as he sifted through the brittle pages of a ledger that looked as if it hadn't been opened in decades. The tension crackled around us, a palpable energy that made it hard to focus solely on the task at hand. It felt as if every word we read pulled us deeper into a story woven with intrigue and tragedy—a narrative that was about to entwine our fates.

"Here," Nathan said, his voice barely above a whisper, yet it sliced through the quiet like a bolt of lightning. He pointed to a passage, and I leaned in closer, our shoulders brushing in a way that sent a delightful jolt through me. "This talks about a family—the Hargroves—who lived here before our time. Their property was seized during the land disputes of the late 1800s. There's something... ominous about this." He met my gaze, and I could see the flicker of determination behind his dark eyes.

The mention of the Hargroves sent a shiver of recognition through me. I had heard whispers from my grandmother about a family that had vanished without a trace, their disappearance shrouded in the fabric of local lore. "What if their legacy is somehow connected to the break-ins? What if someone is trying to unearth their buried secrets?" My voice trembled with a mix of excitement and dread.

"Or maybe," Nathan suggested, his voice low and conspiratorial, "someone wants to keep those secrets buried." His words hung heavy in the air, each syllable pulsing with the weight of unspoken fears. The atmosphere shifted, thickening with the realization that we were unraveling something far more significant than we had anticipated.

A chill crept down my spine, but I couldn't suppress the thrill that ran through me at the prospect of adventure.

We poured over the records, ink and dust intertwining in a chaotic dance. Page after page revealed fragments of a story—marriages, land grants, and a bitter feud that had once divided the community. But it was the mention of the 'curse of the Hargroves' that truly caught my attention. My heart raced as I read aloud, "It is said that the Hargrove lineage was tainted by betrayal, and those who sought their land would face misfortune until justice was served."

"Now that's dramatic," Nathan smirked, the corners of his mouth curling into a playful grin. "What's next? A ghost appearing at midnight to curse the unworthy?" His attempt at levity only partly masked the tension coiling in my stomach. "But seriously, what if this curse is why people are breaking in? They could be searching for something they believe will lift it."

"Or they could be trying to bury the truth," I countered, my mind racing with possibilities. "What if the break-ins are just the tip of the iceberg? There's got to be something more behind this, something that someone is willing to kill to keep hidden." The weight of our discovery pressed on me, a heavy mantle that I was not yet ready to bear.

Nathan leaned back in his chair, his expression shifting from playful to serious. "We need to dig deeper. Let's find out more about the Hargrove family and the circumstances surrounding their disappearance." His determination ignited something within me—a spark that urged me forward into the unknown.

We spent hours poring over more records, uncovering snippets of information that painted a picture of a once-thriving family living in the shadow of a bitter feud. The town had thrived on the bones of its history, but we were now chasing shadows. With every entry, the air thickened with unanswered questions, and the tension between us escalated, crackling like static electricity. Nathan's intensity was magnetic, and I found myself caught between the thrill of discovery and an undeniable attraction.

"Do you think anyone else knows about the Hargroves?" I asked, breaking the heavy silence. "Someone must have uncovered these secrets before."

"Or tried to bury them," he replied, a shadow flickering across his face. "People don't like to talk about the past, especially when it's filled with pain." He shifted closer, and I could feel the warmth radiating from him, a comforting presence amid the weight of our findings. "But we can't let fear silence us. We owe it to the Hargroves to uncover the truth."

I nodded, my heart racing not just from the thrill of the chase, but also from being so close to him. The moment felt charged, as if the universe had momentarily paused to watch us breathe, share, and consider what lay ahead. "Then let's do this," I said, the determination in my voice surprising even myself. "We'll find out what really happened."

With renewed vigor, we dove back into the records, our minds a whirl of theories and speculations. I could hardly concentrate, though, with the brush of Nathan's arm against mine igniting a fire within me. Each fleeting touch felt electric, heightening my senses as we worked side by side, piecing together fragments of history.

As we sifted through the records, I caught snippets of conversation from the librarians nearby, their hushed voices buzzing like bees around a hive. "Did you hear about the old Hargrove place? Rumor has it, it's been vandalized again," one murmured, her tone laced with intrigue. "People say it's haunted."

"Haunted or cursed," the other replied, "the only thing I know is that it's a place best avoided." The weight of their words settled over me like a heavy fog, intensifying my curiosity.

"What if we visit the Hargrove place?" Nathan suggested, his eyes brightening with excitement. "It could hold more clues about what we're dealing with."

The thought sent a thrill through me, a mix of fear and exhilaration. "Are you crazy? That place is a death trap!" I shot back, a grin breaking through my mock protest. "But then again, what's the worst that could happen? A ghost might leap out and tell us all their secrets."

"Or we could stumble upon a hidden treasure," Nathan countered, his expression turning serious, yet a playful glint danced in his eyes. "Besides, what's an adventure without a little risk?"

I had to admit, there was something appealing about the idea of storming into the unknown with Nathan by my side. The connection we were forming felt undeniable, a force pulling us closer with every challenge we faced. And as the afternoon sun dipped lower in the sky, casting long shadows through the library's windows, I knew that whatever lay ahead, I wanted him beside me, ready to unravel the mysteries that held us captive.

The sun dipped below the horizon, painting the sky in a riot of orange and purple hues, and I felt as if we were on the brink of something monumental. With each clue we unearthed, it became increasingly clear that the shadows of the past were not merely relics of history but living entities, entwined with the fabric of our present. Nathan's presence beside me felt both grounding and exhilarating, an anchor amidst the swirling storm of our discoveries.

As we exited the library, the crisp evening air wrapped around us like a cool embrace, washing away the mustiness that clung to our clothes. The streetlights flickered on, casting pools of light that illuminated the cobblestone path leading to the Hargrove property. A shiver ran down my spine as I glanced at the overgrown garden—wild and unkempt, it spoke of neglect and secrets buried deep within its tangled roots.

"Are you ready for this?" Nathan asked, his tone light, yet I could sense the seriousness beneath it. He looked at me with an intensity that made my heart flutter, a mixture of excitement and apprehension reflected in his gaze.

I hesitated, feeling a cocktail of fear and thrill bubble in my stomach. "Ready as I'll ever be, I suppose. Just remember, if we get chased by a ghost, it's every man for himself," I replied, forcing a grin despite the trepidation brewing inside me.

"Great plan. I'll distract the ghost while you make a run for it," he quipped, laughter dancing in his voice. It eased the tension, if only slightly, and I took a deep breath, steeling myself for whatever lay ahead.

As we approached the property, the air grew thick with an eerie stillness, broken only by the rustling leaves and the occasional creak of the old wooden gate. The house loomed before us, a shadow of its former self. Once grand, it now stood as a testament to decay, its windows like dark, hollow eyes staring into our souls. I could feel the weight of history pressing against me, urging me to turn back, yet the pull of the unknown was far too compelling.

"This is it," Nathan whispered, more to himself than to me. He stepped forward, and I followed, our footsteps muffled by the thick carpet of fallen leaves that blanketed the ground. A part of me wanted to grab his hand, to feel that connection solidify against the encroaching darkness, but another part whispered caution, reminding me of the mystery that lay ahead.

The front door hung ajar, a gaping mouth that invited us in. Nathan exchanged a glance with me, his expression both reassuring and resolute. "Shall we?" he asked, an eyebrow raised in challenge.

"Only if you promise to keep the ghost at bay," I replied, my voice wavering slightly. I stepped into the foyer, the air inside thick and stale, like a secret waiting to be unearthed. Shadows danced along the walls, flickering in the dim light that spilled through cracked windows.

"Hello? Any spirits home?" Nathan called out, a playful lilt to his voice that did little to mask the tension. I rolled my eyes, half-amused and half-anxious, and together we ventured further into the heart of the house.

The interior was a labyrinth of dust-covered furniture and faded photographs. Framed portraits lined the walls, capturing moments frozen in time—faces with solemn expressions that seemed to watch our every move. I couldn't shake the feeling that we were intruding, unwelcome guests in a home that had long since turned its back on the world.

"Look at this," Nathan said, his voice barely above a whisper as he pointed to a small table tucked away in a corner. An old, leather-bound book sat there, its cover cracked and worn, as if it had been neglected for years. I approached cautiously, the air thickening with anticipation.

As I reached for the book, a sudden sound echoed through the room—a creak from the floorboards above. My heart raced, and I shot a glance at Nathan, whose eyes were wide with surprise. "Did you hear that?" I asked, my voice low.

"Yeah," he replied, scanning the dimly lit space. "Maybe it's just the house settling... or maybe it's the ghost trying to make a dramatic entrance." He attempted a lighthearted chuckle, but it fell flat against the backdrop of our increasing anxiety.

"Let's not stick around to find out," I suggested, a nervous smile on my face as I flipped open the book. The pages were filled with handwritten notes and sketches, revealing a tapestry of the Hargrove family's history—weddings, births, and even hints of the feud that had ultimately led to their downfall. As I read, a chill crept up my spine, and the hairs on my arms stood on end.

"They were trying to protect something," I murmured, the words slipping from my lips as I flipped through the pages. "It's all in here—the names of those involved in the disputes, the losses they suffered... it's as if they knew danger was coming."

Nathan leaned closer, his breath warm against my neck, igniting a spark of something I could barely comprehend. "So, it wasn't just about land. It was about legacy... and betrayal," he said, his voice hushed, as if fearing to disturb the spirits that lingered in the shadows.

My eyes widened as I turned a page, revealing a faded drawing of the house, scrawled with the words "Cursed by Betrayal." "There it is again," I breathed, the weight of those words crashing over us like a wave. "What if this really is a curse? What if those who sought to claim this land are doomed to suffer the consequences of their greed?"

"Or perhaps it's a warning," Nathan suggested, his brow furrowing in thought. "A call to action for someone willing to listen."

Just then, a loud crash echoed from the upper floor, sending us both stumbling back. My heart raced, the blood pounding in my ears. "Okay, that definitely wasn't the house settling," I gasped, adrenaline surging through me.

"Maybe we should investigate?" Nathan said, his voice a mixture of excitement and apprehension.

"Right, because walking into a potential haunted death trap is a brilliant idea," I retorted, my pulse racing. Yet, as I looked into his eyes, I knew I couldn't turn back. This was the moment we had been chasing, and despite the fear that gripped me, the desire for answers was stronger.

Together, we climbed the creaking staircase, each step reverberating through the silence like a heartbeat. The air grew colder as we ascended, thick with the weight of history and unspoken truths. We reached the landing, and I felt a strange sense of foreboding wash over me, as if the walls were whispering secrets I wasn't yet ready to hear.

As we stood before the door at the end of the hall, I turned to Nathan, my heart pounding. "What do you think is behind this door?"

"Only one way to find out," he said, his voice steady despite the uncertainty in the air.

He reached for the handle, and with a swift turn, the door swung open, revealing a room cloaked in shadows and dust. The remnants of the past lay scattered across the floor—broken furniture, shattered glass, and... something glinting in the corner. My breath caught in my throat as we stepped inside, the weight of our discoveries hanging heavily over us, entwined with the secrets of the Hargrove family, beckoning us deeper into the web of their tangled history.

The room was cloaked in shadows, illuminated only by the fading light that seeped through the cracks in the walls. As we stepped inside, the air felt charged with the weight of unspoken stories, secrets lying in wait, eager to be unearthed. My heart raced, caught in the thrilling anticipation of what we might discover. Nathan moved cautiously, his every gesture deliberate, as though he were aware that we were intruding upon a fragile realm where time stood still.

"Looks like a storm blew through here," he remarked, taking in the scattered debris and the dust that coated every surface. "Or maybe a family of raccoons decided to throw a wild party." His attempt at levity brought a smile to my face, even as the unease twisted in my gut.

"Whatever it was, it left a mess," I replied, eyeing a toppled chair that lay on its side, as if it had fallen during some chaotic event. "But I can't shake the feeling that something important is hidden in this room."

As I moved deeper inside, I spotted the glint of something metallic in the corner. I approached cautiously, every instinct telling me to tread carefully. The room seemed to breathe with me, as if it were alive and aware. There, beneath a thick layer of dust, lay an ornate box, its surface covered in intricate carvings that hinted at a time long forgotten. "Nathan, look at this," I called, my voice barely a whisper.

He joined me, his eyes widening as he examined the box. "It's beautiful," he said, reaching out to brush away the dust with careful fingers. "What do you think it holds?"

"Only one way to find out," I said, excitement bubbling up within me. "But we should be cautious." I hesitated, the weight of our discoveries pressing down on me. "Whatever is in here could tie back to the Hargrove family, to everything we've uncovered."

With a shared glance that spoke volumes, we carefully pried open the lid, the hinges creaking like an old door giving way to the secrets of the past. Inside, we found a collection of yellowed letters, their edges frayed and brittle with age. My heart raced as I gingerly lifted one from the box, the paper crumbling slightly under my touch.

"What does it say?" Nathan leaned closer, his breath warm against my cheek, sending a rush of heat through me. I glanced up, momentarily distracted by the intensity of his gaze before focusing on the letter.

"Dear Thomas," I began to read aloud, "If you're reading this, then my fears have come to pass. The feud with the Wainwrights has escalated, and I worry for our safety. They have threatened our family's legacy, and I fear they will stop at nothing to take what is rightfully ours." My voice trembled as I continued, the chilling implications settling in.

"Sounds like they were embroiled in something serious," Nathan commented, his expression darkening. "This doesn't sound like a simple land dispute."

I nodded, scanning the rest of the letter. "There's more," I said, and with each sentence, the tension in the room tightened. "I beg you to hide this letter and protect our secrets. The curse has already claimed so much, and I can't bear to think of what they would do if they found it."

Nathan's eyes met mine, a mix of fear and determination etched on his features. "If the curse is real, we need to be careful. This could explain the break-ins—someone might be searching for these letters, for the truth that could finally settle the score."

Before I could respond, the floor creaked ominously behind us, the sound reverberating through the room. We turned in unison, the tension coiling tighter as we peered into the darkened hallway beyond. "Did you hear that?" I whispered, my heart pounding in my chest.

"Yeah," Nathan replied, his voice low, a shadow of concern crossing his face. "We're not alone."

I felt the air thicken, the hairs on my arms standing at attention. "What if it's the ghost?" I half-joked, trying to lighten the mood even as panic clawed at my insides. But my attempt at humor fell flat against the growing dread that filled the space between us.

"Let's not stick around to find out," Nathan said, urgency edging his words. "We should move. Now."

As we hurried to gather the letters, the darkness seemed to pulse around us, almost alive. Suddenly, a loud crash echoed through the house, sending us both leaping back against the wall. "What the hell was that?" I gasped, my heart racing.

"I don't know," Nathan replied, glancing back at the doorway, his eyes wide. "But we need to get out of here."

We hastily shoved the letters back into the box, our movements frantic. As we turned to leave, the door creaked open slowly, revealing a figure shrouded in shadow, their features obscured by the dim light. My breath caught in my throat, a mix of terror and disbelief flooding my senses.

"Who are you?" Nathan demanded, stepping protectively in front of me.

The figure remained silent, their presence unnerving. I could feel the tension crackling in the air, a standoff between the past and the present, and my instincts screamed that we were about to uncover a truth far more dangerous than we had anticipated.

"Get out," the figure finally rasped, their voice hoarse and chilling, slicing through the silence like a knife. "You don't belong here."

I felt the weight of those words settle over us, the finality of them pressing down like a heavy fog. My heart raced as I exchanged a panicked glance with Nathan, the reality of our situation crashing down around us. We had come seeking answers, but instead, we were stumbling into a confrontation that could change everything.

As the figure stepped closer, the shadows danced around them, and I braced myself for whatever revelation lay ahead. The air crackled with tension, anticipation sparking like electricity, and as I opened my mouth to speak, the world around us seemed to freeze, teetering on the brink of an unknown abyss.

Chapter 10: A Fractured Past

I stepped into the dimly lit café, the faint scent of roasted coffee beans enveloping me like a warm embrace. It was a haven away from the cacophony of the bustling street outside, where the sound of hurried footsteps and distant car horns blended into an urban symphony. The place had an eclectic charm, its walls adorned with mismatched art and photographs that seemed to tell stories of their own. I spotted Nathan seated at a small table in the far corner, his brow furrowed in concentration as he scribbled notes in a worn leather notebook.

His presence was magnetic, drawing my gaze as if he were the only source of light in the room. I took a moment to appreciate the way the light caught the tousled strands of his dark hair, framing his face in a halo of soft glow. There was something profoundly captivating about him, a rawness that made my heart race with both anticipation and dread. As I approached, I noticed the slight tension in his shoulders, the way his fingers drummed against the table in a rhythm that mirrored my own heartbeat.

"Sorry to keep you waiting," I said, sliding into the chair across from him. I tried to sound casual, but the tremor in my voice betrayed me.

He looked up, his piercing blue eyes meeting mine, and for a fleeting moment, the world outside faded into insignificance. "Not a problem. I needed some time to gather my thoughts." There was an undercurrent of weariness in his voice, a reminder that we were treading into dangerous waters.

I leaned in, curiosity bubbling within me. "What did you want to share?"

He hesitated, his gaze flickering toward the window, where rain began to patter softly against the glass. "You know, I've never been one to open up," he began, his voice barely above a whisper. "It's like

I've spent my whole life building these walls, brick by brick, and now I'm not sure how to take them down."

The vulnerability in his words struck a chord within me. I wanted to reach out, to comfort him, but I knew that this was a dance of trust we both had to navigate carefully. "You don't have to if you're not ready," I replied softly, hoping to ease the weight of his decision.

Nathan chuckled, a sound that was both bittersweet and genuine. "You're just as stubborn as I am. But maybe... maybe it's time to crack open a few of those walls." He took a deep breath, as if summoning the courage to confront ghosts from a long-buried past.

"My childhood was... different," he began, his fingers tracing the outline of his notebook. "I grew up in a neighborhood where shadows held secrets, where every corner could tell a tale of someone's heartache. My parents had their own battles, and I learned early on how to navigate the chaos."

I leaned closer, the world outside forgotten as his words wove a tapestry of emotion and experience. "What do you mean by that?"

"Let's just say I became a spectator of life rather than a participant. I learned to listen rather than speak, to observe rather than act. It was safer that way." His eyes were distant, haunted by memories he had yet to fully confront.

"What about your friends? Did you have any?" I asked, wanting to pull him back from the precipice of his recollections.

"Not really. There were people around, sure, but we were all isolated in our own little bubbles. I remember sitting alone on the playground, watching the other kids play. It felt like a window into a world I didn't belong to."

A pang of empathy surged within me, sharp and unwavering. "That sounds lonely."

"It was," he admitted, the hardness in his gaze softening slightly. "But I found solace in stories—books were my escape. They allowed me to step into lives I could only dream of living. I lost myself in their pages, and in some ways, I think that's why I became a writer. I wanted to create worlds where people could truly connect."

"I get that," I said, feeling a connection to his words. "It's a beautiful way to cope, to find meaning in the chaos."

As the conversation flowed, the café became a sanctuary of shared confessions and unguarded moments. I felt myself unraveling alongside him, our shared vulnerabilities intertwining like threads in a rich tapestry. But just as I began to let my own defenses down, the atmosphere shifted, charged with an unsettling energy.

A shadow flitted past the window, a flicker that sent a chill racing down my spine. My heart quickened, instinctively alert to the sense that we were not as alone as we believed. Nathan seemed to notice the change as well, his expression sharpening as he caught sight of my unease.

"What is it?" he asked, concern etching his features.

I shook my head, unwilling to voice the fear creeping into my mind. "Nothing, just... a feeling."

"Feelings can be important," he said, his voice low and steady, urging me to trust my instincts.

I drew in a breath, trying to shake off the sensation that loomed like a dark cloud. "It's just that... sometimes I feel like there's something lurking just out of sight. Like a shadow waiting to reveal itself."

His eyes narrowed slightly, and I could see the flicker of recognition in them. "You're not the only one who senses it. There are things in my past that refuse to let go, shadows I've tried to outrun."

The weight of his words hung heavy between us, a stark reminder that our pasts were like chains, binding us to a history we could not escape. I wanted to press further, to uncover the darkness he hinted at, but I felt a deep-rooted hesitation, knowing that some stories were better left unspoken.

The rain outside intensified, drumming against the café's roof, mirroring the tempest of emotions swirling within me. In that moment, surrounded by the warmth of our conversation and the chill of looming uncertainty, I realized that while we were uncovering layers of our pasts, the present held its own mysteries—unseen, waiting just beyond the edges of our awareness.

The café continued to hum with life around us, yet an unshakeable tension lingered in the air, like a tightly coiled spring waiting to snap. I could sense Nathan's heartbeat echoing my own—a silent pact formed in the shadows of our shared vulnerabilities. As the rain drizzled relentlessly outside, the world beyond the glass blurred into a watercolor of gray and silver. It felt fitting, somehow, to discuss our hidden depths amid such murky weather, where secrets could hide just out of sight.

"Why do you think those shadows still linger?" I asked, testing the waters of our growing intimacy. "I mean, you've moved on. You're here, right?"

He looked thoughtful, his fingers tapping the edge of his notebook rhythmically as if counting out an answer. "Moving on is a curious thing. It's like carrying a backpack filled with stones. You can set it down, but the weight is still there, and sometimes it feels more comforting to hold onto it than to risk letting it go."

"Sounds like you could use a new backpack," I teased, attempting to lighten the atmosphere, but the seriousness of his words lingered like an uninvited guest.

"Perhaps a suitcase would be better. A large one. I could just pack up the entire experience and ship it off to the moon," he replied, a flicker of humor sparking in his eyes. "Though I suspect it would find its way back to me, floating down like confetti at a parade."

I chuckled, appreciating the wit that danced around his grief. "Well, if you ever do get a rocket ship, let me know. I'd be more than happy to join you on that cosmic escape."

A smile tugged at his lips, but the shadows didn't dissipate. "You know, it's strange how the past never truly lets go, even when we think we've buried it. There are moments that resurface unexpectedly, like a terrible song stuck on repeat. Sometimes I hear a certain melody, and it's as if I'm transported back to those days of watching everyone else live."

"Do you remember the lyrics?" I asked, my curiosity piqued. "What song haunts you the most?"

He hesitated, his gaze drifting to the rain-soaked street beyond the window. "It's not a song, really, more like a lullaby that my mother used to hum. It was meant to soothe me, but it now feels like a dirge. I remember feeling so small, like I could disappear into the fabric of the night, unseen and unheard."

"That's heartbreaking," I said softly, feeling the weight of his recollection. "But you're not invisible anymore. You're here, sharing this with me."

"True, but I often wonder if that little boy is still inside, peeking through the cracks," he confessed, his voice barely above a whisper. "Every so often, when things get too close to the surface, I can feel him wanting to break free. And that scares me."

"Why does it scare you?" I pressed, sensing that this was the crux of his struggle.

"Because the truth can be terrifying," he said, his expression solemn. "What if the boy inside me doesn't want to be saved? What if he prefers the shadows?"

The café's ambiance shifted with a new urgency. The chatter of patrons and the clinking of cups faded into a dull murmur as I mulled over his words. There was something profoundly relatable about the fear of confronting one's past. "We can't let fear dictate our lives, Nathan. There's a balance to be struck, a way to acknowledge the past without letting it consume us."

He met my gaze, and for a brief moment, the world around us dimmed, leaving only the warmth of our connection. "You make it sound so simple. But you don't know what it's like to face those demons, to look into the darkness and see what you might find."

"Maybe not," I conceded, "but I do know that keeping those shadows at bay is exhausting. And if you let them out, perhaps you'll find they aren't as terrifying as you think."

He chuckled softly, and for a fleeting moment, the tension between us eased. "I appreciate your faith in me. But not all shadows are born equal, you know. Some hold secrets that could shatter everything."

As his words hung in the air, I sensed a shift, a subtle change in the atmosphere that sent a shiver down my spine. My instincts flared, alerting me to the presence of something lurking at the edge of our conversation. "What if it's not just the past we have to worry about?" I murmured, glancing toward the entrance.

Nathan followed my gaze, his expression tightening as he noticed the figure lingering just beyond the café's glass door. The stranger stood shrouded in the rain, their face obscured by a hood. A sense of foreboding enveloped us like a thick fog, and the air crackled with unspoken tension.

"Do you see that?" I whispered, my heart pounding.

"Yeah," Nathan replied, his voice low and cautious. "What are they doing out there?"

"I don't know," I breathed, straining to get a better look, but the figure remained elusive, watching us with an unsettling intensity. "It's like they're waiting for something... or someone."

Nathan's gaze shifted back to me, a mix of concern and determination etched on his face. "We should go. It feels wrong to stay here."

"Agreed," I replied, the urgency in his tone sending a chill through my veins. I glanced at the barista, who was blissfully unaware, absorbed in their tasks behind the counter. We gathered our belongings, and as we stood to leave, the door swung open, the bell above it chiming an ominous warning.

The figure stepped inside, water dripping from their clothes like a ghost emerging from a storm. Their presence loomed over the café, casting a long shadow that reached into every corner. I froze, my heart racing as the air turned thick with tension.

"Who are you?" Nathan demanded, stepping protectively in front of me.

The stranger pulled back their hood, revealing a face that sent shockwaves of recognition through me. It was someone from my past, a fleeting memory now standing solidly before us, and as our eyes locked, I realized that the shadows we had tried to escape were far more intertwined than either of us had anticipated.

The stranger's face was a canvas of familiar features painted with years of untold stories. A deep breath escaped me as I stepped back instinctively, clenching my bag tightly. Nathan's protective stance beside me felt both reassuring and unsettling, like standing on the edge of a cliff with no clear view of the ground below.

"Emilie?" the figure said, their voice a whisper that wrapped around me like an old, forgotten melody. The sound sent a shiver down my spine, a jolt of recognition that sent a flood of memories crashing through my mind—each one tinged with the bittersweet hue of nostalgia and regret.

"What are you doing here?" I managed, the words tumbling out, betraying a mix of shock and disbelief.

The person before us was a ghost from my past, a former friend who had drifted away like leaves on the wind, leaving behind echoes of laughter and unfinished conversations. I had thought I'd buried those memories, but here they were, rising to the surface with a vengeance.

"I've been looking for you," they said, their gaze darting between Nathan and me, as if weighing our connection against their purpose. "There are things you need to know."

"About what?" Nathan interjected, his voice steady, though I could see the tension knotting his jaw.

"About the investigation you're involved in," they replied, their eyes darkening with urgency. "It's bigger than you think. You're not just chasing shadows; you're getting too close to the truth, and that truth is dangerous."

The café seemed to shrink around us, the soft murmur of voices fading into the background as I absorbed their words. "What do you mean dangerous?" I asked, my voice a shaky whisper, anxiety threading through my thoughts.

"They don't want you to find out," the stranger said, taking a step closer, a raw desperation spilling from their eyes. "I didn't just come back to haunt you. I came because I want to help."

Nathan shot me a sidelong glance, his eyes searching for answers in my own. The bond we had started to forge felt fragile, like glass poised on the edge of a table, ready to shatter with the slightest nudge. "Who are 'they'?" he asked, crossing his arms, a protective stance that sent a flicker of warmth through me, even amidst the encroaching fear.

A flash of frustration crossed Emilie's face. "You need to trust me. It's hard to explain, but there are people who will do anything to keep their secrets hidden. I saw things I shouldn't have. I can't stay in the dark anymore."

Nathan's protective nature flared. "If you want to help, you'd better start spilling. We don't have time for riddles."

The intensity of the moment felt almost electric, the air thick with unspoken words and possibilities. Emilie's face softened for a moment, and I saw a flicker of the girl I once knew, someone who wore laughter like a second skin. "I didn't want to bring this to you, but I didn't have a choice. I found something—something that ties back to our past. And it's coming to a head now."

I felt the walls around me close in, the weight of her confession heavy on my chest. "What did you find?"

Emilie hesitated, glancing at the café's door as if afraid someone might overhear. "There's a file. A file that contains names, dates, everything linked to the events we thought we'd left behind. It's connected to both of us, and if it falls into the wrong hands…" Her voice trailed off, leaving the threat lingering in the air like smoke from a dying fire.

"And you think we're in danger?" Nathan asked, his brows furrowing as he assessed the situation.

"Yes," she replied, her tone grave. "There are forces at work that don't want this information to see the light of day. You have to understand, once you know, there's no going back."

A chill snaked down my spine, and I exchanged a glance with Nathan, the unsaid words heavy between us. What if our investigation had already crossed a line? What if we were being watched?

"I need to see this file," Nathan said, his voice steady but filled with determination. "If what you say is true, we can't afford to ignore it."

"Fine," Emilie said, her eyes flickering with a mix of hope and fear. "Meet me tonight at the old library—there's a basement storage area where I've hidden it. But you must promise to be careful. They've been watching me."

"Watching you?" I echoed, a knot of dread tightening in my stomach. "Who, exactly?"

Her eyes darted around the café, as if the shadows themselves had ears. "I can't say more here. Just trust me. Please."

Nathan and I nodded, but I felt the weight of uncertainty settle over us. "What if it's a trap?" I blurted out, the fear bubbling to the surface.

"Then you'll need to be ready for anything," she replied, her voice steely with resolve.

A silence fell between us, each heartbeat amplifying the tension. I could feel the weight of our past pressing down like a heavy shroud, mingling with the specter of danger that had now enveloped our present. As we moved to leave, the atmosphere buzzed with an electric tension, and I couldn't shake the feeling that we were stepping into a deeper darkness than we had anticipated.

Emilie turned to me, her gaze piercing. "You have to trust your instincts, Emilie. This isn't just about the investigation anymore; it's about survival."

I swallowed hard, uncertainty clawing at my throat as I nodded, but inside, doubt gnawed at me like a ravenous beast.

As we exited the café into the dreary rain, I felt a strange mixture of fear and exhilaration wash over me. The world felt different now, its edges sharper, more defined. Shadows stretched long and twisted around us, twisting and curling like smoke, reminding me that danger lurked just out of sight.

"I can't shake this feeling," Nathan murmured as we walked side by side. "There's more at play here than we understand."

I looked up at him, my heart racing with a mix of admiration and fear. "Are you ready for this?"

"More than ever," he said, his expression resolute. "But we need to be smart about it."

We made our way to the library, the rain drenching us to the bone, but I didn't care. It felt like we were stepping into a storm far greater than the weather. Each step echoed with the promise of revelation and the threat of destruction. As we approached the heavy wooden doors of the library, the air thickened with anticipation, and a sense of foreboding settled deep in my bones.

The moment we crossed the threshold, I felt it—the unmistakable shift in the atmosphere, the realization that we were not alone. And just as I opened my mouth to voice my concern, a figure stepped out of the shadows, blocking our path. "You shouldn't have come here," they said, their voice low and menacing, sending icy fingers of dread creeping up my spine.

Chapter 11: Night Terrors

The shadows in my room felt thicker than the fabric of my dreams, twisting and curling like tendrils of smoke that seeped through the cracks of my subconscious. I had been deep in sleep, lost to the comforting hum of nighttime, when an unidentifiable noise shattered the calm. It was an unsettling sound, an unfamiliar rustling that seemed to creep into my bones, drawing me into the wakeful world with a cold jolt. My heart thundered, each beat echoing in my ears like the relentless drumroll of an impending storm.

As I blinked into the dark, the shapes around me took on a sinister quality. The familiar contours of my bedroom morphed into an alien landscape, cloaked in shadows and uncertainty. I rolled over, my fingers brushing against the smooth sheets, the warmth of my bed suddenly feeling like a thin barrier against the icy dread lurking outside. The noise persisted, a scritch-scratch against the window that set my nerves alight, urging me to investigate. With a reluctance that felt almost tangible, I swung my legs over the side of the bed, my feet meeting the cool hardwood floor with a gasp.

I crept to the window, each step deliberate as if I were traversing a minefield of nightmares. Peering through the thin curtain, I squinted into the night, searching for the source of the sound. The streetlamp flickered like a half-hearted sentinel in the oppressive darkness, casting eerie shadows that danced along the pavement. It was there, beneath its sickly glow, that I saw him—a figure, indistinct and still, like a wraith summoned from my darkest fears. The man's features were obscured, but the outline of his form sent a chill skittering down my spine.

A wave of panic surged through me, relentless and blinding. My instinct was to retreat, to flee back to the sanctuary of my bed and drown in the safety of the covers, but the sight of him anchored me in place. I felt exposed, vulnerable, like prey beneath the gaze of a predator. I fumbled for my phone, fingers trembling as I dialed Nathan's number. I couldn't shake the sensation of being watched, a sinister presence that wrapped around me like a shroud. My voice, usually steady and sure, quaked as I spoke. "Nathan, please, you need to come. There's someone outside."

He arrived in a flurry of urgency, the sound of his car tires crunching on the gravel driveway breaking the stillness of the night. The moment he stepped through the door, an invisible weight lifted slightly from my shoulders, his mere presence a balm against my fears. Nathan exuded an intoxicating blend of strength and warmth, and I found myself instinctively gravitating toward him, seeking the safety that radiated from his being.

"Where?" he asked, eyes narrowing as he took in my anxious demeanor. The sharpness in his voice cut through the fog of terror clinging to my mind, grounding me in the moment.

I gestured toward the window, breath hitching as I recalled the figure lurking beneath the lamp. "Right there," I whispered, a sense of dread washing over me anew as I peeked through the curtain again. But the street was empty now, the figure evaporated into the shadows like a ghost retreating to the depths from whence it came.

Nathan's gaze followed mine, his brow furrowing. "Are you sure? You saw someone?"

"Absolutely. I swear," I insisted, clutching his arm as if he were the only thing tethering me to reality. My heart raced, each pulse reminding me of the fleeting image that had ignited my imagination into a frenzy. The feeling of safety he brought was intoxicating, a welcome respite from the grip of fear that had encased me moments before. But with the figure gone, the night felt deceptively tranquil, the kind of stillness that made my skin prickle with unease.

Nathan's presence transformed the atmosphere, the chill in the air shifting as he moved closer, his warmth seeping into the very marrow of my bones. "Let's check outside," he suggested, and though apprehension clawed at my insides, I nodded, eager to banish the shadows lurking in my mind.

Together, we stepped outside, the cool air wrapping around us like a cloak. The world felt muted, the usual sounds of the night swallowed by an unsettling quiet. The streetlamp stood sentinel, illuminating our path but casting long shadows that stretched into the unknown. Nathan surveyed the area, his posture taut with vigilance. I felt like a child hiding behind a parent, a role reversal that both reassured and unsettled me.

"I don't see anything," he said, though his voice held a note of caution. "Maybe it was just your imagination."

"Or maybe it was something more," I countered, peering into the darkness. The thrill of fear slithered up my spine, not entirely unwelcome; it was a reminder that I was alive, that I felt, that I was capable of facing whatever awaited me in the shadows.

A gust of wind rustled the leaves overhead, and I shivered, my skin tingling as if the universe itself was warning me. I wanted to dismiss the feeling, to shrug it off as the product of my overactive mind, but a part of me knew better. Something was out there, lurking just beyond the periphery of my understanding, and it was only a matter of time before it revealed itself.

"I wish you would let me be your protector more often," Nathan said, a wry smile breaking through his concern. "You know, I come armed with all sorts of protective charms."

"Like your rugged good looks?" I shot back, a playful banter igniting the tension in my chest.

"Exactly! That and a wicked sense of humor." He chuckled, and for a fleeting moment, the weight of fear lifted, replaced by the comforting warmth of our connection. Our eyes locked, and in that shared gaze, the world around us faded—just for a moment—into the comforting embrace of possibility.

But then reality crashed back in, and the shadows deepened once more. The night held its breath, and I felt the chilling grip of dread return, lingering like an unwelcome guest refusing to leave. I clung to Nathan, my heart thundering in my chest, the dark swirling around us, reminding me that the figure beneath the lamp had vanished, but the feeling of dread remained, gnawing at my insides like a hungry beast.

The night had stretched on, every minute tinged with a mix of adrenaline and uncertainty that kept my senses on high alert. Nathan stood beside me, our silhouettes framed against the faint glow of the streetlamp. The air buzzed with tension, thick like fog, yet oddly comforting in its shared vulnerability. "I should have brought my night vision goggles," he quipped, attempting to slice through the palpable unease. "You know, for these midnight stakeouts. Very CIA of me."

I couldn't help but smile, the corners of my mouth twitching upward despite the unsettling atmosphere. "I'd settle for a flashlight, Agent Nathan. I don't need you breaking into a covert operation while I'm just trying to figure out if I'm going crazy." The moment felt intimate, two allies against the unknown, and I relished the way his laughter wrapped around me, like a warm blanket on a chilly evening.

"Let's not jump to conclusions here. Maybe it was just a raccoon. They can be surprisingly stealthy." He glanced around the yard, his expression a mix of playfulness and concern. "I mean, I wouldn't put it past them to be plotting some kind of takeover."

"Right, the raccoons are definitely after my collection of vintage cereal boxes. I just can't seem to keep them away." I chuckled, but the humor did little to mask the tightening knot in my stomach. The shadows seemed to pulse, the branches swaying like gnarled fingers reaching out for something—or someone.

Yet, there was a lingering question hanging in the air like smoke: Who had been standing there? I needed to find out, to push past the fear that held me captive. "I think we should investigate the yard. You know, for peace of mind—or to catch a raccoon red-pawed."

Nathan raised an eyebrow, a mock-serious expression settling over his features. "You're suggesting we hunt down a potential intruder in the middle of the night, with nothing but our wits and questionable jokes? I'm all in." His bravado was infectious, and I found my heart racing for reasons beyond mere fear.

Armed with nothing more than Nathan's confident stride and my resolve, we ventured into the yard. The grass felt damp underfoot, each blade glistening as if the earth had held onto the remnants of the rain that had passed earlier in the day. I peered into the bushes lining the edge of the property, half-expecting a furry bandit to leap out and start reciting Shakespeare.

"Okay, I'll check over here," Nathan whispered, gesturing toward a cluster of azaleas that swayed in the night breeze. I could see the tension in his shoulders, a tightly coiled spring ready to unleash at the slightest provocation. "If you hear a scream, just assume it's a raccoon. Or maybe me finding out you really did have a pet ghost."

"Funny, I could have sworn I felt a chill when you mentioned that." I forced a laugh, but the sound felt thin against the thick blanket of silence.

As Nathan crept toward the bushes, the shadows danced around him, and I felt an inexplicable urge to protect him, despite the absurdity of the situation. "Be careful," I called out softly, my heart fluttering. "Those raccoons are known for their cunning tactics."

"Don't worry, I'm a trained professional." He waved dismissively over his shoulder, stepping cautiously as if the ground might open up beneath him.

Just then, I caught a glint of something metallic in the grass, a flash that didn't belong. My stomach dropped. I knelt down, brushing away the leaves and dirt to reveal a small knife, its blade gleaming under the streetlamp's light. It felt out of place, a stark reminder of the danger that seemed to hover just beyond the edges of our reality.

"Nathan!" I called, urgency propelling my voice into the night. "You need to see this."

He was at my side in an instant, the humor stripped away from his face as he knelt beside me. "Where did you find that?" His voice was low, the weight of the moment pressing down on us both.

"Right here," I said, holding it up for him to see. "This was just lying in the grass. It looks new, but it shouldn't be here." The air grew heavier, the tension palpable as we both processed the implications.

"Someone was definitely here," he muttered, his gaze hardening as he scanned our surroundings. "And it wasn't just a raccoon."

A flicker of movement caught my eye near the fence. A shadow darted, a flicker of darkness that sent a shiver racing down my spine. "Did you see that?" I whispered, gripping the knife tightly, its cool metal a reassuring weight in my palm.

"Yeah, I did," Nathan replied, his voice barely above a whisper. "Stay close."

We moved cautiously toward the fence, where the shadows seemed to congeal, the night thickening with every step. My heart raced with adrenaline, the thrill of the chase igniting something primal within me. There was a rush in being on the edge of something dangerous, a sweet tang of fear that stirred my senses.

"What are we looking for?" I asked, my voice trembling slightly as we drew nearer to the fence. "Do we just confront whoever it is? Or should we call the police?"

Nathan's eyes were locked onto the darkened corner of the yard. "Let's not escalate things yet. I'd rather not scare off a raccoon and its entire family." He cracked a grin, and I couldn't help but smile back, the camaraderie easing the tension just enough.

Then, as if responding to our whispers, the figure re-emerged. The dark shape slipped into the light, revealing a silhouette that was all too familiar. "What are you two doing out here?" Clara's voice sliced through the air, laced with mockery.

I blinked, disbelief washing over me. "Clara? What are you doing here?"

"Nice to see you too, best friend." She crossed her arms, a playful smirk dancing on her lips. "And don't tell me you thought I was a murderer lurking in the bushes."

"No, but I was about to file a missing persons report on your dramatic entrance," I replied, relief flooding through me, though the tension lingered.

Nathan chuckled, shaking his head. "You scared the hell out of us, Clara. Do you always sneak around people's yards at night?"

"Only when I'm trying to find out if my friends have turned into paranoid hermits." She rolled her eyes but her playful tone belied the concern behind her words. "Seriously, though, what's going on? I saw your lights flickering like a disco party and thought I'd come check on you."

"Just a minor security breach," I said, glancing at Nathan, who nodded in agreement. "But we're all good now." The knife felt heavier in my hand as Clara's presence began to shift the atmosphere, the absurdity of the situation settling in.

"Right, because nothing says 'everything is fine' like a knife in the grass," she retorted, raising an eyebrow as she stepped closer. "Care to enlighten me on the rest of the story?"

I exchanged a glance with Nathan, the tension slowly dissipating as the absurdity of our predicament settled around us like a soft blanket. The night was still alive with unseen dangers, but in that moment, with Clara's laughter echoing in the darkness, it felt like we were weaving a protective cocoon against the unknown, each of us ready to face whatever shadows dared to encroach on our world.

Clara's presence transformed the tension in the yard, her bravado slicing through the suffocating quiet. I glanced from her to Nathan, who wore an expression of disbelief that mirrored my own. "What do you mean you were lurking in the shadows?" I asked, half amused and half exasperated. "You really know how to make an entrance, don't you?"

"Hey, I thought you two were in trouble!" She put her hands on her hips, her defiance palpable. "Someone had to come rescue you from whatever spooky specter was haunting your dreams."

Nathan leaned back, arms crossed. "We didn't need a superhero, but the company is appreciated. I'd have just preferred it not to involve a knife in the grass."

Clara rolled her eyes, dismissing our worries with a wave of her hand. "It's a prop, isn't it? If you guys are putting on a haunted house, I'm all in. I brought popcorn."

I chuckled, but the laughter didn't completely banish the unease that lingered. "It was definitely not on the agenda. But at least we have the knife if any raccoons decide to attack."

"Right, let's sharpen it and wait for the Great Raccoon Wars to begin," she quipped, taking the knife from my hand and examining it with a mock seriousness. "You never know when you'll need to defend your cereal box collection."

Despite her lightheartedness, I could sense that Clara was picking up on the undercurrents of anxiety swirling around us. "So, what's the real deal?" she asked, her tone shifting slightly. "You're not out here for some nighttime mischief, are you?"

"No," I admitted, glancing toward Nathan, whose expression had turned grave. "I saw someone standing outside. Someone who shouldn't have been there."

Clara's eyebrows shot up, and she glanced over her shoulder, as if expecting the shadowy figure to leap out from behind the azaleas.

"You're serious? A person? Not a shadow or a figment of your imagination?"

Nathan stepped forward, his voice steady and calm, though I could see the tension lining his jaw. "We found this knife in the yard. Someone was definitely here."

Clara's eyes widened as she took in the gravity of the situation. "And you thought it would be a good idea to hunt them down yourself?"

"We were going to check if the raccoons had an underground lair," I shot back, but my attempt at humor fell flat. "I mean, I just needed to know what was happening."

"I can't believe you both!" Clara exclaimed, throwing her hands up in exasperation. "This is not a scene from a horror movie! You can't just go chasing shadows."

"Look, if something was out there, we can't just sit back and hope it doesn't come back," Nathan replied, his voice resolute. "This is our home, and we have to protect it."

Clara hesitated, her bravado wavering as she looked between us. "Okay, but we need a plan. Let's not go charging into danger without backup. I'm not ready for a bloodbath involving raccoons and crazy intruders."

"Are you volunteering to help?" I raised an eyebrow, not entirely convinced.

"Absolutely," she said, crossing her arms defiantly. "But only if we do this the smart way. No reckless decisions. And for heaven's sake, keep the knife away from me. It's giving me anxiety."

We huddled together, Clara brainstorming ideas while Nathan stood vigilantly, scanning the perimeter. A rush of gratitude surged through me as I realized how lucky I was to have friends who would stand with me against the shadows. Yet, the fear that something darker lurked just out of sight kept gnawing at the edges of my mind.

"I say we set a little trap," Clara suggested, her eyes lighting up with determination. "We can leave some of your cereal out and see if anything—or anyone—takes the bait."

"Brilliant," I replied, half-serious. "The perfect lure: cereal. You might be onto something, Clara."

"Hey, if it works, I get to say I'm a genius," she shot back, grinning. "And if it doesn't, well, at least we'll have breakfast ready."

The plan solidified quickly, each of us playing our part. Nathan collected the cereal from the kitchen while Clara set up her phone to record any suspicious activity. I felt a rush of excitement mixed with apprehension as we laid out our little trap. We stationed ourselves behind the safety of a tree, the moon casting eerie shadows that danced with our movements.

"Just don't let the raccoons know we're here," I whispered as we crouched down, peering through the branches. "They'll plot a coup."

"Coup de raccoon, coming to a yard near you," Nathan said with a wink, and for a moment, the absurdity of the situation drew a laugh from me.

The seconds stretched into minutes, the air thickening with anticipation as we waited in silence, the stillness pressing against our ears like a heavy weight. The shadows around us seemed to grow deeper, creeping in like a fog. My heart thrummed in my chest, the thrill of the unknown electrifying.

Just when I thought the night might drag on forever, Clara's phone buzzed, the screen lighting up as it detected movement. "It's recording!" she whispered urgently, her excitement palpable.

"Is it the raccoons?" I leaned forward, straining to see through the branches.

"Only one way to find out," Nathan replied, eyes glinting with determination.

As we held our breaths, the darkness shifted, and a figure emerged from the shadows, slipping into the weak glow of the streetlamp. The moonlight revealed a face I recognized instantly—a face I hadn't expected to see again.

"Zara?" I gasped, disbelief flooding through me. "What are you doing here?"

"Looking for you," she said, her voice steady yet laced with an urgency that sent a shiver down my spine.

Before I could process her presence, I caught sight of a shadow behind her, a looming figure that stepped into the light, a gleam of steel flashing in the night. My heart raced, panic clawing at my throat as reality twisted, and the night became a living nightmare.

"Run!" I screamed, the warning ripping from my lips just as everything erupted into chaos, the night holding its breath as danger closed in around us.

Chapter 12: The Stranger

The bar was a dimly lit enclave tucked away from the bustling streets, its ambiance a curious mix of smoky nostalgia and cheap beer. The walls, adorned with sepia-toned photographs of bygone eras, whispered secrets of a time when laughter came easier and the worries of the world felt distant. I took a seat at a scarred wooden table, the surface sticky with remnants of hasty drinks and conversations, while Nathan slipped into the seat across from me. His presence was a beacon, a warmth that both calmed and thrilled me in equal measure.

"Do you think he'll show?" I asked, my fingers tracing the rim of a chipped glass, my mind racing. The fluorescent lights overhead flickered, casting intermittent shadows that danced like specters along the walls.

"He will," Nathan replied, his voice steady but laced with a tension that matched the tightness in my chest. The air was thick with the scent of spilled liquor and fried food, an olfactory cocktail that threatened to drown out my thoughts. It was the kind of place where stories lingered long after the last patron had left, and I felt like I was on the precipice of one.

As the minutes dragged on, the chatter around us swelled, punctuated by bursts of laughter and the clinking of glasses. It felt like a world apart from the urgency that gripped us. My mind flitted back to the notes we had discovered—cryptic, unsettling. They hinted at danger lurking just beyond our reach, and yet we were sitting here, waiting for a man who could either guide us to the truth or plunge us deeper into uncertainty.

"I don't like this," I muttered, leaning closer to Nathan, lowering my voice as if the shadows themselves might eavesdrop. "What if he knows more than he's letting on? What if he's the reason for all this?"

His eyes met mine, an intense storm brewing within them. "That's why we need to hear him out. He might be the key to understanding what's really happening here."

Just then, the door swung open, creaking like an old hinge that had witnessed too much. A gust of cold air swept into the room, momentarily cutting through the humidity. In stepped a man cloaked in a leather jacket, his silhouette stark against the dim lighting. He paused, scanning the room with an air of predatory calm, before locking eyes with us. There was an undeniable weight to his presence, a gravitational pull that seemed to draw everyone's attention, if only for a moment.

"He's here," I whispered, a shiver racing down my spine as the man approached.

"Let me do the talking," Nathan instructed, his voice a low rumble.

I nodded, though my heart hammered against my ribcage like a caged bird desperate for escape. The stranger slid into the booth beside Nathan, his demeanor relaxed yet alert, as if he were both predator and prey in this game we didn't quite understand.

"Thanks for coming," Nathan said, his tone steely. "We have questions, and we hope you have answers."

The man studied us for a moment, his eyes narrowing as if weighing our worth. "You're deeper in this than you realize," he said finally, his voice smooth and low, a dark melody that sent ripples of unease through me. "And I can't promise you'll like what I have to say."

"Just tell us what you know," I interjected, emboldened by a mix of fear and determination. "We're not here to play games."

A sly smile crept across his face, the corners of his mouth twitching as if he found my bravado amusing. "Games? Oh, sweet girl, this isn't a game. This is a labyrinth, and you're already lost."

Nathan leaned in closer, his fists clenched on the table. "Stop with the riddles. We need to know about the notes. Who sent them? Why us?"

The stranger's gaze flickered to the side, his expression darkening. "The notes are a warning. They're tied to something ancient, something that has been buried for far too long. You've stumbled into a web woven by those who would rather see you dead than have the truth uncovered."

"Why us?" I pressed, feeling the walls of the bar close in around me. "What do we have to do with any of this?"

"You're part of a legacy, dear," he replied, his tone now a whisper, drawing me closer into his orbit. "Your past holds the key to your future, but it also carries the weight of the danger that follows you."

My heart raced, the implications settling like a stone in my stomach. "You don't even know us," I challenged, my voice trembling despite my resolve.

"I know enough," he said, his smile fading as he regarded me with an intensity that left no room for doubt. "The past is a restless beast, and it has a way of finding those it deems worthy—or unworthy—of its attention."

Before I could respond, Nathan surged forward, his frustration spilling over. "Enough with the cryptic nonsense! What do we need to do to get out of this alive?"

The man leaned back, amusement glinting in his eyes. "Survival is easy; you just have to play your cards right. But you'll need to trust each other, and trust is a fragile thing, easily broken."

As he spoke, the bar around us faded into the background, the laughter and clinking glasses becoming a dull hum. It felt like the three of us were suspended in time, hovering on the brink of revelation or catastrophe. I caught Nathan's eye, and in that shared glance, we both understood the stakes had risen, the game had changed, and we were already in over our heads.

FADING ECHOES   117

"Trust is a fragile thing, easily broken." The stranger's words hung in the air like smoke, curling and twisting in the dim light as if they were more than just an ominous warning. I shifted in my seat, the worn leather sticking to the back of my thighs, and tried to shake off the unsettling weight of his gaze.

"So, what's it going to take for you to share the real story?" Nathan demanded, his voice steady but tinged with urgency. The tension between us was palpable, electric, and I could feel the simmering anxiety bubble just beneath the surface, ready to burst.

"Patience, my friend," the stranger replied, his eyes glinting with a mix of amusement and something darker. "You'll need it if you want to survive this."

I leaned in closer, intrigued despite my better judgment. "What exactly do you mean by 'survive this'? Are we in danger?"

He chuckled softly, a sound that didn't quite reach his eyes. "Danger is relative. The real question is how much you're willing to risk for the truth. Some people lose everything in the search; others gain more than they ever imagined. It's a delicate balance."

"Great," I muttered, shooting a glance at Nathan, whose jaw was clenched tight enough to crack. "So we're basically playing poker with our lives on the line."

"Exactly," the stranger replied, clearly enjoying my attempt to simplify the situation. "And from the looks of it, you're not very good at bluffing."

I shot him a glare that could have melted steel. "Is that a challenge? Because I can bluff with the best of them."

Nathan placed a reassuring hand on my arm, grounding me. "What do you know about the notes? Who sent them, and why us?" His tone was commanding, demanding answers while my impatience simmered just beneath the surface.

"Those notes are a call to action," he replied, his gaze penetrating as he assessed our reactions. "Someone wants you to dig deeper, but they've chosen to cloak their intentions in riddles. It's clever, really. Keeps the weak from interfering."

"Great," I replied, rolling my eyes. "So we're in a riddle contest now. Why not throw in a treasure hunt while we're at it?"

The stranger leaned back, a smirk playing at the corners of his lips. "I like your spirit. But you might want to temper that enthusiasm with caution. Not everyone finds this game amusing."

"And what about you?" Nathan interjected, his tone sharper than before. "Are you one of those who finds it amusing?"

"I'm just an observer," he said, his voice deceptively calm. "But I know enough to recognize when someone is playing a dangerous game."

My heart raced at the implications of his words. I could almost feel the walls of the bar closing in, the laughter of the other patrons fading into a distant echo. "What's our next move?" I asked, my voice steadier than I felt.

"Follow the threads," he said, his eyes narrowing, suddenly serious. "But remember, not all threads lead to the truth. Some are designed to ensnare you." He paused, letting his words sink in. "And if you're not careful, you might find yourself tangled in a web far more sinister than you can imagine."

A heavy silence settled between us as his words hung like a dense fog. I exchanged a glance with Nathan, his brow furrowed in thought, and I could almost see the gears turning in his mind. The tension in the air was almost suffocating.

"Tell us what we need to do," Nathan insisted, his voice low and firm, a command rather than a question. "If we're going to uncover whatever's going on, we need a plan."

The stranger leaned forward, his demeanor shifting, seriousness replacing the earlier levity. "You'll need to speak to someone who knows more—someone who can give you insight into the past. They're not easy to find, and even harder to convince."

"Why not just point us in their direction?" I pressed, frustration bubbling up again. "Why all this mystery? Just tell us what we need to know."

"Because, sweet girl," he said, leaning back with an enigmatic smile, "the journey is as important as the destination. If I simply gave you the answers, you'd never learn the real lesson."

I scoffed, crossing my arms defiantly. "And what lesson is that? To be cryptic and annoying?"

"Close," he said, his tone playful. "To trust your instincts and to understand that the people you think you know may not be who they seem. In this game, everyone has their agenda."

"Great," I replied, the sarcasm dripping from my words. "A lesson in trust from a total stranger in a bar."

"Consider it a warning," he shot back, the amusement fading from his eyes. "Not everyone will want you to succeed. Be prepared for betrayal; it often comes from unexpected places."

My skin prickled at the suggestion. I turned to Nathan, his gaze sharp and calculating as he processed the stranger's words. "Do we trust him?" I whispered, my voice barely above a breath.

He hesitated, weighing his words carefully. "I think we have to. For now, at least. But we need to keep our guard up."

I nodded, a wave of anxiety washing over me. The stakes had risen significantly, and I couldn't shake the feeling that we were on the precipice of something far greater than I had anticipated.

"Your first step is to visit the old bookstore on Maple Street," the stranger said, breaking the silence. "Ask for Evelyn. She holds the keys to many doors. Just remember: not all doors should be opened."

With that, he rose, the movement fluid and deliberate. "I've said enough for now. Good luck, and remember—trust is a fragile thing. Handle it with care."

As he slipped away into the crowd, I felt a mix of relief and apprehension. The air had shifted, the weight of his words settling heavily on my shoulders. I turned to Nathan, who was still deep in thought, his brow furrowed.

"Do you think we can really trust him?" I asked, uncertainty creeping into my voice.

Nathan took a deep breath, his expression resolute. "Trusting him might be our only option right now. But we'll need to stay sharp. The moment we let our guard down could be the moment we lose everything."

A chill ran down my spine, but alongside it surged a flicker of determination. We were in this together, and as daunting as the path ahead might be, I wasn't going to back down. The truth awaited, tangled in shadows and riddles, and we were going to uncover it, one step at a time.

As the door to the bar swung shut behind the stranger, I took a deep breath, letting the air cool the heat of uncertainty that clung to me like a second skin. Nathan remained seated, his gaze fixed on the spot where the stranger had just vanished. The din of the bar slowly returned to life around us, laughter and music blending into a chaotic symphony that felt worlds away from our own tense reality.

"Evelyn," I murmured, the name echoing in my mind like a chant. "What do you think she knows?"

Nathan finally turned to me, his expression serious but softened by a glimmer of hope. "I think it's our best shot. If this Evelyn knows about the notes and the threats, we need to find her."

I nodded, my stomach churning with a mix of anticipation and dread. "Do you think she'll talk to us? The way he spoke about trust—it sounded like we need to earn it."

"Trust is a two-way street," Nathan replied, his tone steady. "We'll have to be careful, but we can't afford to let fear paralyze us. We need to push forward."

We stood up, leaving our sticky table behind, and stepped out into the cool night air. The street was awash in a haze of city lights, each flickering bulb casting long shadows that seemed to dance along the pavement. The world felt alive, vibrant, yet tinged with an underlying tension that echoed the uncertainty in my heart.

The bookstore on Maple Street was only a few blocks away, a quaint little place with a sign that creaked softly in the night breeze. As we approached, I could see the warm glow of the interior spilling out onto the sidewalk, inviting yet intimidating. The door was an old wooden affair, its surface worn smooth by the hands of countless visitors. I paused, my heart racing.

"Ready?" Nathan asked, his voice low and reassuring, though I could see the determination etched on his face.

"Ready as I'll ever be," I replied, forcing a smile despite the knot tightening in my stomach.

We pushed the door open, and the soft chime of a bell announced our arrival. The interior was a haven of bookshelves crammed with volumes that seemed to reach toward the ceiling, their spines like soldiers standing guard over the secrets contained within. The air smelled of aged paper and the faintest hint of coffee.

At a small counter at the back stood a woman with graying hair tied in a loose bun, her glasses perched at the tip of her nose. She glanced up as we entered, her eyes narrowing slightly before brightening with recognition.

"Welcome! It's been a while since I've seen fresh faces," she said, her voice warm yet filled with curiosity. "What can I do for you?"

"Are you Evelyn?" I asked, my voice barely above a whisper, unsure if I should plunge straight into the heart of the matter.

"Yes, that's me," she replied, stepping closer with a welcoming smile. "And you are?"

"I'm—" I started, but Nathan interjected.

"We need your help," he said, cutting to the chase. "We're looking for information about some notes we found. They're tied to something dangerous, and we think you might know more about it."

Evelyn's demeanor shifted instantly. The warmth faded, replaced by a guarded expression. "Dangerous is a relative term. What do you think you know?"

I exchanged a glance with Nathan, sensing the tension between the two. "We know someone is threatening people in the neighborhood," I said, my voice steadying. "And we've been warned to tread carefully. We're just trying to understand what's really going on."

Evelyn studied us for a long moment, her gaze searching our faces as if trying to determine our intentions. "You're right to be cautious. The world is filled with shadows, and not everyone emerges from them unscathed. But if you're willing to risk it, I may have something that could help you."

"What is it?" Nathan asked, leaning forward slightly, his eagerness palpable.

Evelyn gestured for us to follow her to a secluded corner of the bookstore, where a small table was adorned with an assortment of dusty tomes and mysterious artifacts. "This was left in my care many years ago," she said, brushing her fingers over a worn leather-bound book, its cover embossed with symbols I didn't recognize. "It contains the stories of those who have come before you—individuals who faced similar threats. But beware, not all of them ended well."

"What do you mean?" I asked, feeling a chill crawl up my spine.

"This book holds more than just stories. It has the power to reveal hidden truths, but it can also lead to great peril," she replied, her voice low and filled with foreboding. "The paths you take will define your fate. Choose wisely."

I glanced at Nathan, who seemed equally captivated and cautious. "What kind of truths?" I pressed, needing more clarity.

"The kind that could change everything," Evelyn said, her eyes narrowing with intensity. "But remember, knowledge can be both a weapon and a shield. It's up to you how you wield it."

The weight of her words settled over us like a thick fog. "Can we see it?" Nathan asked, his voice steady despite the storm of emotions swirling within me.

With a nod, Evelyn carefully opened the book, its pages yellowed with age. Symbols and illustrations leaped to life before us, each one more mesmerizing than the last. I leaned in closer, scanning the ancient script, feeling as if I were peering into a world that had long been forgotten.

"This," she said, tracing a finger over an illustration of a sprawling map, "could lead you to places that hold the answers you seek. But you must be cautious; others are searching for the same knowledge, and they will stop at nothing to keep it hidden."

A shiver ran down my spine at the thought of someone else hunting for answers. "Who?" I whispered, my voice catching in my throat.

Evelyn paused, her expression grave. "There are forces at play that you can't begin to comprehend. The people behind the notes have deep connections, and they will not hesitate to eliminate threats. You've already attracted attention simply by seeking the truth."

The weight of her warning settled heavily on my shoulders. "What should we do?" I asked, anxiety knotting my stomach.

"Follow the map," she instructed, her voice a whisper, her eyes flashing with intensity. "But be prepared for what you might uncover. Sometimes the truth is more terrifying than the lies we tell ourselves."

Before I could respond, a loud crash echoed from the front of the bookstore, shattering the fragile bubble of safety we had just begun to build. The door burst open, and a figure rushed in, panting, wild-eyed. "You need to get out! They're coming!"

A rush of adrenaline surged through me as I exchanged a panicked look with Nathan. "Who's coming?" I demanded, my heart racing.

The figure looked around frantically before their gaze landed on Evelyn. "I saw them—black suits, dark cars. They're looking for you!"

Fear gripped me, a vise tightening around my chest. "We need to leave. Now!" I shouted, adrenaline coursing through my veins.

As Nathan grabbed my hand, the urgency of the situation ignited a fire within me. I could feel the ground shifting beneath our feet, the world spiraling into chaos. We had been thrust into a game of shadows, and as we raced toward the back exit, I couldn't shake the feeling that the real danger was just beginning. The thrill of the chase pulsed through me, but so did the chilling realization that not everyone would make it out alive.

The door slammed shut behind us, but the weight of what lay ahead loomed larger than ever, an uncharted territory fraught with peril. And in that moment, as we plunged into the darkened alleyway, I knew we were not just seeking answers—we were running for our lives.

Chapter 13: The Dance of Deception

The gala unfolded like a dream, a whirlwind of color and sound that danced in harmony with the cool autumn breeze whispering through the open windows. Golden chandeliers hung above like stars captured in glass, their light cascading onto the elegantly clothed guests, transforming the room into a shimmering sea of silk and satin. The air was thick with laughter and the intoxicating aroma of delicate hors d'oeuvres, mingling with the sweet notes of an orchestra playing a soft waltz in the background. As I stood at the edge of the ballroom, my emerald gown swished around my ankles, a vivid splash of color against the more muted tones of the crowd.

Nathan's presence beside me was like a steady heartbeat in this chaotic atmosphere. He looked dashing in a tailored black suit that accentuated the broadness of his shoulders, his dark hair neatly styled, every inch a picture of sophistication. Our eyes met, and for a fleeting moment, the weight of our mission slipped away, leaving just the thrill of the night and the unsaid words lingering in the air between us.

"Ready for our grand performance?" he asked, a mischievous glint in his eye. His voice was low, almost conspiratorial, weaving through the noise like a soft thread in a grand tapestry.

"Only if you promise not to step on my toes," I shot back, my smile playful yet my heart raced with the knowledge of the danger that lay ahead.

As we made our way deeper into the throng of elegantly dressed patrons, the rhythm of the music pulled us toward the dance floor. The swirling couples moved as if caught in an elaborate ballet, and we were swept along, Nathan's hand firmly clasping mine. The moment we stepped into the circle of twirling bodies, I felt the world around us dissolve into an array of vibrant colors and shapes.

"Just follow my lead," he instructed, his grip tightening slightly as he guided me into a graceful spin. I laughed, the sound mingling with the music, the sheer joy of movement releasing the tension that had settled in my chest. I let myself be swept away, allowing the rhythm of the waltz to carry us.

"Are you sure this isn't just a clever ploy to get me to admit I'm a terrible dancer?" I teased, stepping lightly in time with the music, exhilaration coursing through me.

"Trust me, your dancing is the least of my worries," Nathan replied, his expression shifting as he focused on my movements. "Just keep your eyes on me. We need to maintain our cover."

With every turn, I felt the electric charge between us intensify, a magnetic pull that made the surroundings fade into a blurred backdrop. His eyes locked onto mine, and in that moment, the chaotic chatter of the gala dimmed into a distant hum, leaving just the two of us suspended in a world of our own making.

But as the music soared, so did the nagging reminders of our precarious situation. We were here to uncover secrets, to navigate a labyrinth of deception where each smile could mask ulterior motives and every laugh could hide whispered threats. The atmosphere crackled with tension, a palpable energy that made the hairs on the back of my neck stand on end.

As we spun around the floor, I caught glimpses of the other guests, their laughter ringing hollow in my ears. A group of men in crisp suits lingered near the bar, their hushed conversations punctuated by furtive glances. I couldn't help but wonder what secrets they were hiding, what dangerous alliances were being forged under the guise of celebration.

Just as the thought crossed my mind, Nathan leaned closer, his breath warm against my ear. "Stay alert. I've noticed some unusual movements near the entrance."

"Unusual how?" I asked, a chill creeping down my spine, my senses heightening.

"Let's just say, not everyone here is who they claim to be," he replied, his expression shifting from playful to serious in an instant.

The dance continued, but my heart raced for a different reason now. I scanned the crowd, trying to discern the truth hidden behind their smiles. A woman in a red gown caught my eye, her laughter too loud, too bright. She spoke animatedly with a man whose posture seemed overly relaxed, as if he was savoring a moment far too delicious to share.

"Keep your head in the game," Nathan urged, pulling me closer as the music swelled. "Focus on our cover, and let's gather what we can. There's bound to be more happening than we see."

Just as I opened my mouth to respond, the music shifted to a faster tempo, and Nathan led me into a lively twirl. My heart raced, a mix of exhilaration and anxiety coursing through my veins as we danced amid the chaos. The world spun around us, but Nathan's gaze remained steady, anchoring me in this whirlwind.

Suddenly, I spotted an old acquaintance across the room, a familiar face that sent a wave of dread crashing over me. James, an investigative journalist known for his keen eye and relentless pursuit of truth, stood at the edge of the dance floor, surveying the crowd. If he recognized me, all our careful planning could unravel in an instant.

"Nathan," I hissed, tension creeping into my voice. "We need to make ourselves scarce. James is here."

His expression shifted, alert and focused, a hint of concern flickering across his face. "Where?"

"There, by the grand staircase," I whispered, nodding discreetly in his direction.

Nathan glanced over his shoulder, the weight of our secret hanging between us like a taut string ready to snap. "We can't blow our cover. Stay close, and don't make any sudden moves."

The dance continued, but the joy of our earlier steps had transformed into a precarious balancing act. With each twirl, my heart raced, the stakes rising higher as we navigated this dance of deception, where every smile concealed secrets, and every turn brought us closer to a revelation that could shatter everything we had built.

The momentary thrill of the dance began to wane, a subtle tension threading through the air as Nathan and I maneuvered through the sea of shimmering dresses and sharp suits. My heart thudded in my chest, each beat echoing the pulse of the gala's relentless energy. I forced myself to focus, scanning the crowd while keeping the rhythm of the music alive in my body. The strains of the orchestra twisted through the room like a whisper, both inviting and ominous, a reminder that our masquerade was far from over.

"Do you think anyone notices?" I murmured to Nathan, the dance carrying us ever closer to the bar, where shadows seemed to linger more heavily. "I feel like a fish out of water, and yet I'm swimming with sharks."

"Just keep smiling," he replied, his voice steady, but I detected a flicker of uncertainty in his eyes. "The more they see us enjoying ourselves, the less they'll suspect we're up to anything."

I laughed lightly, the sound almost lost among the swirling conversations. "Enjoying ourselves? I feel like I'm in a high-stakes game of poker, and I'm not sure I know the rules."

Nathan leaned in closer, his breath warm against my ear. "Then we better bluff our way through."

With a quick pivot, he led me toward the bar. The air thickened with a sense of intrigue, and as we approached, I noticed a pair of guests deep in conversation, their voices low and urgent. The tension in their stance spoke volumes; they were clearly discussing matters of importance, perhaps even danger. My curiosity piqued as I strained to catch their words, but the cadence of the orchestra swelled, drowning out their hushed tones.

Nathan paused momentarily, his gaze drifting toward the men. "You catch that? Looks like they're sharing more than just pleasantries."

"What do you think they're talking about?" I asked, my voice barely above a whisper, the thrill of our covert mission sending tingles up my spine.

"Only one way to find out."

He nodded toward the bar where a flurry of champagne flutes glimmered under the soft lighting, drawing us closer like moths to a flame. I felt the weight of my gown against my skin, its luxurious fabric swaying gently with each step, amplifying the sensation of being both elegant and vulnerable.

As we reached the bar, Nathan ordered two glasses of champagne with a casual confidence that belied the underlying tension crackling between us. I took a moment to steal another glance at the two men, now gesturing animatedly, their expressions hardening. A knot of apprehension tightened in my stomach.

"Here's to our stealthy escapades," Nathan said, handing me a flute. The bubbly liquid caught the light, sparkling like tiny stars trapped within the glass.

I raised my glass, attempting to match his playful tone. "To blending in and not getting caught. And to my dazzling dance partner, of course."

"Flattery will get you everywhere," he replied, a smirk playing at the corners of his mouth.

Just then, the rhythm of the gala shifted. A sudden hush fell over the crowd as the lights dimmed momentarily, drawing the guests' attention toward a stage at the far end of the room where a tall figure emerged. He was a man dressed in a crisp white suit, his demeanor both commanding and charismatic, instantly capturing the room's attention.

"Ladies and gentlemen," he boomed, his voice smooth as silk, "welcome to an evening of secrets and revelations."

A chill ran through me, and I exchanged a quick glance with Nathan, our shared concern palpable. It felt like an omen, a darkening sky before the storm.

"The night promises surprises," the man continued, a sly grin spreading across his face. "But first, I invite you all to join me in an exhilarating game of chance."

He gestured dramatically to a large roulette wheel that had been wheeled onto the stage, and the crowd erupted into a mix of excited chatter and laughter. I could sense the undercurrents of fear swirling beneath the surface, yet many were drawn in, intrigued by the prospect of danger laced with thrill.

"Should we?" I asked Nathan, my heart racing. The wheel spun like a portal to another world, beckoning with the allure of mystery.

"I don't like the sound of this, but it could be a chance to gather intel," he replied, his brow furrowing as he assessed the situation. "Let's keep our wits about us."

With a shared nod, we moved toward the stage, the crowd parting for us as if we were characters in some fantastical play. The excitement in the air buzzed around us, charged with the electric anticipation of what was to come.

As we approached the wheel, I could see the men from the bar now standing to the side, their faces tight with apprehension, watching closely as the game began. The host spun the wheel with a flourish, the colors blurring together, and I felt an involuntary shiver at the sudden shift in energy.

"Step right up, folks!" the host called, his voice booming over the chatter. "Take a chance, but remember: fortune favors the bold!"

"Bold is definitely one way to describe this," I muttered to Nathan, eyeing the wheel warily.

"Let's get in on it," he said, stepping forward, and before I could object, he pulled me along with him. "What's life without a little risk?"

"Life without a little risk is life with a lot less chaos," I shot back, my heart racing with equal parts excitement and dread.

As we placed our bets—a seemingly harmless nod to the thrill of the night—my mind raced with questions. What secrets were entwined in this game? And what awaited us on the other side of the spinning wheel?

The host began to spin again, his voice rising in fervor. "One lucky winner will walk away with more than just a prize tonight! They'll unlock a mystery that lies hidden within these walls!"

A ripple of excitement spread through the crowd, and as I glanced around, I saw the same men from the bar inching closer, their faces shadowed with intent.

"Do you sense that?" I murmured to Nathan, my senses heightened. "It feels like they're hunting for something—like we're all just pieces on a chessboard."

Nathan's expression hardened, his hand tightening around my wrist as he leaned closer. "Keep your eyes open. This isn't just a game anymore."

The wheel slowed, the anticipation mounting, and my heart raced as it ticked toward its fate. In that moment, I realized we weren't just dancing with deception; we were about to plunge headfirst into a game where the stakes were higher than we could have imagined. The tension hung heavy, wrapping around us like a shroud, and I knew we were teetering on the edge of something dark and thrilling, the line between friend and foe blurred in the kaleidoscope of the night.

The wheel slowed, the vibrant colors blurring together, and the crowd erupted in an ecstatic cheer, the tension amplifying with each passing moment. My heart raced, caught in the whirlwind of excitement and apprehension, the anticipation thickening the air around us. I caught Nathan's gaze, his eyes reflecting both determination and a flicker of mischief, as if he reveled in the chaos we had stepped into.

"Looks like everyone's a little too invested in this game," he remarked, his voice low, barely cutting through the exuberant noise. "We need to stay alert. This might be the distraction they're counting on."

I nodded, acutely aware of the shifting dynamics in the room. The men from the bar had now formed a small huddle, their expressions grim, as they whispered urgently among themselves. The enthusiasm of the gala-goers stood in stark contrast to the tension radiating from that corner, as if the very air around them crackled with unspoken threats.

"Did you catch that?" I whispered, trying to focus on the unsettling energy emanating from the group. "They're not here for fun; they're plotting something."

Nathan's gaze sharpened, scanning the crowd. "Let's keep our distance for now. If they sense we're onto them, it could ruin our cover."

The wheel finally stopped with a loud click, and the host shouted the winning number. Cheers erupted around us, a cacophony of jubilation that echoed through the grand hall. I watched as a young woman in a stunning silver gown jumped up, clapping her hands and practically glowing with excitement as she made her way to the stage. But the exuberance of the crowd was lost on me, my focus zeroed in on the men, who had abruptly fallen silent, their attention now solely on the new victor.

"Is it just me, or do they look like they've seen a ghost?" I murmured, drawing Nathan closer as the cheers faded into an uneasy murmur.

"I'd say that's our cue," he replied, tilting his head slightly toward the bar, where the two men now stood with tight expressions, their earlier camaraderie replaced by a palpable sense of urgency.

With the excitement fading, I felt a creeping chill, the night taking on a more sinister tone. The gleam of the chandelier's crystals overhead felt oppressive now, like the weight of our impending discovery pressed against my chest. As the crowd cheered for the winner, I grabbed Nathan's arm and steered him toward a quieter corner, just beyond the reach of the main festivities.

"What if we confront them?" I suggested, adrenaline coursing through me, a mix of fear and bravado. "If they're up to something, we can't just sit back and watch."

He raised an eyebrow, amusement dancing in his eyes. "And what's your plan, fearless leader? Ask them nicely to share their secrets over a glass of champagne?"

"Touché," I conceded, running a hand through my hair, trying to rein in my rising anxiety. "But we need to figure out what's happening before it spirals out of control."

"I'm all for being proactive, but we can't tip our hand just yet. Let's observe for a moment."

As I leaned against the wall, scanning the crowd, I couldn't shake the feeling that we were being watched. The men seemed to have zeroed in on the girl at the stage, their previous expressions of anxiety replaced by a calculating interest. I tried to focus on the chatter around us, half-listening to the jubilant voices, but the undercurrent of fear persisted.

"You're thinking too loudly," Nathan said, breaking through my thoughts with a chuckle. "Relax a little. You're making me feel anxious."

"Right, because I'm the only one with a reason to be concerned," I shot back, though I couldn't help but smile at his lightheartedness amidst the tension.

"Okay, what's the plan?" he asked, shifting his stance and folding his arms. "Are we waiting for them to reveal their evil plot? Or do we have to lure them into a trap? I can be very convincing."

I rolled my eyes, suppressing a grin. "I'm sure you are. But let's keep it simple for now. We need to get close enough to hear what they're saying without being seen."

As we edged toward the edge of the crowd, the man in the white suit continued to entertain the guests, his voice booming with exaggerated enthusiasm. "And now, let's move on to the next round! Who's feeling lucky?"

The laughter and cheers returned, but my attention was drawn back to the men, who had now stepped away from the bar, moving with purpose. They were closer now, their postures tense, as if they were preparing for something big.

"Here we go," Nathan murmured, nudging me gently. "Time to play our part."

The crowd shifted, and we found ourselves pulled into the flow of guests eager to engage in the next round of the game. I felt my heart race as the host waved his hands dramatically, signaling for everyone to gather around the wheel.

"Join in, folks! Let's see who has the luck tonight!" he declared, grinning from ear to ear.

As we mingled with the crowd, I caught snippets of conversations swirling around us. Excitement crackled through the air, but beneath that veneer of joy, I sensed something darker, a current of treachery lurking just below the surface.

"Just keep your eyes on them," Nathan whispered, nodding subtly toward the men. "Let's see what they do next."

But as I turned my attention back to the men, a shadow crossed my vision. A woman in a sleek black dress, her face partially obscured by a delicate mask, slipped into our line of sight. Her presence was magnetic, an unexplainable pull that drew the attention of the crowd. She moved with purpose, her eyes scanning the room with a calculated intensity.

"Who is she?" I asked, my voice barely above a whisper.

Nathan's expression shifted, the playful spark replaced by concern. "I don't know, but she seems to have a vested interest in this event."

As the woman approached the men, their postures relaxed, an air of familiarity evident in their body language. I felt a pang of unease as I watched their interaction unfold. The conversation seemed casual, but the undertones were charged, and my instincts screamed that we were teetering on the edge of a revelation that could change everything.

"Stay close," Nathan urged, his hand brushing against mine, grounding me amidst the chaos. "I don't like this."

Suddenly, the woman turned, her eyes locking onto mine, and I felt a jolt of recognition ripple through me, as if she could see right through my facade. A smirk played on her lips, and just as I opened my mouth to ask Nathan if he felt the same unease, the air erupted with tension.

"Ladies and gentlemen," the host called again, his voice rising above the noise. "I have an announcement! The next player on our roulette will take home not just a prize but access to information that could change the course of this evening!"

The crowd gasped, a collective intake of breath as curiosity morphed into apprehension. I felt Nathan stiffen beside me, his eyes narrowing as he assessed the situation.

Before I could fully process the weight of the moment, the room plunged into darkness. The lights flickered violently, and chaos erupted as screams pierced the air. The wheel spun wildly, a blinding blur of color and sound, the guests around us falling into a panic.

"Now what?" I shouted over the chaos, my pulse quickening as I clutched Nathan's arm.

"We get out of here!" he replied, his voice firm and urgent.

Just as we turned to navigate through the crowd, I felt a sharp grip on my shoulder, pulling me back into the chaos. A voice hissed close to my ear, "You shouldn't have come here."

I gasped, adrenaline surging as I locked eyes with the woman in black. Her mask glinted in the dim light, and I could feel the weight of her words hanging ominously between us, a threat wrapped in enigma. The world around us spiraled into pandemonium, but her gaze held me captive, the promise of danger hovering just beyond our reach, and I knew that this night was far from over.

Chapter 14: A Dangerous Revelation

The chandelier above glimmered like a thousand trapped stars, each crystal catching the light in a dizzying dance of colors that reflected the glamour of the gala. Laughter mingled with the clinking of glasses, a symphony of high spirits and frivolity that should have enveloped me in its warmth. Yet, as I moved through the throng of elegantly dressed guests, my senses were alert, the evening's frivolity a thin veneer over a reality that was growing darker by the second.

I had donned my favorite dress, a deep emerald green that cascaded down to my ankles, the fabric whispering against my skin as I navigated the crowd. But the laughter around me felt hollow, like the empty echoes of a shell washed ashore. I caught glimpses of familiar faces—smiling, swirling, engrossed in conversations that felt far removed from the truth I had uncovered. My heart raced, not with excitement but with a gnawing anxiety that clawed at my insides, urging me to remain vigilant.

Then I spotted Nathan across the room, his dark hair tousled just so, a perfect match for the crisp lines of his tailored suit. He stood amidst a group of our friends, a magnetic presence as he animatedly recounted some story, and for a fleeting moment, I longed to be enveloped in that warmth, to escape the encroaching shadows that had been creeping into my thoughts. But duty called louder than desire, and I pushed through the crowd, feeling the heat of their mingled perfume and cologne swirling around me like an invisible barrier.

"Hey, can I steal you for a moment?" I interrupted, tugging gently at Nathan's sleeve, my voice barely rising above the din. His eyes flicked to mine, filled with the bright warmth that had always made me feel safe.

"Sure," he replied, his gaze steadying as he sensed my urgency. "What's up?"

I took a breath, steadying the tremor in my hands. "I overheard something—two guests were talking about the break-ins. They know more than they're letting on." The words spilled out, each syllable laced with the gravity of what I had just learned. The laughter around us faded, replaced by the suffocating weight of our shared concern.

Nathan's expression shifted, the easy charm of the evening melting away as he leaned closer, his voice dropping to a whisper. "What did they say?"

"They mentioned something about a connection to someone who lives in the neighborhood," I replied, my voice barely above a breath. "It was like they were discussing a plan, and they sounded... almost familiar with the whole situation. This isn't just petty theft, Nathan. There's something bigger going on, something dangerous."

His brow furrowed, and I could see the gears turning in his mind as he processed the implications. "Did you recognize either of them?"

"No, they were just two strangers, but the way they spoke—there was a confidence there, like they knew exactly what they were doing." I scanned the room, my heart pounding as I realized the enormity of what we might have stumbled upon. "We need to find out who they are. I can't shake the feeling that we've stepped into something we can't handle."

Nathan's jaw clenched, and he nodded. "Let's keep our distance for now. We can't tip them off. But we need to keep an eye on them."

As we spoke, a gust of cool air swept through the ballroom as the heavy doors opened, a fleeting glimpse of the world outside. For a moment, the chatter faded, and all I could hear was the fluttering of my own heartbeat echoing in my ears. There was a certain beauty to the chaos, but underneath it, the danger lurked like a coiled snake, ready to strike.

The night pressed on, but I felt an electric tension tightening around me. Nathan and I fell into an easy rhythm, moving through the crowd, all the while keeping our eyes peeled for the two strangers. The contrast between the vibrant party and the shadows I felt creeping ever closer was maddening. I couldn't shake the feeling that the joy around us was just a mask, and beneath it lay a world of deception and intrigue.

"Hey, over there!" Nathan gestured discreetly, tilting his head toward a cluster of guests gathered near the far wall. "Those two."

I followed his gaze to where the two figures stood, laughter spilling from their lips, a gleam of something in their eyes that sent a chill racing down my spine. They were casual in their demeanor, yet something about the way they leaned toward one another suggested intimacy beyond mere acquaintance. I felt a knot form in my stomach; it was as if they were sharing secrets that could unravel the very fabric of this gala.

"What do you think they're discussing?" I whispered, a mix of curiosity and dread swirling within me.

"Whatever it is, it's more than just idle chatter," Nathan replied, his brow furrowing deeper. "We need to get closer, without being obvious."

We edged toward the group, blending into the crowd, each laugh and clink of glass amplifying the heartbeat thrumming in my ears. I could feel Nathan's presence beside me, a grounding force amidst the uncertainty. Yet as we approached, the tension between us thickened, charged with the unspoken fear that whatever lay ahead could change everything we thought we knew.

And just as I felt we were on the brink of uncovering something monumental, the laughter ceased abruptly. The two strangers exchanged a quick glance, a fleeting moment of realization that sent a ripple of unease through me. I held my breath, the world around us fading away, caught in that moment where the truth seemed to teeter on the edge of revelation.

"Did you hear that?" one of them said, their voice low and conspiratorial, laced with urgency. My pulse quickened as I leaned in, straining to catch every word. "We can't let them get in the way. This has to go smoothly. No loose ends."

I exchanged a glance with Nathan, a shared understanding dawning between us. This wasn't just about the break-ins anymore; we had unwittingly stumbled into a web of deceit that threatened to ensnare us both. The air thickened with unspoken tension, and I realized that the night had only just begun to unravel its dangerous secrets.

The atmosphere buzzed with energy, but it felt like static electricity, as if the air was charged with tension. I watched the two strangers, their laughter still echoing faintly in my ears, but now it sounded more like a cruel joke than a celebration. My heart raced as I tried to piece together what I had just overheard. A tangled web of connections flitted through my mind like shadows dancing on the edges of reality, leaving me feeling both intrigued and utterly unmoored.

"Do you think we should confront them?" Nathan asked, his voice low and steady, grounding me in the moment. His dark eyes were sharp, scanning the crowd as if he could pinpoint the heart of the mystery lurking among the festivities.

"Confront them?" I echoed, incredulity lacing my words. "That sounds like the worst idea in history. What are we supposed to say? 'Excuse me, do you happen to be involved in the crime wave plaguing our neighborhood? Oh, and by the way, could you share your secrets while you're at it?'"

A faint smile tugged at the corners of Nathan's lips. "You've got a point. Maybe more of a stealth approach is in order."

"Stealth? You mean like ninjas? I'm not exactly dressed for stealth missions." I gestured to my shimmering dress, the fabric reflecting the light with every slight movement, betraying my every intention. "More like a disco ball on the dance floor."

"Maybe that's our advantage. You distract them with your dazzling presence while I sneak in and eavesdrop," he quipped, his tone light but his gaze serious.

I shot him a playful glare. "As tempting as that sounds, I'm not sure I want to be the diversion in a potentially dangerous situation. But I do like the idea of you being the sneaky one."

We both chuckled softly, but the laughter did little to ease the unease knotting my stomach. The air thickened with uncertainty, the jubilant ambiance around us a stark contrast to the tension building inside. We needed to find out more, but how to navigate this charade without drawing attention?

"Maybe we could break off into pairs," Nathan suggested, a spark of inspiration lighting his expression. "I can pretend to engage someone else while keeping an ear on our two friends. You can work the crowd a bit, keep your eyes on the exits, and if things escalate, you can alert me."

"Ah, the classic 'divide and conquer' strategy. Sounds like a plan," I agreed, although trepidation lingered in my chest. "Just remember, if you get into trouble, I'm not coming to save you unless you're wearing a superhero cape."

"Deal," he said, offering me a reassuring nod before moving away to position himself closer to the duo.

I felt a rush of adrenaline as I made my way through the crowd, weaving between elegantly dressed guests who were blissfully unaware of the storm brewing beneath the surface. My mind raced as I scanned the faces around me, looking for anyone who might provide a clue, a hint of the intrigue lurking just beneath the glitzy facade.

Moments turned into eternities as I attempted to engage in casual conversations, all the while keeping an ear tuned to Nathan and the strangers. I caught snippets of laughter and idle chatter, but nothing that felt remotely connected to the gravity of what we had unearthed. I took a deep breath, reminding myself to remain calm, to be a part of the celebration even as I felt like an unwitting participant in a thriller.

Then, my attention was drawn to a woman across the room, her striking red dress standing out among the sea of pastels and blacks. She moved with an effortless grace, and for a moment, I was captivated by her elegance. Yet there was something about her that made me uneasy. The way her eyes darted around, calculating, as if she were assessing every person in the room.

Curiosity piqued, I made my way over, feigning interest in a conversation with a nearby guest. Out of the corner of my eye, I could see Nathan shifting closer, his posture relaxed, but I could sense the tension radiating off him like heat waves.

The red-dressed woman turned her head slightly, and I caught a glimpse of her profile. Something clicked in my mind, a jarring connection to the whisper I had overheard earlier. The name danced at the edge of my memory—a name I had heard in connection with the break-ins. My heart raced as I tried to focus on the current conversation while the threads of possibility tangled in my mind.

Just as I felt the urge to approach her, Nathan's gaze shot to mine, a silent warning in his expression. I could see it then, the two strangers had drawn closer, their demeanor shifting from casual banter to something far more sinister.

"We need to move," Nathan mouthed, urgency lacing his expression. I nodded, my pulse quickening as I followed him through the throng of guests, my heart pounding in my chest like a war drum.

"Do you think they've noticed us?" I whispered as we slipped out of the main ballroom into a dimly lit corridor. The music faded to a murmur, and the clinking of glasses transformed into a distant echo.

"I don't know, but we can't afford to wait around and find out," he replied, glancing back toward the ballroom entrance. "We need to gather our thoughts and plan our next move. If they're in on this together, we might not be safe here."

"Great, so we're not just dealing with thieves; we might be up against a whole syndicate," I said, trying to keep my tone light even as fear clawed at my insides. "Should we call the police or something?"

Nathan paused, considering. "No. Not yet. We don't know enough. If we alert them now, they could vanish before we have any real evidence. We need to keep our eyes open and dig deeper."

I nodded, feeling the weight of his words settle heavily on my shoulders. The night had shifted from a glittering gala to a treacherous game of cat and mouse, and I was acutely aware of the stakes. "Okay, but I want to do this together. I don't want to risk either of us getting into trouble alone."

"Together it is," he agreed, a reassuring smile breaking through the tension. "Let's keep an eye on our targets and find out just how deep this rabbit hole goes."

We stepped further into the shadows of the corridor, hearts racing in sync, ready to uncover the secrets lurking in the dark corners of the night. As we positioned ourselves, I couldn't shake the feeling that we were on the precipice of something monumental, and the stakes were climbing higher with every whispered conversation and knowing glance exchanged behind closed doors.

The dimly lit corridor felt like a lifeline, pulling us away from the swirling chaos of the gala. As we stepped further into its embrace, the muted laughter and music faded to an echo, replaced by the unsettling sound of our own hurried breaths. My heart was a war drum, thudding against my ribs as if reminding me of the urgency of our mission. Nathan and I exchanged furtive glances, our minds racing in unison, piecing together the fragments of danger that had snaked their way into our evening.

"Do you think we can follow them?" I whispered, trying to keep my voice steady, though the tremor betrayed me. "They've got to have some sort of plan, and I want to know what it is."

"Let's see if we can spot where they're headed," Nathan replied, his expression thoughtful as he scanned the hallway. "We'll need to keep our distance. If they catch wind that we're onto them, this could turn messy."

I nodded, every nerve in my body thrumming with anticipation. We tiptoed down the corridor, hearts racing as we edged closer to the entrance of the main ballroom. The tension hung thick in the air, almost tangible, as if the walls themselves were holding their breath, waiting for the truth to unfold.

Peering around the corner, I caught sight of the two strangers—now standing in earnest conversation with the woman in red. Their postures were aggressive, animated gestures punctuating the air between them. I strained to hear the words floating back to us, fragments of their conversation whispering on the edge of my understanding.

"This is becoming a liability," one of them said, his tone sharp, like glass shards littering the floor. "We can't afford any mistakes. If they connect us to the break-ins, it's over."

I exchanged a wide-eyed look with Nathan, adrenaline surging through my veins. We were onto something much more profound than we had anticipated. These weren't just petty thieves; this was an operation intricately woven into the fabric of our community.

"What's our play here?" Nathan murmured, his voice barely above a whisper.

"Find out what they're after," I replied, determination bubbling up inside me. "Maybe we can gather enough evidence to go to the police."

He nodded, but I could see the wheels turning in his head, weighing the risk against the potential gain. "You're right. But let's be cautious. If they catch us listening, we could end up in over our heads."

We continued to edge closer, my heart racing as the pieces began to fall into place. With every word I strained to catch, the picture became clearer, a sinister tapestry woven with threats and hidden motives. I could feel the weight of our inquiry pressing down on us, the gravity of what lay ahead looming large.

Just then, the woman in red stepped back, her voice rising above the others. "We need to act quickly. I don't trust those two snoops. They're asking too many questions, and if they connect the dots..." Her voice trailed off, eyes narrowing as she glanced over her shoulder.

Nathan and I instinctively ducked behind a potted palm, the foliage providing a flimsy shield as our hearts raced. The woman's gaze scanned the room, suspicion etched across her face. I held my breath, praying she wouldn't lock onto our hiding spot.

"Keep it together," Nathan whispered, the heat of his breath brushing against my ear, grounding me amidst the tension.

"I'm not panicking," I replied, perhaps a little too defensively. "Just... enjoying the scenery."

Nathan smirked, the corners of his lips twitching as he fought to suppress a laugh. "Right, because nothing says 'relaxation' like eavesdropping on criminals at a high-society event."

We waited, hearts pounding, until the strangers resumed their conversation, seemingly unaware of our presence. "Let's meet at the usual place after the gala," one of them said, his tone low and conspiratorial. "We can finalize the plans then. But until then, keep your eyes peeled. I don't want any loose ends."

"Understood," the other replied, glancing back toward the ballroom entrance. "Let's not attract any unwanted attention."

The three of them exchanged a few more hurried words before breaking apart, each one slipping into the crowd as though they were mere partygoers. Nathan and I watched them go, tension coiling tighter around us like a noose.

"What do you want to do?" I asked, urgency creeping into my voice. "Should we follow?"

"Let's see where they go," Nathan replied, his eyes narrowing as he scanned the ballroom. "But we have to stay out of sight. If they catch on to us, we might find ourselves at the center of whatever mess they're involved in."

We fell into step behind them, the crowd parting like the Red Sea as we navigated our way through clusters of animated guests. My pulse quickened as we trailed them down the hallway, past a series of opulent rooms adorned with gilded mirrors and extravagant floral arrangements. The distant strains of music echoed behind us, a haunting reminder of the revelry that felt worlds apart from the intrigue unfolding just beyond the ballroom doors.

As we approached a quieter corner of the mansion, the strangers paused to exchange hushed words beneath the muted glow of a flickering chandelier. My breath hitched in my throat as I leaned closer, eager to catch every word. "We're running out of time," the woman said, her voice a sharp whisper. "We can't wait until after the gala. We need to act now."

"Act?" one of the men shot back, his expression incredulous. "You want to risk everything because of two nosy bystanders?"

"Those 'bystanders' could ruin everything if they get too curious. They're already digging where they shouldn't. We need to eliminate the threat before it escalates."

I felt a chill run down my spine, the implications of her words sinking in like a stone. Eliminate? The weight of her threat hung heavy in the air, suffocating the breath from my lungs. Nathan's hand found mine, squeezing gently but urgently, as we exchanged terrified glances. This wasn't a petty crime we were up against; this was a matter of life and death.

Just as I began to formulate a plan to retreat, a loud crash echoed from the ballroom, puncturing the tension like a pinprick in a balloon. The trio's heads snapped in unison toward the noise, eyes wide with alarm.

"What was that?" the other man demanded, his voice rising with panic.

"I don't know, but we can't be seen here!" the woman hissed, glancing back toward us.

With adrenaline surging through my veins, I pulled Nathan further into the shadows, just as they began to move. My mind raced as the urgency of the moment enveloped us. We had to stay hidden, but I couldn't shake the feeling that we were about to stumble into a confrontation that would change everything.

Then, without warning, a figure burst through the ballroom door, silhouetted against the vibrant lights and chaos inside. My breath caught in my throat as recognition hit me like a punch to the gut. It was someone I knew, someone I hadn't expected to see here tonight, and the implications sent a wave of dread crashing over me.

As the familiar figure stepped into the dim light, I realized we were standing on the brink of an unraveling mystery that was far more dangerous than I could have ever imagined. The night was just beginning, and with each pulse of adrenaline, I felt the world shift beneath my feet, ready to plunge us into the depths of uncertainty.

Chapter 15: Echoes of the Past

The air was thick with the scent of damp earth and age as we ventured deeper into the estate's overgrown gardens, the wild flora tangling around us like the whispers of a long-forgotten world. Ivy clung stubbornly to the weathered stone walls, intertwining with remnants of opulence—stone gargoyles stood sentinel over the decaying grandeur, their expressions a mix of disdain and sorrow. Each step we took disturbed the fragile silence, the crunch of fallen leaves underfoot sounding like the gentle chime of a distant clock, reminding us that time was, indeed, slipping away.

"Did you ever imagine we'd be doing this?" Nathan's voice cut through the stillness, a soft laugh laced with disbelief. He brushed his fingers along a vine, momentarily distracted by the lushness of life reclaiming its territory. The sun streamed through the leaves overhead, casting dappled patterns on his face, illuminating the determination etched in his brow.

"Honestly? I thought you'd be busy saving the world in some corporate boardroom," I shot back, unable to resist the banter that had become our lifeblood. "Not traipsing through the underbrush like some kind of—"

"Adventurer?" he interjected, grinning, his confidence blooming like the wildflowers sprouting defiantly between the cracks of the old stone path. There was a spark in his eyes that I hadn't seen before, a glimmer of excitement that masked the tension beneath.

"More like a misguided archeologist," I teased, but the playful exchange was a thin veil over the deeper undercurrents thrumming between us, echoing the estate's ghostly past. It was as if the very air we breathed was heavy with unspoken histories, urging us to uncover what lay beneath the surface.

With each corner we turned, we stumbled upon remnants of lives once lived—faded photographs trapped in cracked frames, their subjects gazing back at us with expressions both haunting and hopeful. I picked up a dusty silver locket, the intricate engraving obscured by years of neglect, and turned it over in my palm, feeling the weight of memories trapped inside. "Do you think they were happy?" I mused, the question hanging in the air like a forgotten prayer.

Nathan knelt beside me, brushing his fingers across the locket, his touch tender, almost reverent. "Happiness is complicated," he replied, his tone shifting from playful to serious. "Sometimes the facade is more comforting than the truth."

I met his gaze, the depth of his words settling into my bones. There was a vulnerability in him, an openness I hadn't expected. "Is that how you feel about your family?"

His laugh was devoid of humor, a brittle sound that shattered the moment. "My family is a minefield of expectations and regrets. I learned early on to navigate it with a smile."

Before I could probe deeper, a creaking sound echoed through the hall, startling us both. "Did you hear that?" I whispered, my heart pounding in my chest, the sudden tension pulling us closer together.

"Yeah, let's check it out," Nathan said, his protective instincts flaring again as he stepped in front of me. The shift in his demeanor was palpable; he was no longer the carefree partner in crime but a guardian of sorts, ready to confront whatever lurked in the shadows.

We crept down a narrow corridor, the air thickening with the scent of mold and decay. Faded wallpaper peeled away like the layers of history we were unearthing, revealing bare wood beneath—old scars of a house that had seen better days. A heavy door at the end of the hallway stood slightly ajar, the hinges groaning as we approached, a muted invitation to uncover the unknown.

"After you," Nathan said, a mock bow accompanied by an exaggerated grin. But there was a challenge in his eyes, a dare to breach the threshold and confront whatever lay beyond. I pushed the door open, the creak echoing in the silence like a call to adventure.

Inside, the room was cloaked in shadow, the sunlight battling to penetrate the dust-laden air. Our eyes adjusted, revealing a small parlor, its furniture draped in white sheets that resembled specters frozen in time. As I stepped further in, I felt the chill of the past wrapping around me, pulling me into its embrace. I reached for one of the sheets, ready to unveil the secrets beneath.

"Wait," Nathan cautioned, his voice low and urgent. "Let me." He moved beside me, his breath quickening as he reached for the fabric. Together, we lifted it, the dust swirling around us like tiny fairies caught in a dance, and the sight that met our eyes sent a shiver down my spine.

A small table lay beneath the sheet, its surface littered with trinkets—a porcelain doll with glassy eyes staring blankly into the void, a journal bound in cracked leather, its pages yellowed with age. As Nathan reached for the journal, a chill swept through the room, a gust of wind that seemed to carry with it the whispers of the past.

"Careful," I warned, my heart racing. "What if it's cursed?"

He chuckled softly, a sound that was both reassuring and filled with unease. "Or it could just be filled with boring entries about tea parties and gossip." But there was a flicker of tension in his smile, a shared acknowledgment that we were trespassing in a world that was not ours.

With a deft movement, he opened the journal, and the pages fluttered like startled birds, revealing cursive scrawls and sketches that brought the past to life. As he read aloud, I was entranced by the stories unfolding—tales of love and loss, of laughter and heartache, the echoes of lives once vibrant now reduced to ink and paper. Each word resonated deep within me, awakening something long dormant, a yearning to understand the fragility of our existence.

As Nathan read on, I found myself leaning closer, captivated not just by the words but by the man beside me, his voice weaving a spell that blurred the lines between our realities. In that moment, I understood: the past wasn't just an echo; it was a living, breathing part of who we were. And in the midst of crumbling walls and fading memories, I felt an unexpected bond growing between us—a shared curiosity that would drive us deeper into the shadows, into the heart of the mysteries that had ensnared our lives.

The atmosphere in the parlor shifted as Nathan continued reading from the journal, his voice a gentle murmur that echoed off the peeling walls. Each entry revealed a fragment of a life intertwined with joy and despair, the words painting vivid images in my mind. I could almost hear the laughter of children playing in the garden, feel the warmth of sunlight streaming through the windows, and sense the weight of secrets buried beneath the floorboards, waiting for someone to uncover them.

"Listen to this," Nathan said, his brow furrowing as he read an entry filled with a kind of melancholy that wrapped around us like a shroud. "It talks about a hidden room, a sanctuary from the outside world where secrets were kept safe." He paused, glancing at me with a spark of mischief in his eyes. "Should we go treasure hunting?"

"Treasure hunting? In a decrepit old house? What could possibly go wrong?" I replied, my voice dripping with sarcasm, but the thrill of adventure coursed through me. The idea of seeking out hidden treasures within this labyrinth of a mansion sent a shiver of excitement down my spine, a flicker of the same daring spirit that propelled me to explore the estate in the first place.

We set off, the journal now cradled in Nathan's arm as if it were a sacred relic. The shadows cast by the late afternoon sun danced across the walls, illuminating our path as we retraced our steps, peering into every nook and cranny. Each room was a portal into the past, filled with remnants of forgotten lives—an ornate mirror cracked with age, a dusty piano, its keys silent, yet whispering of melodies long gone.

"Over here," I called out, my eyes catching the glimmer of something behind a heavy curtain that swayed gently in the breeze. Nathan joined me, his curiosity piqued. Together, we pulled back the fabric, revealing a narrow door concealed within the wall, its edges worn and faded.

"This must be it," I breathed, excitement bubbling up within me. "The hidden room!"

"Or a place where they kept the family secrets locked away," Nathan said, half-joking but with an edge of seriousness that gave me pause. "Let's just hope it's not filled with skeletons."

"Please, if there were skeletons, they'd have to be more interesting than the ones in my closet," I quipped, trying to lighten the tension. But even I could sense the weight of what lay beyond that door.

With a deep breath, Nathan pushed it open, revealing a narrow staircase spiraling down into darkness. The air was cool and musty, a stark contrast to the warmth of the sunlit rooms above. "I'll go first," he said, a hint of protectiveness threading through his words.

"Of course you will," I replied, feigning annoyance as I nudged him aside. "You think I'm going to let you have all the fun?"

"Fun is a stretch when we're possibly descending into a dungeon," he countered, but there was a hint of a smile on his lips as he stepped back.

The first few steps creaked ominously beneath my weight, but I pressed on, a mixture of fear and exhilaration propelling me forward. Nathan followed closely, his presence a comfort against the encroaching darkness. As we descended, the world above faded away, replaced by the faint sound of dripping water and the distant echo of our footsteps against stone.

At the bottom, we emerged into a low-ceilinged chamber, the air thick with dampness. The walls were lined with shelves, their contents obscured by layers of dust. "What do you think we'll find?" I whispered, the anticipation thrumming in my veins.

"Only one way to find out," Nathan replied, his tone shifting to something more serious as he began to sweep the dust off the nearest shelf.

"Whoa, hold on," I said, suddenly feeling the weight of the moment. "Shouldn't we be careful? What if these are family heirlooms or—"

"Or a collection of horror-movie memorabilia?" Nathan quipped, a smirk dancing at the corners of his mouth. "I'll take my chances with the ghosts of great-aunts past."

Laughter bubbled up, dissolving the tension that had threatened to engulf us. Together, we began to sift through the items, uncovering remnants of lives lived long ago—an old clock that had long ceased to tick, a collection of delicate porcelain figurines, and a trunk bound in rusty chains, each discovery steeped in mystery and the weight of forgotten stories.

"What if there's something truly valuable in here?" I mused, running my fingers over the trunk. "Like a lost treasure or—"

"—a map to the fountain of youth?" Nathan finished for me, arching an eyebrow. "If you find that, I'm totally in."

I couldn't help but roll my eyes, but his humor had a way of lightening the air, the banter a balm against the unsettling atmosphere. "You just want to be young enough to have more bad hair days."

He laughed, a genuine sound that reverberated through the chamber. "Touché. But seriously, what if there's something here that could change everything?"

As he spoke, a flicker of something caught my eye from the corner of the room. I turned, and there it was—a small, ornate mirror set into the wall, its glass surprisingly clear amidst the dust. The frame was intricately carved, vines and flowers twining together in a dance of artistry.

"Hey, check this out," I called, drawn to it like a moth to a flame. As I stepped closer, the air shifted again, a sensation creeping over my skin like the chill of an impending storm. I reached out, my fingers grazing the cool surface, and in that moment, the world seemed to shift.

"What is it?" Nathan asked, his curiosity piqued.

"It's just a mirror, but... it feels different," I said, unable to shake the feeling that it was more than just a reflection staring back at me. My heart raced as I studied my own image, but something in the glass shimmered, flickering like the ghost of a memory just out of reach.

Before I could say another word, the light in the room dimmed, shadows lengthening and curling around us. "Nathan, I think—"

Suddenly, the air crackled with tension, the weight of the past bearing down on us. The mirror glowed with an otherworldly light, illuminating the room as if it were alive, and I felt a surge of energy coursing through me, tugging at my very soul.

"What is happening?" Nathan shouted, his voice strained as he moved closer to me, our connection a tether in the growing chaos.

"I don't know!" I cried, my gaze locked on the mirror as it shimmered with possibilities.

In that moment, I realized: we had unwittingly awakened something within these walls, something that demanded to be acknowledged. As the echoes of the past surged forth, I felt the boundaries between time and reality blur, pulling us into a whirlwind of history, secrets, and untold stories, forever changing the path that lay ahead.

The mirror's glow enveloped us, casting ethereal shadows that danced like wisps of smoke. It was as if the glass had become a portal, a doorway to a reality that lay just beyond the veil of our own.

My heart raced, caught between exhilaration and fear as I grasped Nathan's hand, the warmth of his touch grounding me amidst the chaos swirling around us.

"Can you feel that?" I whispered, my voice barely above a breath. "It's like... it's alive."

Nathan's expression shifted from curiosity to caution, his brow furrowing as he stepped closer, drawn into the mirror's light. "Whatever it is, it feels intense. Maybe we should—"

Before he could finish, the light flared, illuminating the chamber in a blinding flash that made us squint. I felt an electric pulse vibrate through the air, a resonance that connected us to the echoes of the past we had so eagerly sought. The world around us faded, the dusty shelves and creaking floorboards melting away until all that remained was the mirror, pulsating with an energy that felt both inviting and foreboding.

Suddenly, the reflection began to shift, images swirling like a storm within the glass. I leaned in, breathless, as scenes from another time unfolded before us. A lavish ballroom shimmered in the distance, filled with elegantly dressed couples swirling in a waltz, laughter echoing through the air like music. The clinking of glasses, the rustle of silk gowns—it was a glimpse into a world untouched by the decay surrounding us.

"Is that...?" Nathan started, his voice laced with disbelief.

"It looks like a party," I breathed, captivated. "But how can we see this?"

"Maybe it's a memory," he suggested, his fascination evident. "What if the mirror is a conduit for what once was?"

As if responding to his words, the scene intensified, focusing on a single couple at the center of the dance floor. Their faces were blurred, but the connection between them radiated warmth and longing. The woman wore a gown of deep emerald, her hair swept up in delicate curls, while the man, tall and handsome, held her close, his eyes reflecting an adoration that transcended time.

"This is incredible," I murmured, entranced by the sight. "What if we could step into that moment? What if we could—"

"Cecilia!" Nathan's urgent voice snapped me back to reality. He pulled me closer as the mirror began to ripple, the scenes shifting violently. The couple's laughter twisted into cries of despair, their joyful expressions morphing into horror as shadows loomed over them, dark figures creeping into the edges of the scene.

"What's happening?" I asked, panic rising in my throat as the shadows grew larger, consuming the light.

"I don't know, but we need to get out of here!" Nathan urged, his grip tightening on my hand. He turned to retreat, but the moment he stepped back, the mirror's glow flared brighter, casting an unyielding light that held us in place.

"No!" I protested, straining against his hold. "We can't leave yet! There's something here, something we need to understand!"

As I spoke, a voice echoed from within the mirror, soft yet commanding, slicing through the chaos like a blade. "You must remember. You must choose."

"What does that even mean?" Nathan exclaimed, frustration mingling with confusion. "Choose what?"

The mirror trembled, the images swirling faster now, the ballroom dissolving into darkness, replaced by flashes of memories—a child's laughter, a woman crying, an argument echoing against the walls of a grand home. With each new scene, the air grew thicker, suffocating in its urgency.

"Cecilia, we can't stay here!" Nathan insisted, his voice rising above the cacophony of sounds. I could see the strain in his face, the shadows of fear that flickered in his eyes.

But the voice persisted, almost pleading. "The choice must be made. The past cannot remain buried."

In that moment, the world shifted again. The mirror split, revealing two distinct paths: one leading back into the ballroom, where the couple danced obliviously, and another descending into a cavern of darkness, filled with the distant echoes of despair and longing. The choice was palpable, heavy with the weight of countless lives intertwined in sorrow and joy.

"Nathan, what do we do?" My voice trembled as I turned to him, searching for answers in his eyes.

"I—" he hesitated, the uncertainty pulling us apart even as we stood side by side. "We can't change the past. But maybe we can understand it."

With a rush of adrenaline, I made my decision. "Then we go into the darkness. We need to know what happened."

He looked at me, a mixture of admiration and dread in his gaze. "You're sure about this?"

"More than anything," I replied, conviction settling deep within me. We had uncovered too much already; the past was not something we could ignore. The shadows beckoned us, promising secrets that had long been silenced.

As we stepped closer to the darkened path, the voice from the mirror resonated once more. "The choice will bind you. Choose wisely."

A chilling gust of wind swept through the chamber, extinguishing the last vestiges of light as we crossed the threshold, plunging into a world unknown. The darkness enveloped us, thick and suffocating, and I could feel Nathan's hand clasping mine tightly, anchoring me to the only certainty I had.

Just as the darkness began to pulse with an energy all its own, a sudden realization hit me—a terrifying thought that sent shivers racing down my spine. What if, in choosing to confront the past, we unwittingly unleashed something far more dangerous than we could have ever anticipated?

The ground beneath us shifted, an unsettling tremor that echoed the turmoil in my heart. The mirror's voice faded, replaced by a low rumble that vibrated through the very essence of my being. And just as the shadows coalesced around us, I heard the faintest whisper, a haunting reminder that the echoes of the past would always find a way to emerge, even when we least expected it.

Before I could catch my breath, the darkness surged forward, pulling us into its depths, the weight of countless secrets crashing over us like a tidal wave. My heart raced, uncertainty clawing at the edges of my mind as we were thrust into an abyss, a swirling chaos of memories and shadows that threatened to consume us whole.

With one final gasp, the darkness enveloped us, and the last remnants of light flickered out, leaving nothing but the echoes of our choices reverberating in the silence.

Chapter 16: The Shadowed Threat

The air crackled with an intensity that mirrored the electric storm brewing overhead. A low rumble of thunder reverberated through the old estate, sending a shiver down my spine that had nothing to do with the chill of the night. Shadows danced along the walls, flickering as the waning light of day surrendered to the creeping darkness. My heart raced, not merely from fear but from the heady rush of adrenaline that coursed through me as Nathan pulled me closer, his grip firm yet reassuring.

"Stay quiet," he whispered, his breath warm against my ear, igniting a spark that spread through me like wildfire. The world around us faded; it was just the two of us against whatever menace lurked in the shadows. The echoes of footsteps grew louder, each one a portent of danger, making the hair on the back of my neck stand on end. We weren't alone.

The estate was a sprawling maze of forgotten corridors and secret chambers, its history whispering through the cracked walls. I had spent countless hours exploring its creaking bones, drawn by a sense of nostalgia and intrigue, but nothing could prepare me for this chilling revelation. The flickering candlelight cast eerie patterns, creating ghostly shapes that seemed to reach out for us as we navigated through the dimly lit hall.

"Nathan," I breathed, my voice barely above a whisper, "do you think it's them? The ones from the reports?" I could hardly believe the rumors of the estate being haunted were true, yet I felt a sinister presence lurking just out of sight.

He glanced down at me, his expression a mix of determination and worry. "If it is, we need to find a way out. Fast." His brow furrowed, eyes narrowing as if trying to pierce through the darkness that enveloped us. I felt the warmth of his body close to mine, a reminder that I wasn't alone in this terrifying moment.

The footsteps stopped abruptly, and a suffocating silence enveloped us, punctuated only by the distant rumble of thunder. I strained to hear, my senses heightened, every tiny creak of the floorboards sending my heart racing. My imagination spun wild tales of what could be lurking just beyond the reach of our feeble light, conjuring images of spectral figures and hidden dangers.

Just as I opened my mouth to suggest we retreat, a shadow flitted past the doorway, a dark shape that made my breath hitch in my throat. Nathan reacted instantly, pulling me behind a heavy velvet curtain, our bodies pressed tightly together. I could feel his heartbeat racing in sync with mine, a chaotic rhythm that drowned out the world. The smell of his cologne—earthy with a hint of something sharp—wrapped around me like a comforting blanket.

The figure moved slowly, cautiously, almost deliberately. I peered around the curtain, my heart hammering as I caught a glimpse of the intruder. A man, tall and cloaked in darkness, moved with an unnerving grace, his features obscured by the shadows. My mind raced with possibilities. Was he friend or foe? I could feel the tension coiling in my stomach, a tight knot that threatened to unravel me.

"Is he looking for something?" I whispered, my voice trembling. Nathan's jaw clenched, and he nodded subtly, his eyes darting between me and the figure.

"We can't stay here. We need to move," he replied, a fierce resolve igniting in his voice. The urgency of the situation hung between us, a palpable force that pushed us into action.

As we slipped from our hiding place, the atmosphere shifted. The house felt alive, every creak of the floorboards echoing like a heartbeat. We darted into the nearest hallway, our footsteps muffled by the thick carpet, each step resonating with the unspoken understanding that we were now players in a game far more dangerous than we had anticipated.

FADING ECHOES 161

Nathan led the way, his instincts sharp and unwavering. I trailed closely, adrenaline fueling my every move. The thrill of the chase mingled with fear, sending a rush of heat through my veins as I stole glances at him. The storm outside raged, rain slashing against the windows like nature's own warning, but we pressed on, navigating the labyrinth of the estate, trying to shake the looming threat that stalked us.

"Do you think he saw us?" I asked, my voice a mere whisper as we turned a corner, our backs pressed against the cold wall.

"Let's hope not," Nathan replied, the tension in his voice evident. His gaze was fixed ahead, and I could see the muscles in his jaw flexing. "We need to find a way out before he alerts the others."

The mention of 'others' sent another chill down my spine. The stories of a clandestine group operating within these walls echoed in my mind, tales I had initially dismissed as mere folklore. But standing there, engulfed in the shadows and secrets of the estate, I began to wonder just how much truth lay within those tales.

A sudden noise drew our attention—a soft thud followed by a muted curse. My pulse quickened, and I felt Nathan's body tense beside me. He glanced back, eyes wide with urgency. "We need to move, now!"

Without waiting for a response, he grabbed my hand, and we sprinted down the corridor, the world around us a blur of shadows and flickering light. Every door we passed felt like a potential escape route, yet I couldn't shake the feeling that each one concealed its own dangers. As we reached the end of the hallway, Nathan skidded to a halt, scanning the area.

"Where do we go?" I panted, adrenaline pumping through me like a rushing river.

He hesitated, his brow furrowing as if weighing options. "There," he finally said, pointing toward a heavy wooden door, its surface weathered and cracked, like the estate itself. It seemed like a gateway to uncertainty, but it was our best shot at evading whatever threat pursued us.

The door creaked open with a ghostly sigh, revealing a narrow staircase that spiraled downward into the bowels of the estate. The darkness seemed to swallow the light, and I hesitated for just a moment, fear battling against the urgency of our situation.

"Come on," Nathan urged, his voice firm yet soothing, a lifeline in the storm of chaos. I took a deep breath, allowing his confidence to bolster my own, and together we plunged into the unknown, the air growing cooler as we descended into the depths below.

The air grew dense as we descended into the darkness, each step down the spiraling staircase a descent into the unknown. The faint glow from the candlelight above flickered like a dying star, but as we plunged deeper, the only illumination came from the spectral glow of my phone screen. I felt Nathan's hand gripping mine firmly, our fingers intertwined, creating a connection that pulsed with urgency and fear.

The staircase opened into a narrow corridor, its walls lined with damp stone that seemed to close in around us, almost as if the estate itself was holding its breath. I could hear the distant sound of dripping water, the rhythm of it echoing my racing heart. Shadows loomed in the corners of my vision, threatening to break free and swallow us whole. Every instinct screamed for us to turn back, but there was no turning back now. The danger was behind us, and whatever lay ahead was our only hope of escape.

"Do you think he followed us?" I whispered, glancing over my shoulder, half-expecting to see a dark figure looming just behind us.

"I don't know," Nathan replied, his voice steady despite the uncertainty etched on his face. "But we can't linger here. We need to keep moving."

His resolve invigorated me, propelling me forward. As we crept along the corridor, I focused on the sound of our footsteps, muted against the cold stone. It felt surreal, like we had stepped into a dream—or perhaps a nightmare—where nothing was as it seemed. My thoughts raced, swirling with questions and possibilities. Who was the intruder? What did he want? And more importantly, how were we going to survive this?

We rounded a corner and stumbled upon a heavy wooden door, its surface marred with scratches and age. It appeared to lead to a room long abandoned, its secrets hidden behind layers of dust and neglect. "This might be our best chance," Nathan said, gesturing toward the door.

"What if it's worse inside?" I shot back, my pulse quickening again at the thought of encountering something even more sinister.

Nathan's brow furrowed, a thoughtful look crossing his face. "True, but we'll be trapped here if we don't take the risk. We can't stay exposed."

With a reluctant nod, I steeled myself, and he pushed the door open. It creaked ominously, revealing a room shrouded in darkness. I flicked on my phone's flashlight, the beam cutting through the shadows and illuminating a scene that felt plucked from a gothic novel.

The room was filled with remnants of the past: old furniture draped in white sheets, like ghosts lingering in a forgotten realm. Cobwebs clung to the corners, glistening in the light, and a large window framed by heavy drapes loomed in the back, offering a view of the storm raging outside. Lightning flashed, illuminating the room for a fleeting moment and casting sinister shapes against the walls.

"What a charming place," I said wryly, forcing a smile to mask the tension that knotted my stomach. "I can almost see us hosting a delightful dinner party here."

Nathan chuckled softly, and the sound felt like a small victory against the creeping dread. "Only if the guests are made of dust and memories."

We stepped inside, and Nathan closed the door behind us with a soft click, plunging us into near-complete darkness once more. The air was stale, heavy with the scent of mildew and something else—something metallic that sent a chill down my spine. My eyes adjusted, and I noticed something glinting on a table in the corner, half-hidden beneath a sheet.

"What is that?" I asked, curiosity momentarily distracting me from our perilous situation.

"Let's find out," Nathan replied, moving toward the table with a purposeful stride. As he pulled the sheet away, a cloud of dust billowed into the air, swirling like a mini-storm, and I coughed lightly, waving my hand in front of my face.

Beneath the covering lay an assortment of old trinkets, but what caught my eye was a brass key, its surface tarnished but still gleaming. "Do you think this opens something?" I asked, picking it up and turning it in my hand, its weight oddly comforting.

Nathan leaned closer, examining the other items. "Maybe. It looks like it could belong to a chest or a door. We should keep it just in case."

As he spoke, a loud crash echoed from the corridor, shattering the fragile calm we had momentarily created. I jumped, heart racing again, and Nathan immediately grabbed my hand, urgency flooding his expression. "We need to hide. Now."

Before I could respond, he pulled me to the side, behind a large wardrobe that loomed in the corner like a sentinel. We crouched low, breaths held tight in our throats. The sound of footsteps grew closer, heavy and deliberate, each thud resonating through the room. I could barely breathe, fear coiling around me, tightening like a vise.

"I'm not sure how much longer I can hold my breath," I whispered, trying to keep my voice steady, though it wavered. "This place really needs a better ventilation system."

Nathan shot me an amused glance, despite the tension. "Always the optimist, huh? Just focus on staying quiet."

The footsteps halted just outside the door, and I felt my heart in my throat as I strained to listen. The sound of heavy breathing filled the air, and I could almost feel the weight of the intruder's presence, looming like a storm cloud.

"What do you want?" a voice growled, low and menacing. My skin prickled at the sound, a chill washing over me.

"I know you're in there," he continued, a taunt lacing his words. "You can't hide forever."

My pulse raced, panic fluttering like a trapped bird inside my chest. "This is not good," I whispered, glancing at Nathan, who remained focused, eyes narrowed in concentration.

"We'll wait for him to leave," he replied softly, his voice steady, but I could hear the tension threading through it.

Just as I settled into the dark shadows of the wardrobe, a sudden crash erupted as the door swung open violently, splintering the air with its force. I squeezed Nathan's hand, every nerve in my body alight with fear and anticipation.

"Where are you?" the intruder called, stepping into the room, casting a long shadow that stretched across the floor like a hungry beast. The adrenaline surged in me, urging my heart to match the chaotic rhythm of my racing thoughts.

I could see the outline of his figure against the flickering light of the storm outside, his features obscured but radiating danger. "You think you can just disappear? I'll find you, and when I do..." His words trailed off, leaving an unsettling promise hanging in the air.

With every second that passed, the tension thickened, coiling around us like a noose. I felt Nathan's grip tighten, his presence grounding me as we both waited for the inevitable clash of shadows to unfold. We were trapped, caught in a web of fear and uncertainty, with only the strength of our connection to pull us through the darkness.

The intruder's silhouette loomed ominously in the doorway, a stark contrast to the chaotic backdrop of the storm outside. I could barely breathe, the weight of fear and uncertainty pressing down on me. Nathan's hand remained firmly clasped around mine, our fingers intertwined in a silent pact of courage. I could sense his muscles tense beside me, every fiber of his being coiled and ready for action.

"What do you want?" The intruder's voice sliced through the air, laden with menace. He stepped further into the room, boots crunching softly against the remnants of dust and memories that carpeted the floor. I felt Nathan's body shift slightly, a silent communication passing between us—a shared understanding that this moment could change everything.

"Just come out, and we can settle this," he taunted, a cruel smirk stretching across his face as he scanned the room. I could see the glint of something in his hand, and my heart raced with trepidation. Was it a weapon? The thought sent a cold chill through my veins, igniting a desperate need to act.

"Now would be a good time to find a different hiding spot," I whispered, my voice barely a tremor as I tried to keep the panic from spilling over. Nathan met my gaze, determination etched on his features, and in that fleeting moment, I could see the resolve in his eyes—a fierce light that pushed back the darkness threatening to engulf us.

Before I could process what was happening, Nathan shifted slightly and made a move to the side of the wardrobe, his body a blur of action as he stepped into the shadows, pulling me along with him. The intruder had turned his back momentarily, his focus still fixed on the room, and in that split second, we darted towards the back of the wardrobe where a small gap revealed a hidden compartment.

"Quick!" Nathan urged, his voice sharp and urgent. We slipped inside just as the intruder's attention flicked back to the doorway, and the door creaked ominously on its hinges. I held my breath, praying the shadows would swallow us whole.

From our cramped hiding spot, I could see the intruder's expression morph into confusion as he peered around the room, frowning at the shadows that danced along the walls. "You think you're clever, don't you?" he sneered, moving further into the room, eyes narrowing as he searched for any sign of movement.

The silence stretched, heavy and suffocating, as we clung to each other in the dim light. My heart thudded in my chest, a relentless drumbeat of anxiety, but beneath it all was a flicker of adrenaline that felt dangerously exhilarating. Nathan's breath was steady beside me, grounding me, yet I could feel the tension radiating off him, an electric charge in the air that set my skin alight.

"What if he finds us?" I whispered, my voice shaking slightly.

"He won't," Nathan replied confidently, though the tremor in his grip suggested he was just as on edge as I was.

The intruder continued to search, moving closer to our hiding spot. I could see the outline of his form looming ominously against the backdrop of the room. With every passing second, my anxiety twisted into dread, visions of what could happen flooding my mind. Just then, he paused, a slow, deliberate turn of his head as if he could sense our presence.

A loud crash erupted outside the window, shattering the tension in the room and sending shards of fear spiraling through me. The intruder whipped around, momentarily distracted. "What the hell was that?" he growled, the menace in his tone palpable.

"Now's our chance," Nathan hissed, his voice low and urgent. With a swift movement, he took my hand, and we bolted from our hiding place, darting for the door just as the intruder turned back, eyes wide with realization.

The door flew open, the wind whipping through the space like a living entity. We plunged into the stormy night, the air electric with the scent of rain and the sound of thunder rolling across the sky. My heart raced as we stumbled out into the gardens, the chaos of nature surrounding us in a cacophony of sound and fury.

"Over here!" Nathan called, leading me through the tangled paths, branches clawing at us as we navigated the overgrown foliage. The moon flickered behind the clouds, casting intermittent beams of light that danced across the ground, guiding our frantic escape.

"Do you think he's coming after us?" I gasped, trying to keep pace as my heart pounded like a war drum in my chest. The thrill of the chase mixed with the fear of what was behind us, creating a whirlwind of emotions that threatened to overwhelm me.

"Just keep moving," Nathan urged, his voice fierce, even as the urgency of our situation weighed heavily upon him. The shadows flickered around us, and the air felt charged, crackling with electricity and danger.

We navigated through the twisting paths of the garden, the sounds of our footsteps muffled by the thick carpet of grass and leaves beneath us. The estate loomed behind us, a dark fortress of secrets and threats. I could feel Nathan's presence beside me, his energy radiating with an intensity that both comforted and excited me.

Suddenly, the sound of crashing footsteps echoed through the garden, a reminder that we weren't alone. I risked a glance over my shoulder, and my blood ran cold as I spotted the figure emerging from the shadows, eyes gleaming with a predatory glint. The intruder was hot on our trail, fury etched on his face, a storm of his own brewing within him.

"Run!" Nathan shouted, urging me forward as we raced toward the edge of the estate, where the trees thickened, offering a potential refuge. I could hear the heavy footfalls of our pursuer, the thud of his boots a constant reminder of the danger we faced. The storm overhead raged, a perfect reflection of the chaos around us.

Branches snagged at my clothing, but I didn't stop. My breath came in ragged gasps, and my legs burned with the effort, but the adrenaline surged through me, propelling me forward. We plunged deeper into the trees, the world around us growing dark and foreboding.

"Where are we going?" I yelled, my voice nearly lost to the wind that howled through the branches.

"To the old chapel!" Nathan shouted back, determination lacing his tone. "It's our only chance!"

The old chapel, long abandoned and rumored to be haunted, flickered into my mind—a haven of lost souls and forgotten prayers. But the thought of seeking refuge there sent a thrill of dread spiraling through me. Still, it was better than facing the fury of our pursuer.

Just as we neared the edge of the trees, a figure stepped into our path, silhouetted against the flickering light of the storm. The flash of a knife glinted ominously in the darkness, the threat sharp and undeniable. My heart dropped as we skidded to a halt, caught between the intruder behind us and the looming danger ahead.

"Not so fast," the new figure sneered, eyes narrowing, predatory and cold. "You've come too far to escape now."

The night felt like it was closing in around us, the shadows pressing tighter as a sense of impending doom settled over me. I turned to Nathan, fear pooling in my stomach as I grasped the weight of our situation. We were trapped, the darkness surrounding us thick and suffocating, and with a single heartbeat, everything changed.

Chapter 17: The Edge of Darkness

The moment the door slammed shut behind us, I leaned against it, pressing my back against the cold wood, feeling the weight of the night's events settle heavily on my shoulders. The sharp inhale of the stale apartment air was laden with a mixture of fear and exhilaration. I turned to Nathan, whose wild eyes mirrored my own, glinting with the remnants of adrenaline and something else—an unspoken bond forged in the furnace of near disaster.

"Did we really just do that?" I asked, breathless, the words tumbling from my lips like a string of broken pearls.

Nathan ran a hand through his disheveled hair, the dark strands sticking up in charming rebellion. "I think we did," he replied, a half-smile tugging at his lips, but the uncertainty hung in the air like smoke from a fire long extinguished.

I glanced out the window, the curtains fluttering slightly in the cool breeze, and I couldn't help but wonder if the shadows in the woods were still watching. "What do we do now?"

"Now?" He took a step toward me, his expression shifting from playful to serious in a heartbeat. "Now we figure out what the hell we stumbled into."

The soft glow of the streetlights illuminated his features, casting a warm light that contrasted sharply with the chill that had settled over me. My apartment, usually a sanctuary filled with the soft hum of familiarity, felt oddly alien after our harrowing escape. The faded walls, decorated with paintings I'd collected over the years, now bore witness to a reality I hadn't anticipated.

"I can't believe you dragged me into that estate," I said, folding my arms defensively, although I knew my words held a playful accusation. "You could have gotten us killed."

"Or discovered a hidden treasure," he shot back, that spark of mischief returning to his eyes. "Think of it as an adventure!"

"Adventure? This was more like a horror movie waiting to happen."

He laughed, the sound rich and warm, breaking the tension that had woven itself tightly between us. "What's life without a little risk?"

I rolled my eyes, unable to suppress a smile. "I like my life a little less... life-threatening."

Nathan stepped closer, his breath mingling with mine, and the atmosphere shifted. The air crackled with an unspoken understanding that we were two souls inexplicably drawn together by circumstances beyond our control. "You're right. We need to be cautious."

The gravity of his words pulled me back to reality, a reminder that beneath the playful banter was a darkness we couldn't ignore. "We need to talk about what we saw in there," I said, my voice dropping to a whisper as if the walls had ears.

"Yeah," he replied, leaning against the kitchen counter, crossing his arms as if to ward off the chill that seemed to envelop us. "The symbols, the chanting... What do you think it means?"

I closed my eyes, the images flooding back—the dimly lit room, the robed figures, the strange symbols painted on the walls. It felt like a half-remembered nightmare, too vivid to dismiss but too bizarre to fully comprehend. "It felt like something out of a cult film," I said, shivering at the memory. "But it was real, Nathan. Those people—what if they're still out there?"

"Then we'll deal with it together," he assured me, his voice steady. "I'm not letting anything happen to you."

His sincerity wrapped around me like a warm blanket, comforting yet unsettling in its intensity. "What do we even know about them?" I wondered aloud, pacing the small kitchen. "What if they're dangerous? What if they want to keep us quiet?"

Nathan's brow furrowed, the weight of my words clearly sinking in. "We need to find out more—about them and about the estate. There has to be something out there, some clue that tells us what we're dealing with."

I nodded, determination igniting within me. "I'm not going back there without a plan, though."

"Smart thinking."

"Plus, I need to dig into the history of that place," I mused, my mind racing. "Maybe there's something in the archives or the library that can shed light on what we saw."

"Library? Now you're talking about the one place I could spend an entire day," he said, a playful grin returning to his face. "It's the only sanctuary in a world of chaos."

"Don't get too comfortable. I'm not letting you turn this into a field trip," I shot back, though I couldn't help but laugh.

The tension between us ebbed as we brainstormed, the pulse of danger simmering beneath our playful banter. Still, the shadows of uncertainty loomed large. What if the figures we had encountered in the woods were not mere figments of our imagination, but a threat that would not fade into the night?

The thought sent a chill down my spine, a reminder that we were still very much in the eye of the storm. But alongside the fear was a sense of exhilaration—an adventure that had turned our ordinary lives into something extraordinary, however terrifying it might be. And as I caught Nathan's eye, the spark of mischief dancing in his gaze, I realized that whatever lay ahead, we would face it together.

The sun hung low the next day, filtering through my living room window in soft, golden rays that seemed to mock the terror of the previous night. I sat cross-legged on my couch, a fortress of blankets piled around me, clutching a mug of steaming tea that did little to chase away the lingering chill in my bones. Nathan paced like a caged lion, the floorboards creaking under his weight as he transformed my small space into his personal arena of thought.

"What if we're not the only ones who saw what happened?" he mused, running a hand through his hair, making it stand even more wildly. "What if they're looking for us?"

I set my tea down, the ceramic cool against the heat radiating from my palms. "That's a distinct possibility," I replied, pushing a stray hair behind my ear. "But what do we do about it? We can't exactly call the police and say, 'Hey, we saw some people chanting in a creepy old house.' They'll think we're delusional."

"Or worse," Nathan added, biting his lip in that way that always drove me crazy, a mixture of concern and determination. "What if they know we were there?"

The thought hung between us, a dark cloud looming over the warm light of the afternoon. I crossed my arms tightly, fighting against a wave of unease. "We need to figure out what we're up against. We need information, and for that, we'll have to go back to the estate."

"Seriously?" he asked, raising an eyebrow. "After last night? You want to go back to the scene of the—what did you call it?—the 'horror movie waiting to happen'?"

I shot him a pointed look, hoping to keep the tension light. "I'd prefer not to be eaten by whatever cultist monsters lurk in the shadows, but we can't just sit here and wait for them to come to us."

Nathan leaned against the wall, his arms crossed defensively. "Okay, so how do we gather intel without ending up in a sacrificial ceremony?"

"Research," I said, letting a sly smile curve my lips. "You have a knack for blending in; you can play the part of a curious college student looking for spooky stories to share with friends."

"And you?"

"I'll be the brilliant sidekick," I replied with mock seriousness. "Every great detective has one. We'll visit the local archives. There must be something written about that estate—its history, previous owners, any scandals."

"Your brilliant sidekick needs a code name," Nathan declared, his eyes sparkling with mischief. "How about 'The Archivist'? It has a nice ring to it."

I laughed, the sound reverberating through the apartment, easing the tension that had coiled around us like a serpent. "And what about you? 'The Dashing Investigator'?"

"Dashing? I'm flattered," he said, mock bowing with exaggerated flair, earning him a playful shove.

With laughter still dancing in the air, we solidified our plan. I gathered my things, a notepad, a pen, and a list of questions I had scribbled in the hazy aftermath of the previous night's events. Together, we ventured into the heart of the city, where the local library stood like a sentinel, its brick façade adorned with climbing ivy that whispered tales of years long gone.

Inside, the scent of old books enveloped us—a mixture of mustiness and wisdom, comforting and daunting. The wood-paneled walls echoed our footsteps as we made our way toward the reference section, where dusty tomes lined the shelves, filled with secrets waiting to be unearthed.

Nathan drifted to a nearby desk, flipping through a few files. "I think I found something," he called out, his voice carrying a hint of excitement.

"What did you find?"

"Just the estate's history—founded in the 1800s by a family of eccentric artists. Apparently, they hosted lavish parties that turned into notorious soirees with rumors of strange rituals," he said, scanning the pages, his brows knitting together in concentration.

"Perfect," I whispered, stepping closer to peek at the documents. "Anything that mentions the current owners?"

He flipped a page, his expression changing from intrigue to concern. "It looks like it's been abandoned for decades, but there are mentions of a mysterious figure appearing in the area, someone claiming to be a 'guardian' of the estate."

"A guardian?" I echoed, incredulity lacing my voice. "What does that even mean?"

He shrugged, his face serious. "Could be nothing, but if that person is watching over the estate, they might have a connection to whatever we saw last night."

My heart raced at the thought. "So we're not just dealing with a haunted house; we might be up against a guardian who doesn't want anyone poking around."

Nathan nodded, the intensity of the moment hanging heavy in the air. "We need to know more about this guardian. If they're protecting something—"

"Or someone," I interrupted, my mind racing. "We could be stepping into a much larger conflict than we imagined."

"Let's dig deeper," Nathan said, determination burning in his eyes. "I'll handle the history section. You check the local newspapers for any strange incidents or sightings connected to the estate."

"Sounds like a plan," I said, my pulse quickening with both excitement and dread.

Hours slipped by as we lost ourselves in research, surrounded by the whispers of the past and the looming shadows of what might still be hidden. As I sifted through the brittle pages of old newspapers, I felt an unsettling sensation wash over me—a sense of being watched. I glanced around, half-expecting to see a pair of eyes lingering on me from behind a shelf.

"Hey," Nathan said, breaking my concentration. "You okay?"

"Yeah, just... a weird feeling." I shrugged, trying to shake off the unease that clung to my skin like a chill. "Let's just find this guardian and get some answers."

"Together," he reminded me, his voice firm yet reassuring.

With renewed resolve, we dove back into our search, the weight of the unknown looming ever closer. Each page turned felt like a step toward unraveling the mystery, a journey fraught with hidden dangers and unexpected revelations. The walls of the library seemed to close in, the air thickening with anticipation as we prepared to confront whatever awaited us in the shadows.

The library's quiet hum buzzed around us, but I was acutely aware of the silence, punctuated only by the faint rustling of pages and the low murmur of distant conversations. Nathan and I worked side by side, a rhythm forming between us as we shared our findings, each discovery more chilling than the last.

"Look at this," Nathan said, leaning over my shoulder, his breath warm against my ear. "There's a whole article about disappearances linked to the estate over the years. The last one was just a few months ago."

I felt a cold wave wash over me, creeping down my spine. "What do you mean disappearances?"

"People who went in and never came out," he replied, his voice barely above a whisper. "There's a pattern—a group of college students went missing last fall, and there are whispers of locals avoiding the area. It's as if the whole town knows to stay away."

"What if the guardian is involved?" I asked, my heart racing. "What if they're not just protecting something; what if they're trapping people?"

"Or worse," Nathan said, his expression grave. "What if the cult we saw is somehow connected to these disappearances? It makes sense—if they're performing rituals, they might need people."

The thought lodged itself in my throat like a stone, heavy and suffocating. "We can't ignore this. If we're going back to the estate, we need to be prepared."

Nathan's brow furrowed, and he took a step back, running a hand through his hair as if trying to comb through the chaos of our findings. "I agree, but how do we prepare for something we don't even fully understand?"

I closed my eyes, recalling the symbols painted on the walls, the chanting echoing in my mind like a distant song. "We find out more about the cult. We need to know who they are, what they believe, and if they're still active. Maybe we can disrupt whatever they're planning."

"Disruption sounds like a solid plan," he said with a teasing grin. "Just let me grab my cape."

"Very funny, superhero." I rolled my eyes, a smile breaking through the tension. "Maybe we should get some flashlights and a map."

"Flashlights, check. And I'm a decent navigator if I do say so myself."

We gathered our findings, a new resolve igniting between us. The library was beginning to feel stifling, as if the walls themselves were aware of our intentions, whispering warnings. As we turned to leave, the weight of our discoveries lingered, casting a long shadow over our thoughts.

Outside, the evening air was crisp, the sky painted with hues of lavender and rose. I shivered, not entirely from the chill, but from the anticipation that hummed in my veins. "You think we can really do this?" I asked, my voice barely above a whisper.

Nathan nodded, a fierce determination in his eyes. "We have to. For those who disappeared, and for ourselves."

As we approached my apartment, the familiar sight felt ominous, the windows dim and foreboding. My heart raced with each step.

I fumbled for my keys, but the metallic clink felt jarring in the otherwise quiet evening. Just as I pushed the door open, the soft chime of my phone broke through the silence.

I glanced at the screen, my heart skipping a beat. Unknown number. "It could be a prank," Nathan said, peering over my shoulder.

"Or it could be someone warning us." I hesitated before answering, an uneasy feeling creeping in. "Hello?"

The voice that came through was low and gravelly, sending a chill down my spine. "You shouldn't have gone there. They're watching you."

"Who is this?" I demanded, my grip tightening on the phone.

"Get out while you still can." The line went dead, leaving only silence in its wake.

Nathan's expression was grave, his eyes wide. "What did they say?"

"Someone's warning us," I said, breath hitching in my throat. "They know we went to the estate."

"Great, so now we're on someone's radar." He ran a hand through his hair, a nervous habit I'd grown familiar with. "What do we do now?"

"Now? We prepare. We go back tomorrow, armed with what we've learned."

"And if they're waiting for us?"

"They might be," I admitted, the reality settling over us like a dark cloud. "But we can't back down. We need answers."

Just then, a loud knock echoed through the hallway, startling us both. I froze, heart pounding, glancing at Nathan who looked equally tense.

"Who could that be?" he asked, his voice low.

"Only one way to find out," I replied, my bravado wavering as I moved toward the door.

I opened it slowly, revealing a figure cloaked in shadows. It was a woman, her face obscured by the dim light. "You need to come with me," she said urgently, stepping into the threshold with a sudden intensity.

"Who are you?" I asked, instinctively moving closer to Nathan.

"There's no time to explain," she insisted, glancing nervously down the hallway. "They're coming for you."

I felt a mix of fear and intrigue; who was this stranger, and how did she know what was happening? "What do you mean they're coming?"

Before she could answer, the sound of footsteps echoed from the stairwell, heavy and purposeful. My heart raced as I turned to Nathan, who looked equally bewildered.

"Trust me, you have to leave now," the woman urged, her eyes darting toward the door as the footsteps grew louder.

I hesitated, torn between the thrill of the unknown and the instinct to run. "I don't even know who you are!"

"The ones who want you are here," she said, urgency creeping into her voice. "You're in danger!"

Just then, the footsteps halted outside my door, and the world felt like it was closing in. The woman grasped my arm tightly, her grip surprisingly strong. "You have to choose—come with me or face them."

As the door rattled under a heavy knock, the decision weighed heavily on me. I looked between Nathan and the stranger, my heart pounding like a war drum, echoing the ominous tension closing in around us. The air felt thick, charged with uncertainty as I prepared to leap into the unknown, not knowing where it would lead.

Chapter 18: Fractured Trust

The moon hung low that night, casting a silvery sheen over the tangled mess of the backyard. Shadows flickered in the gentle breeze, and I could hear the rustle of leaves whispering secrets, teasing at the edges of my consciousness. I stood near the garden, my hands shoved deep into the pockets of my sweater, willing the chill of the night to ease the warmth gathering inside me. It was one of those moments when the world outside seems to hold its breath, and everything felt suspended in time.

Nathan was just a few feet away, his silhouette carved against the glow of the porch light, a beacon of conflicting emotions. His brow furrowed as he leaned against the railing, his broad shoulders tense, the muscles coiling beneath his shirt as if ready to spring into action at any moment. I had come to know that posture well; it was his way of preparing for confrontation, a protective armor he donned when the unspoken weighed heavily between us.

"Do you ever wonder if we're just... running in circles?" I asked, my voice a thread of sound, barely breaking the silence that clung like a thick fog. I could feel the words hanging in the air, a challenge wrapped in vulnerability. My heart raced as I took a step closer, the distance between us feeling like a chasm filled with all the things we hadn't said.

He shifted, his gaze piercing through the dim light. "Running in circles? Or trying to find our way out of the labyrinth?" His voice was low, gravelly, the undertone of something deeper lurking just beneath. I searched his eyes, looking for the flicker of reassurance I craved but found only a reflection of my own doubts.

"I just..." I trailed off, frustration bubbling up. "Every time we get close to understanding each other, it feels like we take a step back. You know, like we're stuck in this endless loop. I want to trust you, but..."

The unspoken "but" hung in the air like a storm cloud, dark and heavy. I watched as his jaw tightened, the familiar warmth of his presence turning sharp and frigid, and my stomach twisted with uncertainty.

"But?" he echoed, leaning forward, a spark of challenge lighting his eyes. "What's holding you back? Is it the past? Or is it the fact that you think I'm hiding something from you?"

His words struck me like a bolt of lightning, igniting the tension that simmered just beneath the surface. "You're not the only one with secrets, Nathan," I shot back, my voice steadier than I felt. "I've got my own shadows, and I'm not sure how much longer I can keep them hidden."

The weight of our shared vulnerabilities hung like an unspoken pact, binding us in a way that felt both exhilarating and terrifying. I could see the flicker of understanding in his eyes, and for a moment, the air between us crackled with the possibility of connection.

"What if I told you I'm scared too?" he said, stepping closer, the warmth radiating from him intoxicating yet disorienting. "Scared that you'll uncover something you can't unsee. I don't want to be that person, but—"

"Then don't be," I interrupted, the words bursting forth before I could hold them back. "Don't keep me in the dark. I need to know if I can trust you."

His silence was deafening, each second stretching into an eternity as the moon continued its slow ascent, illuminating the uncertainty etched across his face. "Trust is a fragile thing, isn't it?" he finally murmured, his voice soft, almost reverent. "Once broken, it's hard to mend."

"Is that what you think this is? A fragile thing?" I challenged, my heart pounding, desperation seeping into my words. "I need to know if I can lean on you. If we can be stronger together rather than alone."

He hesitated, his gaze drifting to the night sky, where stars twinkled like distant promises. "What if leaning on me leads to a greater fall?"

The honesty of his question hit me like a punch to the gut, forcing me to confront the reality of our situation. We were walking a tightrope, teetering on the edge of something that could be beautiful or catastrophic.

"Then I guess we'd have to figure out how to catch each other," I said, my voice steadier now, as if speaking the words out loud somehow solidified my resolve. "Because I'm tired of living in fear. I'm tired of tiptoeing around what we could be."

In that moment, the distance between us shrank. The air pulsed with the weight of unacknowledged feelings, a tension so thick I could almost taste it. I searched his face, hoping to find the reassurance I needed, but instead, I found a flicker of uncertainty that mirrored my own.

"What if we're not ready?" he asked, his brow furrowed in thought, the warmth of his breath brushing against my skin as he stepped closer. "What if the truth fractures us even more?"

"Then we pick up the pieces," I whispered, a newfound determination igniting within me. "But I won't walk away from this without knowing. We owe it to ourselves to try."

His expression softened, and for a heartbeat, the world around us faded. The tension shifted, replaced by a fragile hope, but just as I thought we might bridge the gap that had grown so wide, an unexpected noise shattered the moment—a branch snapped, followed by the rustle of underbrush. We both froze, hearts racing, the silence morphing into an eerie backdrop against our shared uncertainty.

"Did you hear that?" I breathed, my instincts sharpening, the playful banter between us dissolving into the night air. Nathan's eyes darkened, the protective guard instantly rising around him once more. The moment that had felt so promising was now overshadowed by an unfamiliar threat, pulling us back into a world of fear and doubt.

"Stay close," he murmured, his voice low, alert. The distance we had just started to bridge felt precariously close to collapsing, and as the shadows deepened around us, I realized that trust—like love—could be both a sanctuary and a battleground.

The moment hung heavy between us, the air thick with uncertainty as the rustle of leaves gave way to a quiet stillness. Nathan's eyes, usually warm and inviting, were now hard and focused, scanning the shadows that seemed to creep closer with every passing second. I stood frozen, a mixture of fear and curiosity battling for dominance within me. The ambiance had shifted; what had once felt like an intimate revelation now took on a menacing tone, the darkness teasing at our vulnerabilities, coaxing them to the surface.

"What was that?" I whispered, my voice barely a tremor, as if louder sounds would summon whatever lurked beyond the porch light. Nathan didn't answer, his posture tense, muscles coiled like a spring ready to unleash. Instead, he gestured for me to step back, and I felt a pang of frustration. This wasn't the first time I'd been shrouded in secrecy and shadows, and the instinct to press for answers bubbled up like a fizzing soda can.

"It's probably just a raccoon or something," he said, trying to sound casual, though the way his fingers gripped the railing betrayed his calm facade. "But let's not take chances."

"Right, because that's the standard approach to nocturnal wildlife. Let's all just assume the best." I couldn't help the wry tone that slipped into my voice, even as the tension coiled tighter around us. It was my defense mechanism, a way to defuse the simmering unease without breaking down completely. "You know, if I didn't know any better, I'd think you were hiding something far more sinister."

Nathan turned to me, his eyes flickering with a mixture of irritation and amusement. "Hiding something? From you? As if I could." There was an edge of honesty in his tone, yet it was tinged with a playfulness that cut through the tension, reminding me of the moments we'd shared when we'd let our guards down.

"Please, I know your game," I replied, crossing my arms in defiance, my heart racing both from fear and an unexpected thrill. "You're the mysterious brooding type, always lurking in the shadows. It's practically your brand."

"I'm not lurking," he shot back, a smirk creeping onto his lips despite the circumstances. "More like strategically positioning myself for maximum effect."

The corners of my mouth turned upward at his defiance, and for a moment, the threat lurking outside faded into the background. "Strategic positioning, huh? That sounds like something a villain in a bad romance novel would say."

"Oh, so you're saying I'm a villain now?" His voice dipped into mock seriousness, eyes glinting with mischief. "What do I have to do to earn my hero status back?"

"Start by explaining why we're outside in the middle of the night when you could just be in there, sipping cocoa and pretending we aren't in a drama series."

But before he could respond, the sound I had initially dismissed shattered the night's fragile calm—a low growl followed by a rustle that sent a fresh wave of panic coursing through me. Nathan stiffened, his amusement evaporating, replaced by a primal alertness. "Stay close," he instructed, his voice dropping to a low murmur, authority lacing each word.

He moved to stand in front of me, shielding me instinctively. My pulse quickened as I caught a glimpse of something moving beyond the trees—a flash of fur, perhaps, or maybe just a trick of the light.

"Nathan, what if it's not just a raccoon?" I asked, my heart thudding against my ribcage. "What if it's something worse?"

He turned slightly, his gaze still fixed on the shadows. "Whatever it is, we'll deal with it together," he said, his voice steady but his eyes betraying a hint of concern. "You trust me, right?"

"Trust? That's a loaded question," I quipped, though I didn't truly want to push him away. The truth was, in that moment, I wanted to trust him more than ever. There was something protective and fierce about him, a side that made me feel safe despite the encroaching darkness.

As we stood there, tension coiling tighter around us, the shadows seemed to shift and swirl, taunting our fears. Then, out of nowhere, a raccoon emerged, scrabbling through the leaves, its beady eyes shining with mischief.

Nathan exhaled, the tension in his body dissipating like fog under the sun. "See? Just a little thief looking for snacks."

I couldn't help but chuckle, the absurdity of the situation breaking through my nerves. "Just a raccoon, right? Not a secret spy or a werewolf?"

"Not unless it's been training at the gym," he quipped back, and for a moment, the laughter between us dispelled the shadows, weaving a fragile thread of connection amidst our uncertainties.

However, the moment of levity was short-lived. The laughter echoed in the night, and as we exchanged light-hearted banter, I couldn't shake the feeling that we were still standing on the precipice of something profound. The raccoon, no matter how amusing, couldn't erase the weight of our unspoken fears.

"Do you ever feel like we're playing a game, one that could get serious if we aren't careful?" I asked, my tone turning more earnest as the laughter faded. "Like we're just two players moving pieces without knowing the rules?"

His gaze softened, the teasing glimmer in his eyes replaced by a serious contemplation. "Sometimes, I feel like I'm juggling fire. One wrong move, and everything could go up in flames."

I nodded, the gravity of his words sinking in. "Then what do we do? How do we keep it from burning us both?"

He stepped closer, the warmth radiating off him pulling me in. "We communicate. We lay our cards on the table. No more secrets, no more lurking."

The sincerity in his tone tugged at something deep within me, igniting a spark of hope. "What if we're not ready for the cards? What if laying them out just reveals how flawed we really are?"

"Flawed? Please. If I wanted perfect, I'd have stuck to playing solitaire." His grin returned, brightening the atmosphere once more, but I could see the flicker of seriousness beneath.

"I don't know, Nathan. Flaws seem to have a way of complicating things," I said, my heart racing as I weighed the precarious balance between risk and safety. "What if exposing those flaws shatters whatever this is between us?"

"Then we build something new," he replied, his voice a gentle anchor in the storm of my thoughts. "But only if we're both willing to take that leap. Together."

The shadows loomed around us, but for the first time, I felt a sense of determination rising to the surface. It was terrifying and exhilarating all at once, the fear intertwining with the thrill of possibility. I took a deep breath, steadying myself as I faced the unknown. Maybe it was time to stop hiding in the shadows, to step into the light—even if it meant exposing the parts of myself I had kept tucked away for so long.

"Together, then," I echoed softly, and as the words left my lips, I felt the first flicker of trust igniting between us, a fragile flame that promised warmth even in the darkest of nights.

A light breeze stirred the air, carrying the scent of damp earth and leaves, momentarily distracting me from the whirlwind of emotions swirling in my chest. The raccoon had scuttled off, leaving us in a peculiar silence, as if the world itself was waiting for us to move, to decide what came next. Nathan's eyes were locked onto mine, searching for answers, and for a heartbeat, it felt like we stood on the precipice of something monumental, a cliffhanger in our own story.

"Let's just be honest for a moment," I said, my voice trembling slightly with the weight of my words. "What do we really know about each other?"

His gaze flickered, an almost imperceptible crack in his confident exterior. "More than we let on, apparently," he replied, a hint of challenge in his tone, but there was a softness in his eyes that told me he understood the depth of my question.

"Do we, though?" I pressed, my frustration bubbling beneath the surface. "I mean, I know about your penchant for saving stray cats and your fear of the dentist, but those aren't exactly groundbreaking revelations."

He chuckled, the sound rich and warm, like sunlight breaking through clouds. "Well, I think you just revealed a lot more than I did. I was going for the heroic vibe, but now I feel like a dog whisperer."

"Heroic? If anything, that just makes you a glorified cat dad." I rolled my eyes playfully, but the levity felt fleeting, the truth of the matter looming over us. "I'm talking about the real stuff—the things that could break us."

Nathan's expression shifted, the humor fading as he took a step closer, the warmth between us tinged with tension. "The things we keep hidden. Right."

"Yes, exactly. Like the fact that you're always so quick to put yourself between me and danger. Why do you feel the need to protect me like I'm some fragile flower?"

He inhaled deeply, as if he were trying to gather all his thoughts into one coherent answer. "Because I care about you. And honestly? Because I'm scared."

"Scared?" I echoed, a bit stunned by his admission. "Of what?"

"Of losing you. Of not being able to keep you safe."

The vulnerability in his voice struck a chord deep within me. It was an admission I hadn't expected, and it forced me to confront my own fears. "And what about my fears? What if I can't live up to whatever image you have of me?"

His expression softened, the sharp edges of tension smoothing out. "You don't have to live up to anything for me, you know that? I just want you to be you."

The sincerity in his words hung in the air, a fragile yet powerful promise, and for a moment, I felt the weight of our uncertainties lift. But just as the conversation seemed to take a turn for the better, a low growl echoed through the stillness, sending chills racing down my spine.

"What was that?" I asked, my voice dipping into a hushed tone, fear creeping back in like a familiar shadow.

"Stay behind me," Nathan instructed again, his earlier playfulness evaporating into the cool night air.

I stepped back instinctively, but my heart raced with an unsettling mix of fear and curiosity. "What if it's just another raccoon? Or maybe it's the same one, trying to get its revenge."

"Not with that growl," he murmured, eyes narrowing as he scanned the darkness. "We need to—"

Before he could finish, the bushes rustled violently, and something massive emerged from the shadows. My breath caught in my throat as a large figure loomed before us, its form indistinct but unmistakably threatening.

"Nathan..." I whispered, the word barely escaping my lips.

"Get ready," he hissed, his voice low and urgent. "Whatever it is, we need to be prepared."

The adrenaline surged through my veins again, a stark contrast to the previous warmth we'd shared. I had expected a light-hearted banter, but this felt all too real, too dangerous.

"What do you mean, prepared?" I asked, glancing around for something—anything—that could be used as a weapon. "This isn't exactly the setting for a heroic showdown!"

"Just trust me," he replied, his gaze locked on the creature that continued to slink closer, revealing more of its form in the dim light. "And whatever happens, stay close."

A flash of fur caught my eye, and my heart raced as I strained to see. The creature finally stepped into the moonlight, its eyes gleaming with a predatory glint. It was larger than a dog, lean and muscular, with jagged fur that bristled against the cool air. My stomach twisted in fear as recognition flooded my senses.

"Is that... a wolf?" I breathed, panic tightening my throat.

"It's definitely not a raccoon," Nathan replied tersely, his posture shifting into a defensive stance. "And it's not friendly."

"Maybe it's just misunderstood?" I offered, the absurdity of the suggestion making me want to laugh, though the humor felt inappropriate given the circumstances. "Do we really need to fight it? Perhaps we can offer it a cookie or something."

"Now's not the time for jokes," he snapped, though I caught the flicker of amusement in his eyes as they darted toward me. "Just be quiet."

As the wolf approached, the moon illuminated its sleek coat, a mix of gray and black, and I felt a primal fear stir within me. This was not some ordinary animal; it was a predator, keen and aware.

Nathan positioned himself between me and the creature, and in that moment, I felt the full weight of his protectiveness, a tangible shield against the unknown.

"Do you have any idea what we're dealing with?" I whispered, adrenaline sharpening my senses. "Is it even possible to reason with a wolf?"

"Only if it understands human words," he replied dryly, his eyes never leaving the creature. "But let's not test that theory."

The wolf paused, its nostrils flaring as it caught our scent, its eyes narrowing into slits, calculating and predatory. A moment stretched into eternity, and I could feel my heart racing, every beat echoing like a drum in the silent night. I had no idea what would happen next, but I knew we were caught in the crosshairs of something terrifying.

Then, without warning, the wolf lunged forward, a blur of fur and teeth, and I felt time slow as Nathan sprang into action, his body moving in a way that was both instinctual and protective. I had never seen him like this—fierce, focused, and utterly determined.

"Run!" he shouted, and my mind screamed at me to obey, but my feet felt rooted to the ground. I wanted to help him, to do something, anything, but all I could do was watch as the chaos unfolded, a wild dance of instinct and raw power under the haunting glow of the moon.

In that moment, a realization gripped me: trust, once fractured, had the power to bind us closer or tear us apart in an instant. As I stood on the precipice of danger, a new layer of understanding unfurled before me, and I knew this was just the beginning of something far more complicated than I had ever imagined.

With the wolf lunging forward and Nathan ready to defend, the world around us shrank into sharp focus, and I felt the sharp sting of uncertainty. It was now or never, a moment that would define everything we had built together—or tear it all apart.

Chapter 19: The Calm Before the Storm

The sun dipped low on the horizon, casting a warm golden hue over the Battery, as if nature herself conspired to soften the day's earlier tumult. The intricate wrought-iron fences, adorned with delicate curling patterns, stood guard over the manicured lawns, where emerald grass kissed by the late afternoon sun sparkled like a million tiny diamonds. I inhaled deeply, the air rich with the heady fragrance of blooming jasmine, mingling with the briny aroma of the nearby harbor. Each step felt lighter, a delicate dance away from the chaos that had wrapped itself around my life like an unyielding vise.

Beside me, Ethan walked with a relaxed ease that I hadn't seen in weeks. His sandy hair glinted like spun gold in the fading light, and for a moment, I forgot the shadows lurking behind us. We ambled along the historic promenade, the cobblestones beneath our feet whispering tales of a time long past. It was as if the spirit of Charleston itself wrapped us in a gentle embrace, a quiet sanctuary amidst the storm that raged in our hearts.

"So, what's the most ridiculous thing you did as a kid?" he asked, breaking the comfortable silence that had settled between us like an old friend.

I grinned, recalling a particularly embarrassing moment from my childhood. "Oh, that's easy. I once thought I could fly. I climbed to the roof of my garage with a bed sheet tied around my waist like a cape. I was convinced I'd soar into the sunset. Instead, I fell, landed in a rose bush, and spent the next hour trying to explain the thorns to my mom."

His laughter rang out, clear and genuine, mingling with the distant sound of waves lapping against the shoreline. "Did it at least look cool in your mind?"

"Absolutely! I was a superhero, battling the forces of boredom in our suburban neighborhood. I think I took my role a bit too seriously, though. My mom had to rescue me from the thorns. It was rather anticlimactic."

As we continued to share our childhood misadventures, the tension in the air seemed to dissipate, replaced by the comfortable familiarity of shared laughter and stories. The sun sank lower, painting the sky in shades of pink and orange, each hue more breathtaking than the last. In that moment, it felt like the world had paused, granting us a brief reprieve from reality.

Yet, as the shadows stretched, a flicker of unease settled in the pit of my stomach, a nagging reminder that this peace was only temporary. I glanced at Ethan, his features illuminated by the twilight glow, and for the first time in weeks, I felt a glimmer of hope. Maybe we could navigate through the chaos together, forging a path amidst the uncertainty.

"What about you?" I prompted, wanting to pull him into the warmth of nostalgia. "What was your most ridiculous childhood stunt?"

He paused, a thoughtful expression crossing his face. "There was this time I thought I could catch a raccoon. My friends dared me to. I ended up in the bushes, yelling at a raccoon that clearly didn't want to be friends. Let's just say, I learned that wild animals are not as receptive to invitations as you'd hope."

I burst into laughter, picturing the scene: Ethan, a boy of mischief and bravado, grappling with a feisty raccoon in the twilight of his own backyard. "And here I thought you were just the suave, charming guy in a button-up," I teased.

He raised an eyebrow, his smirk teasing the corner of his mouth. "Oh, don't let the shirt fool you. I have a history of bad decisions, just like everyone else."

As the sun dipped below the horizon, casting a deep indigo over the world, we paused at the edge of the Battery, where the grass met the old brick walls worn smooth by time. I took a moment to breathe in the beauty surrounding us, the gentle breeze tousling my hair as if it were trying to coax away my lingering worries.

Yet, as the last vestiges of daylight faded, an uneasy thought crept in. It felt too serene, too perfect. What if the chaos we had left behind came crashing back, uninvited and relentless? I shook my head, trying to dispel the thought, but it lingered like a dark cloud, threatening to obscure the clarity we had found in our laughter.

"Let's sit for a moment," Ethan suggested, pointing to a bench that overlooked the water. I nodded, grateful for the chance to gather my thoughts. We settled down, and the sound of the waves provided a soothing rhythm, lulling me into a false sense of tranquility.

"I'm really glad we did this," I said, my voice barely above a whisper. The golden hour cast a warm glow around us, highlighting the lines of worry etched on Ethan's face. "It's nice to take a break from...everything."

"Yeah," he replied, his gaze fixed on the horizon where the last sliver of sun was disappearing. "It's easy to get lost in the chaos and forget what's important."

I turned to him, the weight of our unspoken troubles hovering between us. "What do you think is important, Ethan?"

He hesitated, a shadow crossing his features before he answered. "Connection. Understanding. Knowing that, no matter how dark things get, we don't have to face it alone."

His words hung in the air, heavy with meaning, and I felt a flicker of something deep within me, something that had been dormant for too long. I wanted to believe him, to grasp onto that hope like a lifeline. But just as I began to embrace the warmth of his sentiment, a sudden chill swept through the air, a prelude to the storm that loomed on the horizon.

A distant rumble echoed, a sound that didn't belong to the natural world around us. The serenity shattered, and in that instant, I knew our moment of peace was fleeting, a calm before an impending tempest that threatened to drown us in uncertainty once more.

The air grew thick with anticipation as the sun melted into the horizon, casting long shadows that danced playfully across the brick path beneath our feet. I sat on the weathered bench, my fingers brushing the cool iron armrest, and watched as Ethan stared out at the shimmering water, his expression contemplative, almost wistful. The evening sky had transformed into a canvas of deep blues and purples, punctuated by the first twinkling stars, and yet a part of me felt an unsettling shift beneath the surface of this idyllic scene.

"Are you sure you're okay?" I asked, my voice barely a whisper, as if the very act of speaking would shatter the fragile peace surrounding us.

He turned to me, his deep-set eyes searching mine. "I'm okay. Just... thinking."

"About what? The raccoon? Or maybe the superhero that fell from grace?" I attempted to lighten the mood, but the edge of concern in his expression remained.

"More like wondering how we ended up here," he replied, his voice low. "How we went from sharing childhood stories to facing a reality that feels far more complicated."

A faint smile tugged at the corner of my lips despite the weight of his words. "A little melodramatic, aren't we? We could always return to our childhoods—just climb a tree and see if we can't fly."

He chuckled, a sound that momentarily lifted the gloom. "I'd prefer not to end up in another bush, thank you very much."

Just as I felt the tension begin to ease, the distant rumble I had sensed earlier grew louder, a deep, ominous growl that seemed to vibrate through the very ground beneath us. The water, once calm and inviting, now churned with an unsettling intensity, waves crashing against the shoreline as if urging us to pay attention.

"Did you hear that?" I asked, the humor evaporating from my voice.

"Yeah. It's like Mother Nature's way of reminding us that tranquility is a fleeting illusion," he said, a hint of sarcasm coloring his words.

Before I could respond, a sudden gust of wind swept across the Battery, swirling leaves and debris around us, creating a mini cyclone of chaos that whipped at our hair and clothes. The jasmine-sweetened air turned sharp and cold, and I instinctively pulled my cardigan tighter around me.

"Maybe we should—" I started, but my words were cut off as Ethan stood abruptly, his posture tense.

"Let's move. We're not staying here if a storm's coming."

We hurried down the path, our earlier laughter forgotten as we navigated the increasingly turbulent atmosphere. The clamor of the waves echoed our urgency, each crash sounding like a warning bell. The vibrant landscape that had offered solace moments before now seemed to darken, the shadows growing deeper, more sinister.

"Do you think we'll make it to the car before it hits?" I called out, trying to inject a note of levity into our retreat.

"Depends on how fast you can run in those shoes," he shot back, glancing at my strappy sandals that were far more suited for a leisurely stroll than a sprint.

I rolled my eyes but felt a spark of adrenaline kick in, urging my legs to move faster. "If only I had known we were in for an extreme weather event, I would have brought my sneakers!"

Just as we rounded a corner, a chilling howl sliced through the air, causing us both to freeze in place. The sound was alien, unnerving, and unlike anything I had ever heard. It was followed by the crack of thunder that rattled the heavens, an echoing reminder that we were at the mercy of nature's whims.

"What was that?" I whispered, my heart pounding against my ribcage like a caged bird desperate for escape.

"Probably just the storm," Ethan replied, though the way he furrowed his brow suggested he wasn't entirely convinced.

I shivered as a drop of rain splattered on my cheek, quickly followed by another, and then another, as if the sky itself had ruptured, releasing its pent-up frustrations. We raced toward the parking lot, the rain turning from a light drizzle to a downpour within seconds, drenching us instantly.

"I've never appreciated getting soaked in public," I shouted over the noise of the rain.

"Tell me about it!" Ethan laughed, his voice barely rising above the symphony of thunder. "At least we'll have a great story for the grandkids."

I couldn't help but smile, the absurdity of the moment eclipsing my earlier worries. "If we make it out of this storm, maybe we can hold off on the grandkids discussion!"

We finally reached the car, and I fumbled with the keys, my fingers slipping against the slick metal. Ethan grabbed them from my grasp, expertly jamming the key into the lock and swinging the door open.

"Get in!" he yelled, his urgency palpable as we both dove into the car, panting and laughing like a pair of children caught in a summer storm. I quickly slammed the door shut behind me, the sound echoing like a gunshot in the confines of the vehicle.

Rain hammered against the roof like a relentless drummer, a cacophony that nearly drowned out the sound of our rapid breathing. I turned to Ethan, water dripping from his hair, his shirt clinging to his skin. Despite the chaos, there was something undeniably captivating about him, an allure that thrummed beneath the surface of our whirlwind evening.

"We survived!" I declared, raising my arms as if I had just conquered a mountain.

"Only to be trapped in a tin can," he retorted, but his smile belied his words.

I settled back into my seat, the adrenaline slowly fading, replaced by a warmth that curled in my chest. "You know, this isn't the worst adventure I've ever had."

Ethan raised an eyebrow, curiosity sparking in his eyes. "Oh? What was?"

"Getting stuck in an elevator with a man who thought he was an amateur magician," I replied, the memory bringing a chuckle to my lips. "He kept trying to pull a rabbit out of his hat while we were waiting for the fire department to rescue us."

"Was he any good?"

"Not a chance! He accidentally revealed the secret behind his 'trick,' which was less magic and more fumbling around. He just kept apologizing to the rabbit he never had."

Ethan burst out laughing, and the sound was like a soothing balm to the chaos surrounding us. In that moment, the storm outside faded, becoming nothing more than a backdrop to the vibrant connection that crackled between us.

But just as I began to feel a sense of calm settle in, a flash of lightning illuminated the sky, briefly illuminating the dark clouds above. My heart raced once more, a reminder that while we may have found laughter in the storm, the tempest was far from over.

The rain pounded against the windshield like an impatient child demanding attention, but inside the car, an unexpected warmth lingered. Ethan and I sat close, the car's interior buzzing with the energy of our shared laughter and the absurdity of our storm-battered adventure. Yet, as the sky flashed bright, illuminating his profile for just a moment, I caught a glimpse of something deeper—something more serious behind his playful façade.

"Do you think it's just a thunderstorm?" I asked, my voice tentative, as if voicing my concerns might summon a more malevolent force.

Ethan turned to me, his expression a mix of mirth and unease. "Well, I doubt it's the welcome committee for a local parade," he replied wryly, his fingers drumming nervously on the steering wheel. "But then again, Charleston is known for its unpredictable weather. A little rain never stopped the party, right?"

I nodded, trying to match his lightheartedness, though my stomach twisted uneasily. "Or maybe it's just a prelude to a torrential downpour of chaos," I muttered, the weight of my worries seeping back in.

He glanced out at the swirling sheets of rain, the streetlights reflecting distorted halos in the deluge. "What do you think we should do?"

"Maybe we should wait it out. Find a café or something until the storm passes," I suggested, already imagining hot coffee and the comforting warmth of freshly baked pastries.

"Good idea. Just as long as it's not some cozy little bistro with ghosts. I've had enough surprises for one night," he said, trying to mask his tension with humor.

"Why do you think there are ghosts? It's a historical city; the past just sticks around, you know?" I replied, my voice teasing.

"Yeah, but if they're anything like the raccoon I almost caught, I'd prefer to keep my distance."

As he laughed, I felt a flicker of hope, the storm outside becoming less of a threat and more a backdrop to our banter. He shifted the car into gear, pulling away from the Battery, and I looked out the window, watching as the world transformed into a blur of lights and rain. Each drop drummed against the glass, creating a rhythm that seemed to echo the racing of my heart.

"Do you believe in signs?" I asked, curiosity sparking as we drove through the rain-soaked streets.

"Like signs from above, or are we talking more along the lines of 'Beware of Falling Branches'?" he replied, a playful glint in his eyes.

I laughed, enjoying the ease of our conversation, but then took a breath to gather my thoughts. "No, I mean real signs—messages that tell you what to do or which direction to take."

He pondered for a moment, the headlights slicing through the darkness ahead. "I think sometimes the universe nudges us in certain directions, whether we like it or not."

The words hung between us, a shared understanding of the choices we faced. "So, what do you think the universe is telling us right now?" I asked, my heart thudding at the weight of the question.

"Probably to keep driving until we can find a decent place to take cover," he replied, his smile faltering slightly. "But if I'm being honest, I think it's telling us that it's okay to be scared, but we shouldn't let that stop us."

The rain beat down in relentless sheets as we turned onto a side street lined with quaint, old homes that seemed to huddle together for warmth against the storm. "Look at that one," I said, gesturing to a charming little café with a flickering sign that read "Open." The warm glow spilling from its windows beckoned us closer, like a lighthouse guiding lost ships to safety.

"Perfect!" Ethan exclaimed, his relief palpable. He pulled into the parking lot, and as the engine turned off, the world outside fell silent save for the rhythmic tapping of raindrops. We exchanged a glance, and an unspoken agreement passed between us—this was a safe haven, a brief respite from the tempest.

The café door swung open, releasing the rich aroma of coffee and freshly baked goods. A bell chimed, a cheerful sound that cut through the remnants of the storm's chaos. As we stepped inside, warmth enveloped us, a cocoon of comfort that immediately eased the tightness in my chest.

"Two coffees, please," Ethan ordered, his voice steadying in the cozy ambiance. I glanced around, taking in the mismatched furniture, walls adorned with local art, and the sound of laughter from a group huddled in the corner. The storm felt miles away.

As we settled into a corner booth, the light from a small lamp cast a warm glow over the table, illuminating Ethan's features. "So, tell me," he said, leaning in slightly, a spark of mischief in his eyes. "What's your most irrational fear?"

I raised an eyebrow, intrigued. "That's a good one! Hmm, probably being trapped in an elevator with a magician."

He laughed again, the sound a sweet melody amidst the café's murmur. "Well, you'd be safe here. No elevators in sight."

"Unless we somehow get transported into a parallel universe where everything is upside down," I replied, leaning back with a grin.

"Okay, now that's a fear worth having," he admitted, shaking his head with a chuckle. "But really, it's good to see you smiling again."

The sincerity in his gaze sent a warmth spreading through me, yet I felt the shift in energy before it fully registered—a sudden chill raced down my spine as I noticed a shadow lingering by the café door. My heart dropped as a figure emerged from the rain, dripping and shrouded in darkness. I squinted, my instincts flaring.

"Ethan," I whispered, my voice barely escaping my lips.

He turned, his brows furrowing as he followed my gaze. The figure stepped into the light, revealing a familiar face twisted with urgency, a wild look in their eyes that sent a shiver racing through me.

"Emma! You need to come with me—now!"

My breath caught as I recognized the urgency in Sarah's voice, the weight of panic wrapping around us like a thick fog. The moment hung in the air, heavy with unanswered questions and the looming threat of the storm outside, as the world within the café faded into the background.

"What's going on?" Ethan asked, but my heart raced with foreboding, every instinct screaming that this was only the beginning of something much darker.

Chapter 20: Threads of Fate

I woke to the sun filtering through my sheer curtains, painting the room in soft golden hues that spoke of a world untouched by chaos. Yet, as I slipped from the warmth of my bed, the delicate illusion of tranquility shattered like glass. There, on my doorstep, lay an envelope—a crisp white square that felt far too heavy for its size. It looked innocuous enough, yet a prickling sensation danced along my spine as I bent down to retrieve it.

I flipped it open with trembling fingers, my heart racing like a caged bird desperate to escape. The words inside were scrawled hastily, a jagged handwriting that sent chills skittering down my arms. "You think you're safe? The truth will find you when you least expect it." I swallowed hard, the taste of fear bitter on my tongue. The message, drenched in ambiguity, wrapped itself around my mind, tangling with the threads of our ongoing investigation. I rushed back inside, my mind racing, my heart a steady drum of alarm.

I had known that our inquiries into the unsettling disappearance of the local historian would not be welcomed by everyone, but I never expected the web of secrets to tighten around me so quickly. Nathan, with his endless resolve and unfathomable charm, had been the one to convince me to dig deeper. His presence was a steadying force, and I needed that now more than ever.

Frantically, I dialed his number, my hands shaking as I paced the length of my apartment. Each ring echoed the tumult in my chest until, finally, his voice broke through, smooth and comforting. "Hey, what's going on?"

I took a breath, steadied by the timbre of his words. "Nathan, I... I found something. It's bad."

Within moments, he was at my door, all tousled hair and urgency. The sun had shifted, casting long shadows in the entryway, and I felt the weight of impending dread settle between us. I led him inside, clutching the note like a talisman against the encroaching darkness. The apartment felt smaller, the walls too close, the air charged with unspoken fears.

"What did it say?" His brow furrowed, and I could see the resolve sharpening in his eyes, an undeniable spark of determination igniting a fire within me. I handed him the note, watching his expression shift as he read. His lips pressed into a thin line, eyes narrowing as he processed the implication of those cryptic words.

"This isn't just a warning," he said finally, his voice low and grave. "It's a message meant to intimidate. They want us to know they're watching."

I nodded, the weight of his words amplifying the sense of peril coiling around me. "What if it's about the historian? What if we're getting too close?"

His gaze remained fixed on the note, brows knitted in concentration. "We need to figure out who sent this. There's more to this story than we realized, and I'm not about to let it pull us apart." His fierce protectiveness ignited a warmth in my chest that warred against the chill of fear.

As we delved into the labyrinthine connections surrounding the historian's disappearance, I could feel our investigation morphing from a simple search for answers into something much more sinister. Each piece we unearthed felt like a thread in a tapestry woven with dark intentions, an intricate design that threatened to ensnare us.

We laid the evidence out on my coffee table—mugs of coffee forgotten, pages of notes scattered, and a map dotted with red marks that mapped out the historian's last known whereabouts. The hum of the city outside faded into a distant murmur as we focused on the tangled lines connecting each clue. A neighborhood map, a faded photograph of the historian at a local event, and newspaper clippings detailing unsolved mysteries from the past.

"There's something here," I said, tapping a finger on a photo of the historian, his friendly smile now tainted by an unsettling aura. "Look at this picture. What's that building behind him?"

Nathan leaned closer, squinting at the image. "It looks like the old library. They say it's haunted."

"Haunted or not, it's definitely linked to our case." The librarian had mentioned strange occurrences tied to the building, whispers of secrets hidden among the stacks, and old tomes that might still hold the keys to long-buried truths.

A sudden noise from the hallway sent us both jumping, hearts pounding. I shot a glance at the door, half-expecting another ominous delivery. Instead, it was just the neighbor's dog, a boisterous golden retriever, barking happily as its owner strolled by. I let out a breath I didn't realize I was holding, but the tension between us remained palpable.

"Let's check out the library," Nathan said, his eyes gleaming with a mix of curiosity and resolve. "We need to confront whatever secrets it's hiding. Together."

I smiled, despite the gnawing anxiety churning in my stomach. Together. It was a word that felt like a lifeline, grounding me even as the storm raged around us. As we gathered our things, the energy shifted; a palpable charge hung in the air.

"Just so you know," Nathan said, an impish grin creeping onto his face, "if we find ghosts, I'm definitely blaming you."

"Fair enough," I laughed, feeling a lightness break through the shadows. "But if you scream, I'm not coming back for you."

His laughter echoed with a richness that made the world feel just a little brighter. As we stepped out into the bustling street, the sun dipped lower, casting a warm glow over everything. Yet, the growing shadows whispered warnings I could no longer ignore. The threads of fate intertwined, binding us together as we moved toward the unknown, each step echoing the haunting words that lingered in my mind.

The library loomed ahead like a sentinel from another time, its gothic architecture casting long shadows against the rapidly fading daylight. The wooden doors creaked open with a reluctance that matched my own apprehension, revealing an interior shrouded in dust motes that danced lazily in the muted light. Old books lined the walls, their spines cracked and faded, whispering secrets of yesteryears, a fitting backdrop for our quest for the truth.

"Welcome to the lair of forgotten knowledge," Nathan quipped, nudging my shoulder as we stepped inside. His eyes sparkled with mischief, but there was a palpable tension in the air that made my heart race. "Try not to trip over any ghosts."

"Ha ha, very funny," I shot back, shaking my head at his antics. The atmosphere was thick with history, a weight I felt pressing down on my chest. This place had witnessed generations of stories, and I couldn't shake the feeling that ours was merely one of many threads woven into its fabric.

We walked deeper into the library, the silence punctuated only by the soft padding of our footsteps on the worn carpet. Rows of shelves towered over us, like ancient trees in a forest, and I found myself peering into the shadows, half-expecting a spirit to manifest and guide us to the answers we sought. Instead, we were met with the gentle hum of fluorescent lights buzzing overhead, which felt almost mocking in their brightness.

"Let's start with the local history section," Nathan suggested, motioning toward a dimly lit corner. "If the historian had something worth disappearing for, it's likely buried in the past."

"Buried is right," I muttered, glancing at the cobwebbed corners of the room. "More like a graveyard for old knowledge."

He laughed, the sound rich and warm, cutting through the chill. "At least we have each other to share the horror of it all."

As we settled into a cozy nook surrounded by towering bookshelves, I felt a flutter of anticipation. With each book we pulled from the shelves, the mystery thickened like a fog rolling in from the ocean. Dust particles swirled in the air, and the smell of aged paper enveloped us like a warm embrace.

"Look at this one," Nathan said, holding up a tattered volume titled Echoes of the Past. "It's like a treasure map of secrets."

"Or a portal to doom," I replied, rolling my eyes playfully. "But I'm game if you are."

With our investigation unfolding like the pages of an ancient tome, we scoured the library for clues. A few titles caught my eye, especially those that hinted at unsolved cases and local legends. As we flipped through pages of faded photographs and meticulous notes, the pieces began to fit together like an intricate jigsaw puzzle.

"This one mentions a series of unexplained disappearances dating back decades," I said, excitement buzzing through my veins. "It seems our historian wasn't the first to vanish without a trace."

Nathan leaned closer, scanning the text. "And there's a pattern," he murmured, his voice barely above a whisper. "Each disappearance coincided with a significant event in the town's history. It's like someone is cleaning house."

My stomach twisted at the implication. "You mean... this isn't just about the historian. Someone wants to bury something—something significant."

"Or someone," he added, and a shiver ran down my spine.

We continued our search, flipping through the pages until my fingers brushed against something unusual—a folded letter tucked between two brittle pages. "Nathan, look at this," I said, carefully extracting it as if it were a rare artifact.

He leaned in, his interest piqued. "What does it say?"

I unfolded the letter, my heart racing as I read the scrawled handwriting that mirrored the note left at my door. "You will find what you seek at the crossroads of truth and fate." I swallowed hard, the déjà vu washing over me, knotting my stomach in a vice grip.

"Crossroads... that sounds ominous," Nathan remarked, his eyes narrowing. "We need to figure out where that is. It could lead us straight to whoever is behind this."

"Let's just hope they don't have a penchant for collecting trophies," I replied, attempting to inject levity into the growing dread.

With renewed determination, we searched for any mention of a crossroads, uncovering old maps and photographs that hinted at a location near the outskirts of town—a place where several roads converged, shrouded in trees and mystery.

"Sounds like a perfect spot for a secret meeting," Nathan said, a glint of excitement lighting his features. "And just the kind of place we could use to lay a trap for our elusive friend."

As we prepared to leave, the library's atmosphere shifted, the heavy air thickening with an unnameable tension. I paused, looking back at the shelves, sensing the weight of history pressing in around me. "What if we're getting in over our heads?" I asked, my voice barely above a whisper.

Nathan turned to me, his expression serious yet somehow reassuring. "Every great story involves a leap of faith. Besides, we've already taken the plunge. Backing out now would be a waste."

The determination in his eyes sparked something within me, igniting a courage I didn't know I possessed. "Okay, let's do this," I said, swallowing my fears as we stepped back out into the evening light.

The sun was dipping below the horizon, casting an ethereal glow across the town. Shadows stretched long and deep, intertwining with the encroaching night. I glanced at Nathan, and the gravity of our journey pressed heavily upon us both, but beneath that weight was an undercurrent of something exhilarating—a connection that went beyond mere partnership.

As we navigated the winding streets toward the crossroads, I could feel the air thickening with possibilities, each moment pregnant with tension and expectation. The realization struck me: our paths were entwined, bound by fate and fraught with peril. And as we drove deeper into the unfolding night, the mysteries surrounding us promised to reveal more than we could ever anticipate, twisting our lives together in ways we had yet to comprehend.

The crossroads unfolded before us, a junction of asphalt and uncertainty, nestled within a dense thicket of trees that loomed like ancient sentinels. As Nathan parked the car, the soft rustle of leaves overhead whispered secrets, urging us to tread carefully. The fading light painted the sky in dusky shades of lavender and crimson, a vibrant farewell to the day that felt like an omen—a dramatic backdrop to the dark unraveling of our lives.

"This place has the charm of a horror movie set," I said, stepping out of the car and glancing around. A chill swept through the air, as if the trees themselves were holding their breath, anticipating what would unfold.

Nathan chuckled softly, trying to lighten the atmosphere. "Well, if we encounter a ghost, I promise to save you first."

"Such gallantry. But if it's a zombie, I'm shoving you in front of me," I shot back, a smile tugging at my lips despite the tension brewing in my chest.

We ventured onto the dirt path that forked in several directions, each way veiled in shadow and mystery. The sound of gravel crunching beneath our feet echoed like a heartbeat, a steady reminder of the danger lurking just out of sight. I could feel the adrenaline coursing through my veins, a mix of excitement and dread that sharpened my senses.

"This is where the historian's trail led," Nathan said, studying the ground as if the earth itself might yield answers. "We need to find something—anything—that connects him to this place."

"Or someone who can tell us what's hidden in the dark," I replied, scanning the surroundings. There was an unsettling beauty to the area, wildflowers peeking through the underbrush and the last rays of sunlight illuminating the leaves in a golden haze. Yet beneath that beauty lay an unease, a sense that the trees held secrets they were unwilling to share.

As we continued along the path, I caught sight of an old wooden signpost, weathered and leaning precariously. "This could be our guide," I said, brushing aside the overgrown vines to reveal the names etched on the wood. "Looks like there are a few trails we could explore."

"Great, because what we need is to get more lost," Nathan joked, but his eyes narrowed, scanning the sign for clues. "Let's head toward that one—it's the most likely to lead us to whatever's going on here."

The further we walked, the heavier the atmosphere grew, as if the very air was thick with unspoken tension. I could sense Nathan's presence beside me, steady and reassuring, a comfort in the midst of the unknown. The path began to slope downward, leading us into a small clearing encircled by towering trees.

In the center, a weather-beaten stone bench sat, its surface carved with initials and cryptic symbols that hinted at countless stories shared beneath the shade. "This feels... familiar," I murmured, my fingers tracing the rough edges of the bench.

"Familiar how?" Nathan asked, tilting his head in curiosity.

"Like I've been here before, in another life or a forgotten dream."

"Maybe it's a sign," he replied, his tone playful but his eyes serious. "Or a warning."

Before I could respond, a low rustling broke the silence, drawing our attention toward the edge of the clearing. A figure emerged from the shadows, stepping into the fading light—a woman, her clothes tattered and eyes wild, as if she had just stumbled out of a nightmare.

"Who are you?" I demanded, heart racing as I instinctively moved closer to Nathan.

"I've been waiting for you," she rasped, her voice barely more than a whisper, yet the urgency in her tone cut through the air like a blade. "You need to leave this place. It's not safe."

"What do you know?" Nathan stepped forward, protective yet intrigued. "What danger are you talking about?"

She scanned the trees, her eyes wide with fear. "They watch from the shadows. They know what you're searching for. You have to turn back before it's too late."

"Turn back?" I echoed, incredulous. "We can't just leave now. We're here for answers."

"You don't understand! The historian... he knew too much. He got too close to the truth." Her voice trembled, and I felt the gravity of her words wrap around me like a heavy cloak.

"Do you know what happened to him?" Nathan pressed, his voice steady despite the growing sense of foreboding.

She hesitated, glancing back at the trees, the wildness in her eyes flickering with uncertainty. "The last place he was seen was here... at the crossroads. You must be careful—"

A sharp crack echoed through the woods, cutting her off mid-sentence. I flinched, instinctively stepping back as the ground seemed to shake beneath us. Nathan took my arm, pulling me closer to him, his grip firm.

"What was that?" I asked, my heart pounding against my ribs.

The woman's expression shifted from fear to panic. "They're coming! You have to run!"

Before we could react, the shadows around us deepened, and figures began to emerge from the trees, their faces obscured by darkness, yet I could feel their intent—an ominous force ready to engulf us.

"Nathan!" I shouted, the urgency in my voice slicing through the chaos. "We need to go, now!"

He nodded, his eyes scanning the clearing, but the way back seemed swallowed by the growing shadows. The woman stumbled backward, her gaze locked on the approaching figures. "You don't have much time!"

With a surge of adrenaline, we turned to flee, my breath quickening as I felt the weight of unseen eyes upon us, the air crackling with an energy that promised danger. As we raced back toward the path, the sound of footsteps echoed behind us, urgent and relentless.

"Don't look back!" Nathan urged, his voice a commanding whisper that pulled me forward.

But curiosity tugged at me like a chain. I cast a glance over my shoulder, and in that split second, I caught a glimpse of their faces—masked, twisted in expressions of anger and determination. The world around me seemed to distort, shadows twisting into forms that shouldn't exist, a nightmare brought to life.

With every step, the clearing behind us grew dimmer, but the sense of dread surged like a tide, and the forest seemed to close in, trapping us within its sinister embrace. I could feel my heart racing, the fear and exhilaration intertwining as we dashed deeper into the trees, the whispers of fate guiding us toward an uncertain escape.

"Stay close!" Nathan shouted, pulling me into a narrow path flanked by thick underbrush, but the weight of the darkness behind us lingered, a chilling reminder that whatever hunted us was still in pursuit, eager to claim its prize. As the last rays of daylight vanished, the world plunged into an abyss of shadows, and I couldn't shake the feeling that we had just crossed a line from which there was no turning back.

Chapter 21: The Heart of the Labyrinth

Navigating the narrow, cobblestone streets of Charleston felt like stepping into a painting, each brushstroke vibrant with life, yet heavy with whispers of the past. The sun hung low in the sky, casting golden rays that danced across the weathered façades, highlighting the intricate wrought iron balconies that leaned over us like watchful guardians. Nathan walked beside me, his presence steadying amidst the growing tension, the weight of our investigation pressing down like the thick, sultry air around us.

"Do you think it's true?" I asked, breaking the heavy silence that had settled between us. The words lingered, thick and heavy, and I could see the muscles in his jaw tighten as he considered the question. We had spent countless hours combing through the town's archives, poring over cryptic journals and historical documents that hinted at something sinister lurking just beneath Charleston's picturesque surface.

"I don't know," he replied, his voice low, barely above a whisper, as if uttering the truth would summon the very shadows we feared. "But if the stories are correct, we're closer than ever to finding the answers." His eyes glinted with determination, yet a flicker of doubt passed through them, as if the truth could slip away at any moment, just like the fleeting light of the setting sun.

We rounded a corner, entering a narrow alley that felt almost alive, the brick walls damp and breathing. Vines snaked their way up the sides of the buildings, wrapping around wrought-iron fixtures as though trying to keep the secrets hidden within. A heavy wooden door stood ajar at the end of the alley, an invitation that sent a shiver down my spine. My instincts screamed for caution, but the thrill of discovery pushed me forward, each step echoing the pounding of my heart.

"Are you ready?" Nathan asked, a hint of mischief in his tone that pulled me out of my thoughts.

"Ready as I'll ever be," I replied, trying to sound braver than I felt. He grinned, and the corner of his mouth curled up in a way that made my stomach flip. There was something intoxicating about our shared adventure—an unspoken bond that had formed through late-night conversations and the thrill of the chase.

We pushed the door open, the creaking hinges protesting like a chorus of ghosts. Inside, the room was dimly lit, filled with an earthy aroma that felt both ancient and fresh, like a forest after rain. Shadows loomed in the corners, their shapes shifting as we stepped further inside. I reached for the flashlight in my pocket, illuminating the space before us. Dust motes danced in the beam of light, and the walls were lined with shelves crammed full of old tomes and peculiar artifacts—each one a remnant of the past, waiting to share its story.

"What do you think this place is?" I asked, my voice echoing off the walls, feeling both intimate and strange in the silence.

"Could be a secret meeting spot," Nathan mused, glancing around. "Or maybe a hideout for someone wanting to keep a low profile. Either way, we're definitely onto something."

As we scoured the room, I felt a growing sense of urgency. Each moment spent searching was a step closer to unearthing whatever hidden truth lay at the heart of our investigation. But with that urgency came an unease, a prickling at the back of my neck that warned me we weren't alone.

"Did you hear that?" I whispered, my heart racing.

Nathan paused, his brow furrowing. "What did you hear?"

"Like... a scratching sound. Over there." I pointed towards a shadowed corner where the light from my flashlight barely reached.

He nodded, moving cautiously toward the source. "Stay behind me," he instructed, his voice low and steady, though I could sense his own tension beneath the surface.

As he approached the corner, the scratching intensified, a rapid, frantic sound that seemed to pulse in time with my heartbeat. I held my breath, bracing for whatever might emerge. Then, out of the shadows, a small figure darted out—a scruffy, half-starved cat, its fur matted and its eyes wide with fear.

"Great, just a cat," Nathan sighed in relief, chuckling softly. "I was expecting something far worse."

I let out a breath I hadn't realized I was holding, laughter bubbling up at the absurdity of the moment. "Maybe it's a guardian spirit, keeping watch over the secrets of this place."

"Or just a really hungry feline," he replied with a grin, kneeling to coax the cat closer. It approached cautiously, sniffing the air before rubbing against his leg, a purr rumbling softly in the quiet. "You know, it's a good sign when animals trust you," he said, glancing up at me. "It means we're on the right track."

I couldn't help but smile at the sight—Nathan, so in tune with this stray creature, momentarily forgetting the weight of our mission. "Well, if the cat thinks we're safe, maybe we really are."

The moment was fleeting, but it brought a sense of warmth to the chilly room. Yet, as I glanced around at the dusty tomes, an inkling of doubt settled back in. We were drawing closer to the heart of the labyrinth, and with each piece we uncovered, I could feel the shadows lengthening, the air thickening with tension. The thrill of discovery was intoxicating, but I couldn't shake the feeling that something dark awaited us—a truth buried so deep, it could change everything.

"Let's see what else we can find," Nathan suggested, his voice steadying the unease swirling within me. As we delved deeper into the labyrinth, I could almost hear the echoes of the past whispering around us, secrets waiting to be unveiled.

Dust motes swirled around us like tiny dancers caught in a spotlight as Nathan and I continued our exploration. The ancient walls seemed to absorb our whispered words, holding onto the echoes of countless conversations that had taken place long before we arrived. A sense of urgency filled the air, urging us deeper into the recesses of the dimly lit room. The cat, now comfortably perched on Nathan's shoulder, blinked lazily, as if it had become the judge of our destiny.

"Alright, feline oracle," I joked, gesturing toward the stacks of books. "What should we read first? The 'How to Summon a Curse' manual or 'Secrets of the Old South'?"

Nathan chuckled, his voice a soothing balm in the charged atmosphere. "Let's skip the curse. I'm not sure I'm ready for a hex today." He reached for a tattered journal that looked older than my grandmother. Its leather cover was cracked and worn, but it still radiated an aura of importance, as if it held within its pages the answers we sought.

As he opened the journal, the scent of aged paper wafted up, mingling with the earthy aroma of the room. "This one seems promising," he said, flipping through the yellowed pages. "It's filled with notes, sketches, and..." He squinted, tracing a faded ink line with his finger. "It appears to be a map."

"Let me see." I leaned in, excitement bubbling up as he held the journal closer. The map was intricate, depicting a network of tunnels and hidden spaces beneath Charleston—an underground labyrinth that could lead us to secrets long buried. I couldn't suppress a gasp. "This is incredible! If we can follow this, we might find what we're looking for."

Nathan's eyes sparkled with a mix of determination and apprehension. "Or we might get hopelessly lost in a maze of darkness. I'm game if you are." He grinned, the tension in the air easing slightly, a shared understanding passing between us. We were partners in this strange dance, navigating not just the city's hidden past but also the unpredictable currents of our connection.

"Then let's find our way," I declared, the thrill of the chase invigorating me. I carefully tucked the journal into my bag, making a mental note to study it further once we were in a safer environment. "Lead the way, brave adventurer."

As we stepped out of the room, the sunlight hit us like a wave, revitalizing our spirits. The sudden brightness cast everything into sharp relief, but a sense of dread still lingered in the air. We paused at the alley's entrance, scanning the bustling street. Tourists meandered along, blissfully unaware of the shadows swirling just beneath the surface. The vibrant sounds of street musicians and the inviting scent of local cuisine filled the air, yet I felt an undercurrent of tension—a reminder that not everything was as it appeared.

"Where do we start?" Nathan asked, breaking the spell. "The map isn't exactly detailed in its instructions."

"Maybe we should retrace our steps to the old tavern. I recall seeing some historical plaques nearby," I suggested. The tavern had been buzzing with tales of old, stories steeped in mystery, and perhaps someone there would have knowledge about the tunnels.

"Sounds like a plan," he replied, his gaze lingering on the crowd. "Just keep your eyes peeled. If we've uncovered this much, it's possible someone else is looking for the same thing."

We made our way through the streets, the map tucked safely in my bag, our senses heightened. With every step, the weight of our mission settled more firmly on my shoulders, but Nathan's presence was a grounding force, a reminder that we were in this together.

The tavern stood before us, its exterior weathered and charming, exuding an air of history that beckoned us inside. The wooden door creaked as we entered, the warmth and noise washing over us like a comforting embrace. The bar was lined with locals, their laughter mingling with the clinking of glasses, while patrons shared tales of the city's storied past.

"Let's find a corner," Nathan suggested, his eyes scanning the room. "We can regroup and figure out our next move."

Settling into a booth, I waved at a waitress who approached, her apron dotted with flour from baking the daily special. "Can I get you two something?" she asked, a friendly smile gracing her lips.

"I'll take an iced tea," I said, my throat dry from anticipation. Nathan ordered a beer, and as the waitress walked away, I leaned closer to him, my voice low. "So, how do we find someone who knows about the tunnels without looking too suspicious?"

"Simple," he replied, a mischievous glint in his eye. "We just need to engage in some casual eavesdropping. You know, act like we belong here."

"Ah, the classic 'blend in and hope no one notices us' tactic," I laughed, shaking my head. "What if they start talking about the cursed pirate treasure, and we can't hold back our enthusiasm?"

"Then we'll just have to improvise. I mean, who doesn't love a good pirate story?" His grin was infectious, and despite the weight of our mission, I felt lighter in that moment, the tension momentarily forgotten.

The waitress returned with our drinks, setting them down with a flourish. "You two look like you're up to something exciting. What's the story?"

I exchanged a glance with Nathan, and before I could speak, he chimed in, "Just hunting for hidden gems in the city. Charleston has quite the history, doesn't it?"

"Absolutely!" She leaned in, intrigued. "You wouldn't believe the tales this place holds. Just last week, I heard a legend about some secret tunnels beneath the city, said to lead to treasures and all sorts of strange happenings."

My heart raced, and I shot Nathan a look that said, "This is our opening."

"Really? What kind of strange happenings?" I asked, leaning forward, feigning casual interest.

"Oh, you know, the usual ghostly apparitions, lost souls wandering through the streets at night, that sort of thing. But the tunnels? They're supposed to connect all the old taverns together. Rumor has it, there's even a hidden speakeasy down there," she replied, her eyes sparkling with the thrill of sharing secrets.

"Do you think anyone's ever found it?" Nathan pressed, his tone playful yet serious.

"Not that I know of," she replied, a hint of mystery in her voice. "But it's just one of those things people talk about over drinks. You'll hear a new story every night."

I exchanged another look with Nathan, our minds racing with possibilities. "Thanks for the info!" I said, hoping to keep the conversation going. "Do you think there's a way to get access to those tunnels?"

"Well, if anyone knew, it'd probably be the old bartender. He's been here longer than the building itself and has some wild stories," she said, nodding toward the bar where an elderly man was polishing glasses with an almost ritualistic precision.

"Great, we'll have to chat with him," Nathan said, his expression shifting from playful to determined.

The waitress moved on to other patrons, and I leaned in closer to Nathan. "Think we should just approach him? Or should we wait until the coast is clear?"

"Let's just go for it. What's the worst that could happen?" His eyes sparkled with mischief again, and I couldn't help but smile. The weight of our investigation felt a little lighter, the promise of adventure ahead pushing us forward into the unknown. As we made our way toward the bar, the ambient noise of the tavern faded into a distant hum, leaving only the anticipation of what lay ahead—the unraveling of secrets long hidden, waiting for someone daring enough to seek them.

The old bartender was a fixture behind the bar, his silver hair catching the soft glow of the overhead lights. His hands moved with the precision of a craftsman, each glass polished to a shine that reflected the world back at us—a world filled with laughter, stories, and perhaps the specters of long-forgotten secrets. As Nathan and I approached, I could feel the weight of history hanging in the air, thick and palpable.

"Excuse me," Nathan began, his tone casual yet firm, "we're curious about some of the local legends—specifically, the tunnels beneath the city."

The bartender paused, lifting his gaze from the glass. His eyes, a striking shade of blue, seemed to bore into us, gauging our sincerity. "Tunnels, you say? Many a fool has searched for those, drawn in by tales as old as the city itself. What's got you interested?"

"Just a bit of curiosity," I replied, adopting a casual demeanor, though inside, my heart raced. "We heard there's a hidden speakeasy down there. Thought it might be a fun adventure."

"Fun, you say? That's one way to put it." He chuckled softly, the sound both light and weighted with meaning. "But the fun runs thin once you're lost in the dark. Those tunnels are not just a tourist attraction; they hold stories you might not want to hear."

"Like ghost stories?" Nathan asked, his interest piqued.

"More like cautionary tales. There's a reason some things are kept hidden," the bartender replied, his expression shifting from amusement to something more serious. "And if you're looking to uncover them, you best be prepared for what you might find."

I exchanged a glance with Nathan, the air between us crackling with the thrill of the unknown. "We can handle it," I said, trying to inject a sense of bravado into my voice. "What do we need to know?"

He leaned forward, lowering his voice as if he were sharing state secrets. "You'll want to look for the old well just outside the tavern. It's not much to look at, but it's one of the few entrances left. Just know that whatever you find down there, it may not be welcoming."

"Thanks for the warning," Nathan said, his tone light, though I could sense the tension beneath the surface. "And the well... Is it marked? Or just hiding in plain sight?"

"Plain sight, yes. Just don't go poking around after dark unless you've got a death wish." The bartender's lips twitched into a smile, but his eyes remained serious, almost sorrowful.

"Noted," I said, my heart pounding with excitement and unease. "We appreciate the heads-up."

As we turned to leave, the bartender called out, "And remember, not all who seek treasure are worthy of finding it." His words hung in the air, a weighty echo that sent shivers down my spine.

Outside, the world felt vibrant, alive with possibility. The golden hour bathed everything in a warm glow, the sun dipping lower on the horizon, casting long shadows that danced at our feet. Nathan fell into step beside me, his presence a comforting constant. "So, a well, huh? Think it'll really lead us to those infamous tunnels?"

"Why not? We're in Charleston, the land of secrets," I replied, my mind racing with the possibilities. "Besides, what's the worst that could happen?"

"Famous last words," he teased, but his smile was genuine, a spark of excitement dancing in his eyes.

We made our way around the tavern, the air thick with anticipation. Finally, we spotted it—the old well, nestled in the overgrown foliage, vines twisting around its stone structure as if trying to reclaim it for nature. The entrance was unassuming, just a circular opening with a rusty iron grate covering the top.

"Here goes nothing," I said, peering down into the darkness. "Do you think it's deep enough to hold all the secrets of Charleston?"

"Or just a few rats," Nathan joked, but his laughter faded as we exchanged apprehensive glances. "You want me to go first?"

"Why do I feel like I'm always the one being offered as a sacrifice?" I retorted, crossing my arms.

"Because I'm a gentleman." He raised an eyebrow, the playful glint in his eyes reassuring. "Besides, I wouldn't want you to lose your sense of adventure before it even begins."

With a roll of my eyes, I nodded. "Fine. I'll follow, but only because I want to be the one to say I told you so if we end up in a dungeon."

Nathan grinned, taking off the grate with surprising ease. The moment it clanked to the ground, a chill wafted up from below, carrying with it the scent of damp earth and something more elusive—perhaps the faintest hint of decay. "Ladies first," he said, gesturing with a flourish that only made me laugh.

I hesitated for a heartbeat, glancing back at the bustling tavern. The noise seemed to fade into the background as I took a deep breath, squaring my shoulders. "Alright, wish me luck!"

As I climbed down the rough-hewn stones, the darkness enveloped me, a shroud that swallowed the world above. The air grew cooler, and the distant sound of dripping water echoed off the walls, a reminder of the labyrinth that lay ahead. Nathan followed closely, his presence a steady reassurance in the growing gloom.

Finally, my feet found purchase on solid ground, and I shone my flashlight around, illuminating a narrow passage lined with uneven stones, the walls glistening with moisture. "Wow, this is… atmospheric," I said, trying to keep the trepidation from my voice.

"Very atmospheric. Let's just hope it's not also very haunted." He chuckled softly, but the humor didn't quite mask the tension in his tone.

We moved deeper into the passage, the air thick with anticipation. The walls seemed to close in around us, but I pressed forward, drawn by an invisible thread that urged me onward. The flashlight beam danced along the walls, revealing the remnants of old graffiti, names scrawled in fading ink, echoes of lives once lived in this hidden space.

"Do you feel that?" Nathan whispered suddenly, halting in his tracks.

I frowned, straining to listen. "Feel what?"

"Like we're being watched."

A chill skittered up my spine. I glanced over my shoulder, the darkness behind us seemingly alive, pressing in with an oppressive weight. "Maybe it's just the ghosts of the past," I joked, attempting to lighten the mood. But deep down, a flicker of fear ignited.

"Very funny," he replied, his voice low and cautious. "Let's just keep moving."

We pressed on, deeper into the unknown, our footsteps echoing against the damp stone. The narrow corridor twisted and turned, and with every step, the weight of the labyrinth bore down on us, the air thickening as if we were diving into a forgotten world.

Suddenly, the passage opened up into a vast chamber, the ceiling lost in shadows, and the ground littered with remnants of what once was—a shattered lantern, rusted chains, and more scrawled names, now indecipherable. The flashlight illuminated something in the corner that made my breath hitch.

"Over there," I pointed, my heart racing as I caught sight of a dusty wooden chest, ornate and battered, sitting forlornly in the shadows. "Do you think it's really treasure?"

Nathan stepped forward, his brow furrowing. "Or it could be a trap."

"Then let's find out!" I exclaimed, moving toward it, the thrill of discovery eclipsing my caution.

As I reached for the lid, a loud crash echoed through the chamber, reverberating off the walls like a thunderclap. My heart leaped into my throat, and I turned to Nathan, wide-eyed.

"What was that?" I breathed, fear pooling in my stomach as the shadows around us seemed to thicken.

"I don't know, but we need to move. Now!" he shouted, his voice laced with urgency.

Just as we turned to flee, a figure emerged from the darkness—a silhouette cloaked in shadow, eyes glinting like daggers. My breath caught, a scream clawing at my throat, but before I could utter a sound, the figure lunged, and everything plunged into chaos.

Chapter 22: The Face of the Enemy

The air crackled with tension, thick and electric, as Nathan and I stood in the dimly lit room, shadows dancing across the walls like ghosts taunting us. A creaking floorboard betrayed our anxious movements, each sound echoing ominously in the stillness. Outside, the world moved on obliviously; leaves rustled in the autumn breeze, a distant car horn blared, but here, time seemed to hang suspended, pregnant with unspoken fears and uncertain futures. My heart thudded loudly in my chest, the rhythm a frantic drumbeat urging me to flee or fight, but fleeing was no longer an option.

"Are you ready for this?" Nathan's voice broke through the suffocating silence, low and gravelly, each word laden with the weight of what was to come. I turned to face him, our eyes locking, and in that moment, the reality of our situation crystallized. This wasn't just about the break-ins, the lurking danger that shadowed us; it was about him. About us. I felt the heat of his gaze, a warm cocoon amidst the chaos, but it wasn't enough to drown out the chill creeping along my spine.

"I don't think there's any way to be ready for what we're about to face," I replied, my voice steadier than I felt. "But we have to confront it. Together." The last word hung between us, a promise wrapped in fear and determination. He nodded, his jaw set in a way that told me he was bracing himself, preparing to shield me from whatever nightmare lay ahead.

As we edged closer to the door, the reality of our situation tightened around us, a vise that threatened to crush our resolve. Nathan's past loomed large, a specter of hurt and betrayal. The person we were about to confront wasn't just a criminal; they were a ghost from his life, someone who knew him intimately. That knowledge churned in my stomach, a mixture of dread and an unexpected surge of empathy. We all had demons, but to have one rise from the ashes of a painful past was a different kind of horror.

"Do you trust me?" Nathan asked, his voice barely above a whisper, his eyes piercing through the dim light.

"More than I trust myself," I admitted, a soft smile breaking through my nerves. It was an uncharacteristic show of vulnerability, yet the sincerity in his gaze mirrored my own.

We stepped through the threshold, the world beyond was painted in shades of gray, the atmosphere thick with the promise of confrontation. The figure was waiting for us, a silhouette against the backdrop of moonlight streaming through the window, casting an eerie glow that danced across the room. Recognition hit me like a slap; it was a face I'd seen only in Nathan's stories, one that spoke of betrayal and old wounds that had yet to heal.

"Ah, Nathan," the voice was smooth, laced with a sickly sweet sarcasm that made my skin crawl. "How quaint to see you again." The antagonist leaned against the wall, arms crossed, exuding a confidence that dripped with malice. "And you've brought a friend. How... adorable."

I felt the urge to shrink back, but I stood firm, a fortress against the rising tide of fear. Nathan stepped closer, his presence a shield that made me feel invincible, even in the face of the unexpected. "What do you want, Alex?" His voice was a low rumble, a storm gathering strength, and I could see the tension in his muscles, ready to spring into action.

"Want?" Alex scoffed, his lips curling into a mocking grin. "I want what's rightfully mine. You, Nathan. You were supposed to be part of the plan, not a rogue element." The words dripped with venom, each syllable a reminder of the betrayal that had forged their connection.

Nathan's fists clenched, and I could sense the storm brewing within him, a whirlwind of emotions teetering on the edge of control. "You lost the right to make plans the moment you decided to betray me." The steel in his voice cut through the air, palpable and fierce.

As they exchanged barbs, a realization struck me like lightning. This wasn't just about Nathan's past; it was about loyalty, choices made in moments of weakness, and the consequences that rippled through lives intertwined like vines in a darkened forest. I could feel the tension mounting, the air thickening with each word, and I knew I had to step in before Nathan lost himself to the rage simmering beneath his surface.

"Enough!" My voice echoed in the charged atmosphere, surprising both men into silence. "We can't change the past, Alex. But we can decide how this ends." I felt the weight of their gazes on me, both incredulous and intrigued. Nathan's eyes widened slightly, a flicker of appreciation mingling with disbelief.

Alex raised an eyebrow, clearly amused. "You think you can dictate how this plays out? You're just a pawn in Nathan's game."

"Maybe so," I replied, stepping forward, my heart pounding with each word. "But every pawn has the potential to become a queen. You underestimate me, and that's your mistake." The defiance in my voice caught even me off guard, but it felt liberating.

Nathan's gaze shifted to me, a mix of admiration and concern. "You don't have to—"

"I want to," I interrupted, the words spilling forth before I could second-guess myself. "This is about us. You're not alone in this fight, Nathan. I refuse to let fear dictate our actions."

Alex scoffed, but his amusement was tinged with uncertainty. "How quaint. A little romance in the face of danger."

"Romance?" I echoed, a laugh escaping me, sharp and defiant. "No, it's more than that. It's about love, loyalty, and the courage to stand up to the past, no matter how twisted it may be."

The shift in the room was palpable. Nathan stepped closer, the warmth of his presence enveloping me, grounding me amidst the chaos. I could see the conflict in his eyes, the struggle between wanting to protect me and recognizing that I was not a damsel in distress. I was a partner, ready to face the storm together.

As the tension crackled like static electricity, I realized this confrontation was only the beginning. The layers of Nathan's past were peeling away, exposing wounds that had festered for too long. But in standing together, we would confront the darkness, not just of our enemies but of ourselves. And perhaps, in the end, we would emerge stronger, forged in the fire of our trials, ready to face whatever came next.

The tension in the room thickened, palpable and electric, as Alex's laughter echoed against the walls, a sound devoid of any genuine mirth. It felt like an affront, a mocking reminder of the chaos he had wrought in Nathan's life. My heart raced, a frantic drum in my chest, matching the tempest of emotions swirling around us. The air hung heavy with unspoken threats, and I could almost taste the bitterness of betrayal lingering in the atmosphere.

"Look at you, Nathan," Alex continued, leaning casually against the wall, a predator surveying its prey. "So quick to defend your little friend. How touching." His eyes narrowed, and I felt the weight of his gaze on me, a scrutiny that made my skin crawl. "But really, darling, you should know better than to meddle in the affairs of men. It rarely ends well."

"Spare me the theatrics," I shot back, surprising even myself with the bite in my voice. "You're the one who's going to regret this." I had never been one for bravado, but the stakes had suddenly shifted. This was no longer just about Nathan's past; it was about our future, a future I was determined to defend with everything I had.

Nathan's hand brushed against mine, a fleeting touch that sent warmth radiating through me, a tether in this storm of animosity.

"You think you can intimidate us?" he asked, his voice low but steady, a steel edge beneath the surface. "We're not afraid of you."

Alex's smile widened, but it held no warmth. "Fear is a curious beast, isn't it? It can turn even the most innocent heart into a weapon. I wonder what secrets you've kept hidden, my dear." He leaned closer, the menace in his words seeping into the room, making the shadows feel alive.

"Careful," I warned, holding his gaze, refusing to back down. "You don't know what you're up against."

"Is that so?" he taunted, pushing off from the wall and stepping forward, the distance between us shrinking with each deliberate stride. "What's a little betrayal in the grand scheme of things? You see, Nathan and I share a history. One that you are unwittingly a part of now."

The chill in his voice froze my blood. I felt Nathan stiffen beside me, his muscles coiling tight as he readied himself for whatever Alex had in store. I had to act fast, to seize the moment before the tension shattered like glass. "Whatever history you two have doesn't matter anymore," I declared, my voice steady, even as adrenaline coursed through my veins. "What matters is the present. You've shown your true colors, and I doubt anyone would want to ally with you now."

Nathan glanced at me, surprise flickering in his eyes, a glimmer of pride amidst the chaos. He was used to shielding others, but I wasn't going to be a damsel waiting for rescue; I was here to fight alongside him.

Alex scoffed, the sound dripping with disdain. "A noble sentiment, but ultimately naïve. I've always admired your spirit, Nathan. It was your weakness that made you a target."

Nathan's jaw tightened, and I could see the rage simmering beneath the surface, a storm ready to break. "You think you can toy with us because of the past? You don't know how far I've come."

"Or how far I've fallen," Alex replied, a hint of something darker creeping into his tone. "What you see as strength can easily become your downfall. And this little escapade? It's only just beginning."

A shiver crept down my spine, and I felt the ground shift beneath us as the reality of his words sank in. What did he mean by that? My heart raced, fear clawing at my insides. But I steeled myself, unwilling to let doubt take root. "If you think we're scared of you, you're mistaken," I shot back, summoning every ounce of courage I could muster.

"I think you're all bravado and no substance," he sneered, the casual menace in his tone underscoring his arrogance. "But let's play your little game for now. I could use the entertainment."

"Why don't you try being less of a cliché villain?" I quipped, crossing my arms defiantly. The words spilled out before I could censor them, fueled by a mixture of adrenaline and the need to reclaim control over the situation.

Nathan's lips twitched into a reluctant smile, a flash of amusement breaking through the tension. "You do have a talent for pissing people off, don't you?"

"Only the deserving ones," I replied, the corners of my mouth lifting in a grin that felt strangely out of place amidst the chaos. But the levity vanished as quickly as it appeared when Alex stepped closer, his demeanor shifting.

"Enough with the games. Let's get down to business." His voice dropped an octave, the playful banter replaced with a chilling seriousness. "You both have something I want. And I'll stop at nothing to get it."

"What do you want?" Nathan demanded, his fists balled at his sides, the muscles in his arms tense and ready for a fight.

"The truth." Alex's gaze locked onto Nathan, a predator sizing up his prey. "You've hidden behind your façade for too long. It's time to reveal your secrets."

I felt the air grow thick as his words lingered in the space between us, the implication heavy. Secrets? Nathan had shared fragments of his past with me, pieces of a puzzle that were still missing many crucial parts. But what was Alex after? What truths did he think Nathan was hiding?

"Maybe you're looking for something that doesn't exist," I said, hoping to deflect the focus from Nathan. "You've already shown your hand, Alex. You're the one with nothing left to lose."

"Oh, but that's where you're wrong," he countered smoothly, his eyes glinting like shards of ice. "I have everything to gain. And you, sweet girl, might just be the key to unlocking it."

An uneasy silence settled in the room, the weight of his words hanging heavily in the air. I glanced at Nathan, searching for reassurance in his gaze. I saw determination flicker there, a resolve that made my heart swell with both admiration and fear. Together, we could face this.

"I won't let you threaten her," Nathan said, his voice firm. "You've already crossed a line. Don't make this worse for yourself."

Alex's laughter rang out, a chilling sound that cut through the tension. "You think you're in control, don't you? But the truth is, you're out of your depth. You're clinging to her like she's a lifeline, but trust me, you're both drowning."

"Then let's take a dive," I said, my voice sharper than I intended, defiance coursing through me. "If you want the truth, let's get it all out on the table. But remember, some truths can be dangerous."

The atmosphere shifted, the stakes rising as I caught a flicker of surprise in Alex's expression. Nathan's grip on my hand tightened, a silent reassurance that grounded me. Whatever lay ahead, we would face it together. I knew we had to stand our ground against the looming shadows of the past.

As the darkness swirled around us, I steeled myself for the truth that would come, ready to confront the monsters both outside and within. We were on the edge of a precipice, and with each heartbeat, the ground trembled beneath us. We were ready to jump, and this time, we would do it together.

The air crackled with an electric tension that seemed to shimmer in the dim light, an unspoken challenge lingering between us. Alex's smirk faded, replaced by a cold glint in his eyes that sent a chill racing down my spine. "You really think you can play the hero here?" he taunted, his voice a smooth whisper that danced through the shadows, wrapping around us like a predator closing in on its prey.

I stood my ground, heart pounding as I met his gaze. "Playing the hero is a lot better than playing the villain," I shot back, surprising myself with the confidence in my voice. "You've made your choices, and now you'll have to face the consequences."

Nathan shifted slightly beside me, the tension in his body radiating like heat from a flame, both protective and precarious. "Consequences?" he echoed, the word heavy with unspent fury. "What consequences are you prepared to face, Alex? Because I promise you, we won't back down."

Alex chuckled, a sound devoid of humor, and for a moment, I could almost see the gears turning in his mind, calculating and cold. "Ah, Nathan. Always so dramatic. It's what made you a target back then. That misplaced sense of loyalty."

"What are you talking about?" My voice slipped out, edged with confusion, but I wasn't about to let Alex see my vulnerability. "You think loyalty is a weakness? That's rich coming from you."

He stepped closer, closing the distance with a predatory grace that was both unsettling and fascinating. "Loyalty can be a double-edged sword. It cuts both ways. And I have always known how to wield it."

The air thickened with unspoken threats as I felt Nathan tense beside me, a storm brewing beneath the surface of his calm demeanor. "You're talking in riddles, Alex," he said, trying to maintain control, though the underlying current of anger pulsed through his words. "Just get to the point. What do you want?"

"Ah, straight to business then," Alex replied, amusement creeping back into his tone. "What I want is to ensure you understand just how far I'm willing to go to reclaim what's mine. You have something I need, Nathan. And I will do whatever it takes to get it."

The implication hung heavy in the air, a dark cloud threatening to burst. I glanced at Nathan, searching for answers in his eyes, but all I saw was a mix of frustration and a fierce determination that stirred something deep within me. "What could he possibly have that you need?" I pressed, wanting to break the tension like a fragile glass under pressure.

Nathan shot me a glance, the flicker of something—fear?—crossing his features before he masked it with stoicism. "This is not just about me," he said, his voice low. "This is about everything I've worked for. Everything I've built."

Alex tilted his head, the corner of his mouth twitching upward in an unsettling smile. "And yet here you are, standing next to your little friend, jeopardizing everything. Isn't it funny how quickly loyalty can turn into a liability?"

The tension in the room spiraled, coiling tighter as I felt the weight of his words sink in. I needed to distract him, to give Nathan a moment to think. "You're delusional if you think your twisted sense of loyalty will win you any friends, Alex," I said, my voice steady despite the storm of emotions raging inside. "You're alone in this, and you'll always be alone if you continue this path."

"Sweet girl, you truly don't understand the game we're playing," he sneered, an edge of menace slipping into his tone. "I'm not alone. I have my allies. And they're closer than you think."

A wave of apprehension washed over me, dread pooling in my stomach. I exchanged a quick look with Nathan, and the understanding between us deepened. Alex's allies? What did that mean for us?

Suddenly, a sound erupted from the hallway—heavy footsteps followed by a hushed murmur, an indication that we were no longer just facing Alex. A rush of adrenaline surged through me, and my instincts kicked into overdrive. "We have to move!" I urged, my voice breaking through the haze of tension that had enveloped us. "Now!"

But before we could react, the door burst open, flooding the room with light. I squinted against the brightness, heart racing as silhouettes spilled into the space. They were figures I recognized, faces I never thought I'd see here, a mix of shock and confusion written all over their expressions.

"Stop right there!" one of them shouted, and I felt the air change, thickening with fear and uncertainty. My heart plummeted as I realized who it was—old acquaintances from Nathan's past, faces I had seen in photographs but never expected to confront.

"You've brought company," Alex remarked, his voice dripping with amusement, and I could see the gleam of triumph in his eyes. "How quaint. I hope you're all ready for the real show."

"Get away from them!" one of the newcomers shouted, stepping forward, a badge gleaming on his chest.

My breath caught in my throat as I processed the chaos unfolding around us. "What do you want?" I demanded, my heart racing, half-prepared for a confrontation that felt more explosive than anything I had anticipated.

"Step away from Nathan!" the officer ordered, confusion flickering in his eyes as he assessed the situation. "We received reports of a disturbance. Are you okay?"

"I'm fine," Nathan replied, his tone low and steely, but I could see the flicker of vulnerability beneath the surface. "But we need to talk about what's happening here."

"Now's not the time for explanations," the officer said, urgency lacing his voice. "You're in danger. We need to secure the area."

The atmosphere shifted again, the stakes rising higher as Alex's laughter filled the air, a dark sound that chilled me to the bone. "You think you can protect them?" he sneered, his gaze darting between Nathan and the officers. "This is just the beginning."

And then it hit me—his allies, the threat lurking just outside our vision. I felt a cold sweat break out across my skin as the gravity of our predicament crashed over me like a tidal wave.

"We need to get out of here!" I shouted, adrenaline surging through me as I grabbed Nathan's hand, pulling him toward the exit. "Now!"

But just as we turned, the door slammed shut behind us with a resounding thud, sealing our fate. The shadows crept closer, and the room pulsed with tension, the threat of what lay beyond wrapping around us like a noose.

Nathan and I exchanged one last look, a silent promise passing between us, as Alex stepped forward, the smile on his face widening like a crack in a mirror, ready to shatter everything we held dear.

"Welcome to the game," he said, his voice dripping with malice, and in that moment, I knew we were far from safe.

Chapter 23: In the Eye of the Storm

The air was thick with the scent of rain-soaked cobblestones and the tang of salt from the nearby harbor, as though the city itself was holding its breath. I could hear the echo of our hurried footsteps blending with the distant rumble of thunder, a drumroll for the chaos unfolding around us. The vibrant colors of Charleston's historic buildings were muted under the heavy gray sky, the once cheerful pastel hues now shrouded in a cloak of impending doom. I glanced over my shoulder, half-expecting to see a ghost rising from the shadows, a remnant of the past come to haunt us.

Nathan's grip tightened around my waist, a lifeline in this tempest of fear and uncertainty. He led me through narrow alleys and under arches draped with ancient vines, each turn taken with calculated precision. There was a fierce determination etched on his face, a flicker of something deeper in his eyes that I couldn't quite place. Perhaps it was desperation or courage—maybe both. My breath hitched as I felt the warmth of his body close to mine, an intimate cocoon that made the chaos outside seem a world away, if only for a heartbeat.

As we slipped into the cool shadows of an abandoned church, the heavy wooden doors creaked shut behind us. The smell of aged wood and dampness filled the air, wrapping around us like a forgotten memory. I could see the remnants of old pews, dust motes dancing lazily in the dim light that filtered through cracked stained glass. There was something eerily beautiful about this sanctuary, a place where hope and despair coexisted in delicate balance.

"Stay close," Nathan whispered, his voice low but steady, laced with an urgency that sent shivers down my spine. I nodded, feeling a flicker of bravery igniting within me, fueled by the palpable tension between us. The storm outside was nothing compared to the tempest brewing in my heart, a mix of fear, excitement, and something I dared not name.

We moved deeper into the church, our footsteps muffled by the thick carpet of dust that had settled over the years. Every creak of the floorboards made me flinch, each sound amplified in the heavy silence. I pressed against the cool stone wall, seeking refuge in its solidity. My heart raced not just from the thrill of our escape but from the electric charge that crackled in the air between us.

"Do you think they saw us?" I asked, my voice barely above a whisper, tinged with both fear and curiosity. Nathan paused, his brow furrowed in thought, and for a moment, I could see the weight of the world on his shoulders.

"They won't stop until they find us," he replied, his jaw clenched as he surveyed our surroundings. The flickering light from a nearby candle cast flickering shadows across his face, illuminating the determination in his eyes. "But we'll find a way out. We have to."

His words were a balm, grounding me in the present moment. I could feel the heat radiating from him, an anchor in the swirling storm of uncertainty. But beneath that steadfast exterior, I sensed a vulnerability, a fleeting glimpse of the man who had once let me in, only to retreat behind walls of his own making.

"Why did you get involved in all of this?" I asked, curiosity getting the better of me. I couldn't help but wonder what had driven him into this dangerous web. "You could have walked away."

He turned to face me, his gaze piercing through the darkness. "And leave you to handle it alone?" His voice was thick with sincerity, and I felt the weight of his words settle around us like a fragile thread connecting our fates. "No. You deserve someone by your side, even if it means diving into the storm."

There was something profoundly touching about his admission, a shared vulnerability that made my heart swell. But before I could respond, the sound of footsteps echoed through the church, shattering the moment. Nathan's eyes widened, and in an instant, he pulled me deeper into the shadows.

We pressed against the wall, the cold stone biting into my back, and held our breath as the footsteps drew closer. I could hear the low murmur of voices, urgency lacing their tones. My pulse quickened, and I could almost taste the tension in the air, thick and electric.

"They're here," Nathan hissed, his voice barely audible. I could see the resolve etched on his face, a fierce determination that both frightened and thrilled me. In that moment, everything else faded away—the danger, the chaos, even the uncertainty of our relationship. It was just us, bound by something far greater than the threats that loomed outside.

The footsteps stopped just outside the door, and I could feel my heart hammering in my chest. I dared to glance at Nathan, and for the briefest moment, our eyes locked in a silent promise. We would fight together, whatever it took.

Suddenly, the door swung open, and a figure stepped inside, silhouetted against the stormy night. My breath caught in my throat, and the world narrowed to a single point of focus. This was no ordinary confrontation; it was the culmination of everything that had brought us here.

"Looking for something?" the figure asked, a wry smile playing on their lips, voice smooth like silk yet laced with a dangerous edge.

I swallowed hard, adrenaline surging through me. There was no turning back now; we were in the eye of the storm, and the winds of fate were swirling around us, fierce and unyielding.

The figure standing in the doorway was cloaked in shadow, but the smirk tugging at the corners of their lips was unmistakably cocky. "Looking for something?" they asked, their voice smooth and inviting, with just a hint of mischief. The words hung in the air like a challenge, daring us to respond.

Nathan tensed beside me, his body a taut line of energy, ready to spring into action. I felt an almost magnetic pull toward him, a connection that defied the chaos swirling around us. The stranger took a step forward, the soft creak of the floorboards echoing like a warning. I was acutely aware of every detail: the way the light glinted off their dark hair, how the fabric of their coat clung to their frame, and the dangerous glint in their eyes that hinted at knowing much more than they let on.

"Just browsing," Nathan said, his tone light, but the steel beneath it was unmistakable. He shifted slightly, placing himself between me and the intruder. I felt a surge of gratitude mixed with a pang of anxiety. Nathan was fearless, and I was grateful for it, yet I also wanted to scream at him to run, to find safety instead of facing whatever this was head-on.

"Browsing, huh?" The stranger leaned against the doorframe, arms crossed casually, as if we were merely discussing the weather instead of being ensnared in a deadly game. "You do know this isn't exactly a place for a leisurely stroll, right? Or did you just think the local ghost tour included a pit stop at an old church?"

The tension in the room thickened, and my heart raced as I searched for words. "We could ask you the same," I shot back, surprising even myself with my boldness. The stranger's eyebrows arched in amusement, and I felt Nathan's hand tighten on my arm, urging me to stay behind him.

"Well, well," the stranger said, their grin widening. "Looks like we have a feisty one here. And you—" They glanced at Nathan, their expression shifting slightly. "You really brought a knife to a gunfight, didn't you? I'm not sure if that's brave or just foolish."

"Let's call it strategic," Nathan replied, his voice smooth, though the tension in his posture betrayed him. "We're not looking for trouble, but it seems like trouble has a way of finding us."

"Trouble? Oh, darling, trouble is my middle name." The stranger stepped forward, their eyes gleaming with a playful light that belied the danger lurking just beneath the surface. "But you should be more worried about your own names. You see, I know who you are, and let's just say, your little adventure is about to get a lot more interesting."

"Interesting how?" I asked, my heart pounding not just from fear but from a reckless curiosity. The air felt electric, buzzing with the potential for something both thrilling and terrifying.

"You're standing at a crossroads, my dear," the stranger said, a hint of theatrics in their tone. "The choices you make tonight will determine not just your fate, but the fates of others, too. A delicate balance of power, don't you think?"

The cryptic warning hung between us like a tightrope, and I exchanged a glance with Nathan. His eyes were filled with a mix of determination and confusion, and I could see the wheels turning in his mind. We were treading on a precarious path, and one misstep could send us tumbling into chaos.

"What do you want from us?" Nathan demanded, his voice a low growl that echoed off the stone walls. "We're not playing your games."

"Oh, but I think you are," the stranger purred, their gaze sharp and calculating. "You already have a taste of the stakes involved. All I'm offering is a chance to level the playing field. You might be surprised at what you're capable of when the chips are down."

Before I could process their words, a loud crash reverberated from the back of the church. My heart leaped into my throat as Nathan instinctively stepped closer, putting himself between me and the sound. The stranger's amused expression flickered, replaced by a glint of interest.

"Ah, looks like your friends have arrived," they said, feigning disappointment. "I was hoping we could have a more civilized conversation, but it seems the night has other plans."

"Who's coming?" I asked, dread pooling in my stomach as the echo of footsteps grew louder, punctuated by urgent whispers.

"An old acquaintance. But don't worry, I wouldn't want you to miss the fun." With a fluid motion, the stranger slipped into the shadows, their laughter lingering in the air like a chilling breeze.

Nathan and I exchanged a frantic look, our breaths coming quick and shallow. We were running out of time. Without waiting for another second, we darted toward the back of the church, hearts racing. The flickering candlelight illuminated the path ahead, revealing a narrow corridor that led deeper into the building.

"Where do we go?" I gasped, glancing at Nathan, who was already assessing our options. His expression was a mix of determination and worry, but he didn't hesitate.

"Just keep moving. We can't let them catch us," he replied, his voice steady even as the world around us spun into chaos.

We ducked into the narrow corridor, the air thick with dust and the scent of dampness. The walls were lined with faded murals depicting scenes of hope and despair, their colors muted by time. I found myself drawn to the art, the stories woven into each brushstroke, but there was no time to linger.

The footsteps echoed louder now, a symphony of pursuit that sent adrenaline coursing through my veins. My heart raced not just from the fear of being caught but from the thrill of the chase, an intoxicating mix that kept me on edge. We rounded a corner, our footsteps muffled by the thick carpet of dust, and entered a small room filled with relics of the past.

"Is this a museum or a hideout?" I quipped, trying to lighten the mood even as my heart hammered in my chest. "I mean, I didn't expect a history lesson on our night out."

Nathan let out a short laugh, shaking his head. "Only you would find humor in this. But I appreciate it."

He stepped further into the room, his eyes scanning for an exit. The flickering light of a lantern caught my attention, casting eerie shadows on the walls. It illuminated a faded tapestry hanging against one wall, depicting a ship battling stormy seas—a fitting metaphor for our current predicament.

"We need to find a way out of here," he said, his voice laced with urgency. "If we can reach the back exit, we might stand a chance."

"Lead the way, Captain," I replied, a teasing lilt in my tone, even as my heart raced at the thought of the unknown dangers lurking just outside. Together, we navigated through the dim light, adrenaline coursing through our veins, ready to face whatever lay ahead.

The dusty room pulsed with a tense energy, the dim light from the lantern casting flickering shadows that danced along the walls. My heart raced as I followed Nathan's lead, my breath shallow and quick. The scent of aged wood and the faint aroma of something floral lingered in the air, remnants of a forgotten time. The tapestry before us, with its depiction of ships braving a stormy sea, felt eerily prophetic, and I couldn't shake the sense that we were caught in a tempest of our own making.

"Let's check over there," Nathan said, motioning toward a door at the far end of the room. My instincts screamed at me to remain vigilant, but the spark in his eyes was enough to keep me moving. Each step felt weighted, as though the floorboards were holding their breath alongside us.

As we approached the door, a heavy silence enveloped us, punctuated only by the distant echo of our footsteps. "Do you ever wonder if we should have just stayed home?" I joked, attempting to mask my nerves. "I mean, pizza and a movie sound a lot safer than whatever this is."

Nathan chuckled, but there was an edge to his laughter, a reminder of the danger lurking just outside. "Yeah, but where's the fun in that?" He paused, placing his hand on the doorknob, tension rippling through his body. "You ready?"

"Ready as I'll ever be," I replied, forcing a brave smile that did little to calm the storm within. With a swift turn, he pushed the door open, revealing a narrow staircase leading down into darkness. The air grew colder as we descended, each step creaking ominously beneath our weight. The flickering lantern light barely penetrated the void, and I felt a shiver race down my spine.

"This place gives me the creeps," I admitted, glancing over my shoulder. The shadows seemed to close in behind us, hungry and watchful. "Do you think we'll find an escape route down here, or just more creepy relics?"

"Only one way to find out," Nathan replied, his voice steady despite the palpable tension. I admired his resolve, even as the uncertainty of our situation gnawed at my insides.

At the bottom of the stairs, we emerged into a small, dimly lit chamber. The air was thick and musty, filled with the scent of mildew. The walls were lined with shelves filled with dusty books and ancient artifacts, a veritable museum of forgotten memories. But it was the large wooden trunk in the center of the room that caught my eye, its surface scarred and weathered, as if it had endured countless storms of its own.

"What do you think is in there?" I asked, nodding toward the trunk. "Treasure? Secrets? An angry ghost?"

"Only one way to find out," he repeated, a mischievous grin tugging at his lips. There was something about the way he said it that made me want to believe we could conquer whatever lay ahead together. He stepped toward the trunk, carefully lifting the lid. It creaked ominously, and I half-expected a puff of smoke to billow forth, revealing an ancient curse.

Inside, the trunk was filled with an assortment of papers, maps, and what appeared to be old photographs. Nathan began rifling through them, his expression shifting from curiosity to intrigue. "These look like they could be significant," he murmured, pulling out a faded map.

"Significant as in 'treasure map' or 'we're walking into a trap'?" I asked, arching an eyebrow. "Because I'm really hoping for the former."

"Let's go with treasure map," he said with a wink, but the underlying tension in his voice betrayed his uncertainty. "It looks like it leads to the old docks. We might find something that can help us."

"Or we might just lead our pursuers right to it," I countered, my heart racing at the thought.

"True," he conceded, looking thoughtful. "But it's a risk we have to take. If we don't figure out what's going on, we're never going to get out of this mess."

As he folded the map and tucked it into his pocket, the atmosphere shifted suddenly. A loud crash reverberated through the chamber, the sound slicing through the tension like a knife. My heart dropped as I spun toward the sound, adrenaline surging through my veins.

"They're getting closer," I whispered, fear creeping into my voice.

"Then we need to move. Now," Nathan said, urgency coloring his tone.

We dashed toward the staircase, the adrenaline propelling us forward. I could hear footsteps thundering above us, accompanied by voices, and I felt the weight of the world pressing down as we climbed. Just as we reached the top, the door swung open, revealing a figure silhouetted against the flickering light—a shadow from our nightmares made flesh.

"Going somewhere?" the stranger from earlier stood there, arms crossed and a smirk on their face, as if they had orchestrated this entire encounter. Behind them, the doorframe filled with more figures, their intentions hidden but their presence ominous.

I exchanged a frantic glance with Nathan, my pulse racing. "What now?" I whispered, panic creeping into my voice.

"Back down!" he urged, but before we could react, the stranger stepped forward, their smile widening into something dangerously charming.

"Why run when you can stay and play?" they taunted, and I could hear the satisfaction in their voice. "This little game of ours is just beginning, and trust me, it's going to be a spectacle you won't want to miss."

"Let us go!" Nathan shouted, the protective instinct in him flaring as he stepped between me and the strangers, his posture fierce.

"Oh, but you're the stars of the show!" the stranger laughed, a sound that sent a chill down my spine. "And I can't have my stars leaving before the grand finale."

Suddenly, the lights flickered violently, plunging us into darkness. Panic surged within me, the absence of light amplifying the dread gnawing at my gut. I reached for Nathan's hand, my fingers trembling as we stood together in the pitch-black void.

"Stick close," he murmured, and I felt the reassuring warmth of his presence beside me.

Then, as if the universe itself had decided to unleash chaos, a loud bang echoed through the darkness, followed by the sound of splintering wood. The door was thrown open, light spilling into the room and revealing a chaotic scene.

I blinked against the sudden brightness, but the sight that met my eyes was far more terrifying than I had imagined. The figures that had been closing in were now engaged in a frantic struggle, chaos erupting as they fought for control. My heart raced as I realized this was our moment.

"Now!" Nathan shouted, grabbing my hand and yanking me forward just as the commotion erupted into a frenzy of shouting and shoving.

But before we could escape, a hand shot out from the chaos, grabbing my arm with a vise-like grip. I gasped as I was yanked back, the world tilting as Nathan turned to face me, panic flashing in his eyes.

"Don't let go!" he shouted, but the grip on my arm tightened, pulling me away from him.

In that instant, time slowed as I struggled against the hold, the chaos of the room swirling around us like a storm. I could feel Nathan's desperation, a tether stretching thinner with each passing second. I caught a glimpse of the smirking stranger as they leaned into the chaos, a satisfied glint in their eyes.

"Didn't you hear?" they purred, their voice cutting through the noise like glass. "This is just the beginning."

With a final, forceful tug, I felt the world slipping away, and as I was pulled into the tumult, the last thing I saw was Nathan's determined expression, a fierce promise in his eyes.

Then everything went dark, and I knew the storm was far from over.

Chapter 24: Love in the Ashes

The morning light spilled through the remnants of the storm, draping the world in a soft golden hue that felt almost ethereal against the darkened backdrop of the city. I leaned against the balcony railing, the cool metal biting slightly into my skin, yet I welcomed the sensation as a reminder that I was alive, that I had weathered the tempest alongside Nathan. The air was heavy with the scent of rain-soaked earth, mingling with the faint traces of salt from the nearby sea. It was a fresh beginning, yet the echoes of our shared trials still lingered, shaping the contours of this moment.

Nathan stood beside me, his silhouette carved against the rising sun. His usual confidence seemed muted, shadows dancing across his face as he turned to look at me. "I never thought I'd see the day when I'd be grateful for a storm," he remarked, his voice a low rumble that sent a thrill through me. "Guess it took some thunder to wake us up."

I smiled, a soft laugh escaping my lips. "Or to remind us that there are worse things than being stuck in a room with someone you can't stand." Our eyes locked, and I felt an undeniable spark, a shift in the air around us, as if the very universe was holding its breath.

The wind whipped gently around us, a playful tug that ruffled his dark hair. I found myself wishing I could reach out and trace my fingers through it, to anchor myself to this moment and to him. There was a vulnerability in Nathan that day, an openness that revealed the depth of his heart, now laid bare after all we had faced together. His past was a labyrinth of shadows, but in those moments of silence, I sensed the light we had both fought to find.

"What do we do now?" he asked, his brow furrowed as he gazed out over the horizon. I could see the thoughts racing through his mind, the remnants of fear and uncertainty battling against the burgeoning hope that flickered like a candle flame between us.

The question hung heavy in the air. I had imagined so many scenarios for how this moment would unfold—resolving our differences, finding closure, or perhaps rekindling the embers of a once-bitter rivalry. Yet standing there, with the sun spilling warmth over the world, I realized that what we truly needed was not just a plan but a shared vision of what lay ahead.

I took a deep breath, inhaling the scents of rain and possibility. "We rebuild," I said finally, my voice steadier than I felt. "Not just our lives, but everything—our trust, our understanding. We can't ignore what's happened, but we can choose to let it guide us."

His gaze shifted from the horizon to my eyes, and for a moment, the noise of the city faded into silence. "You make it sound so simple," he replied, a wry smile tugging at the corners of his mouth. "Like we can just pick up the pieces and start fresh."

"Why not?" I shot back, my heart racing with a mix of defiance and excitement. "Life is messy, Nathan. It always will be. But that doesn't mean we can't make something beautiful from the chaos. Think of all we've survived together. We owe it to ourselves to try."

He stepped closer, the distance between us shrinking until I could feel the warmth radiating from his body. "You're right," he said softly, his voice barely above a whisper. "We've survived a lot. I just... I don't want to lose you again."

The weight of his words settled over me like a heavy blanket, grounding me in reality. It was a risk to open my heart fully, but I couldn't shake the feeling that we were at a precipice, on the edge of something extraordinary.

With a sudden surge of courage, I reached for his hand, intertwining my fingers with his. "Then let's face whatever comes next together," I said, feeling the strength of his grip respond to mine. "We'll learn from our mistakes, and maybe—just maybe—we can find our way through this."

He looked down at our hands, a hint of surprise flickering in his eyes, and then back up at me. "Together," he echoed, as if testing the word on his tongue. "I can work with that."

In that moment, the world around us began to shift. The sounds of Charleston came alive—the distant chatter of people starting their day, the clinking of dishes from the cafés below, the laughter of children chasing each other down the street. It felt like a symphony of new beginnings, each note resonating with the promise of a fresh start.

As we stood there, hand in hand, I couldn't help but imagine what lay ahead. I saw flashes of laughter over cups of coffee, lazy Sunday mornings spent in each other's arms, and quiet evenings filled with whispered secrets. But I also knew there would be challenges—doubts creeping in, the ghosts of our pasts haunting us like shadows, demanding to be acknowledged.

"Let's not pretend it will be easy," I said, breaking the silence. "There will be days when the darkness tries to creep back in, and we might stumble. But I want to be there for you, just as you've been there for me."

He nodded slowly, his expression thoughtful. "I'm not the easiest person to love, you know."

I chuckled, my heart lightening. "Oh, trust me, I've noticed. But I'm stubborn, and I'm not giving up without a fight."

As the sun broke free from the last remnants of cloud cover, its rays illuminated the promise of a new day, I felt a swell of hope rising within me. We were two imperfect souls, scarred yet resilient, daring to forge a future amid the ashes of our past. And as I gazed into Nathan's eyes, I knew I would fight for him—for us—no matter what storms lay ahead.

The day unfolded like a well-loved book, the pages warm and inviting, yet rich with the weight of our shared history. I relished the sunlight flooding into my apartment, painting everything in hues of gold and soft cream. It felt like an embrace, a promise that the storm had not only cleared the air but also birthed a chance for something new and beautiful.

Nathan leaned against the balcony railing, his stance relaxed yet somehow commanding. The muscles in his arms tensed as he shifted slightly, and I couldn't help but admire how the morning light highlighted the contours of his face. There was something in the way he stood, half-turned towards me, that made my heart skip.

"What's the plan for today?" he asked, an amused glint in his eyes that made my stomach flutter.

"Plan? We just survived a storm and a rather dramatic confrontation. I think we've earned a day of rest," I replied, raising an eyebrow. "But knowing you, that means trouble."

"Trouble? Me?" He feigned shock, pressing a hand dramatically to his chest. "I'm merely suggesting we celebrate our new beginning. You know, maybe go for brunch, enjoy some mimosas. Get the city to forget what a hot mess we were just a few days ago."

"Hot mess? You mean, the kind of mess that involved a terrifying confrontation, followed by me almost getting kidnapped?" I quipped, folding my arms playfully.

Nathan laughed, the sound rich and warm, echoing like music through the open air. "Exactly! That's what I'm saying! We deserve some bubbly for our survival skills, don't you think?"

I pretended to ponder his proposal. "As much as I'd love to lounge around in a sun-soaked café, indulging in all things breakfast and sparkling, there's still the matter of the mess we left behind. What if they try to drag us back into the chaos? The world has a funny way of reminding us of our pasts."

He stepped closer, the distance between us vanishing like fog under the sun's relentless rays. "Let them try. We can handle anything together. You've got my back, and I've got yours. Besides, brunch is about enjoying life and forgetting the chaos for a little while. Let's make some memories that don't involve storm clouds or threats."

I felt the weight of his words settle comfortably over me, a warm blanket that pushed away the lingering worries. "Fine, you win. But only if we stop for coffee first. You know I need my caffeine fix to face the world."

"Deal," he said, grinning. "I'll even let you pick the place."

As we made our way downstairs, the air around us felt charged with possibilities. I could hear the distant sounds of Charleston waking up—vendors setting up their carts, the laughter of children as they chased each other down the streets, and the sweet, salty breeze coming off the harbor. It was a city alive with energy, a stark contrast to the quiet chaos we had just navigated.

Nathan walked with a casual confidence, his strides long and purposeful, while I kept pace beside him, my heart racing for reasons I was still trying to understand. "You know," I started, "for a guy who just went through hell, you seem remarkably cheerful."

He glanced sideways, a smirk dancing on his lips. "Why not? Life is too short to dwell in the shadows. I'd rather celebrate the victories, no matter how small."

"True, but let's not forget that sometimes those victories come with a hefty price," I pointed out, feeling a momentary twinge of doubt. "What if our 'celebration' draws unwanted attention?"

"Then we'll give them something to talk about. We'll strut through this city like we own it," he said with a wink, and I couldn't help but laugh at his audacity.

The coffee shop we arrived at was a charming little spot tucked away in a narrow alley, adorned with twinkling fairy lights and potted plants that cascaded down from the windowsills. The scent of freshly brewed coffee mingled with the sweetness of pastries, enveloping us like a warm hug.

"Your place is kind of quaint," Nathan remarked, glancing around as we stepped inside.

I smiled, feeling a surge of pride. "I come here often. The owner is an artist, and every piece of decor has a story behind it."

As we waited in line, a comfortable silence settled between us, punctuated only by the occasional clink of cups and the soft murmur of conversations around us. I felt the warmth of Nathan's presence beside me, a magnetic pull that anchored me in the moment.

"Two coffees, please," I said to the barista, smiling at the young woman with bright blue hair who returned my grin with a knowing look.

"Are you two celebrating something?" she asked, her eyes darting between us, sparkling with curiosity.

"Just surviving," Nathan replied, his tone light and teasing.

"Surviving, huh?" She raised an eyebrow, intrigued. "I'll make sure to make these extra special then."

As she busied herself with our drinks, Nathan leaned closer, his breath warm against my ear. "What do you think? Are we really surviving, or are we just pretending?"

I turned to face him, our noses almost touching. "Maybe a little bit of both. But isn't that what makes life interesting? The act of pretending until we find out what's real?"

"Wise words for someone who claims to need caffeine to function," he shot back, amusement lacing his voice.

"Hey, I'm just trying to navigate this chaotic world with some semblance of sanity," I quipped, enjoying the banter. "Caffeine helps."

The barista returned, setting our coffees on the counter. "Here you go! One espresso and one cappuccino, each with a sprinkle of fairy dust," she joked, winking at us before moving on to the next customer.

Nathan chuckled as he picked up his espresso. "Fairy dust, huh? I like this place. Maybe they're onto something."

We found a cozy table by the window, sunlight spilling over us like a warm embrace. I took a sip of my cappuccino, savoring the velvety texture and rich flavor. "Delicious," I murmured, looking up at him with a smile. "Just what I needed."

He watched me, his gaze intense and thoughtful, as if he were deciphering a complex puzzle. "You really are something special, you know that?"

My heart did a little flip, caught off guard by the sincerity in his words. "I think you're seeing the remnants of chaos and calling it special."

"Chaos can be beautiful, especially when it's part of someone's journey," he replied, his tone earnest. "And you, my friend, have an incredible journey ahead of you."

The conversation flowed easily between us, our laughter mingling with the background hum of the café. With every shared story and playful exchange, the shadows of our past began to fade, replaced by a shimmering light of new possibilities.

And as I sat across from Nathan, a sense of exhilaration washed over me. In that moment, I realized we weren't merely two souls caught in the wreckage of our lives; we were embarking on an adventure, and the open road ahead was filled with countless opportunities to shape our future together.

The café buzzed with the rhythm of morning life, the clattering of cups mingling with the soft chatter of patrons, all blissfully unaware of the tumult that had just settled in my heart. I took another sip of my cappuccino, the frothy foam leaving a delicate mustache on my upper lip. Nathan leaned back in his chair, a lazy smile creeping across his face as he watched me wipe it away with the back of my hand.

"Charming," he teased, his eyes glinting with mischief. "That's one way to start a morning—beauty and grace wrapped up in a coffee cup."

I laughed, shaking my head. "You know, Nathan, for someone who prides himself on being suave, you sure enjoy taking shots at my coffee habits."

"Hey, someone has to keep you humble," he shot back, his grin widening. "But seriously, you're too good at this whole 'waking up to chaos' thing."

With our playful banter, the world around us seemed to blur. We talked about everything and nothing—our favorite childhood memories, the absurdities of modern dating, and our shared love for adventure. I couldn't remember feeling so at ease with anyone before. It was a strange dichotomy; while I felt lighthearted, I could still sense the weight of the past lurking just beneath the surface, like a shadow that refused to fully disappear.

As the conversation flowed, the café door swung open, and a gust of wind swept in, bringing with it a familiar scent of saltwater mixed with the promise of rain. A figure stood at the entrance, a silhouette against the bright backdrop of the city. It was Sophia, my old friend who had vanished from my life after her own chaotic entanglements. The last time I saw her, she had been tangled in her own web of troubles, a reflection of my own past. Her wide eyes locked onto mine, and for a moment, the air thickened with unspoken tension.

"Nathan!" I whispered, my heart racing as I watched her hesitate, glancing around as if unsure of her next move.

"What?" he replied, turning to follow my gaze. His expression shifted instantly, concern knitting his brows together. "Is everything okay?"

"Not sure yet," I said, my voice low. "It's Sophia. I haven't seen her in ages."

Before I could process what was happening, she moved through the café, weaving between tables, her face a mask of urgency. I stood, instinctively drawn toward her, and when our eyes met, a wave of emotions surged between us—relief, apprehension, and a hint of something darker.

"Can we talk?" she asked, her voice barely above a whisper, the weight of her request palpable.

"Of course," I replied, glancing back at Nathan. His eyes were sharp, the protector emerging from the depths of his being, ready to spring into action if needed. I motioned for him to stay put, needing a moment to understand what was happening.

As we stepped outside into the crisp air, the cool breeze felt electric against my skin. I glanced around to make sure we were out of earshot, the chatter of the café fading into the background. "What's going on? You look like you've seen a ghost."

Sophia ran a hand through her hair, her once vibrant curls now muted and frayed. "It's... it's complicated. I didn't think I'd find you here."

"Clearly. You look like you've been running," I noted, worry prickling at my skin. "What's happened?"

She hesitated, biting her lip as if searching for the right words. "I got caught up with some people—bad people. And now they're looking for me."

"Looking for you?" My pulse quickened. "What did you do, Sophia?"

"Nothing I wanted to," she said, her voice thick with regret. "But they don't care about that. I thought I could handle it, but I'm in way over my head."

Just then, Nathan stepped out, concern etched across his face. "You alright?"

I nodded, though my heart was racing. "Sophia's in some trouble. She's being hunted."

"Being hunted?" he echoed, his expression shifting from concern to something more serious. "What kind of trouble are we talking about?"

Sophia shot him a wary glance. "I'm not sure if you should be involved, Nathan. This isn't just some petty crime ring. It's bigger than that."

"Look, I appreciate the concern," he replied, his voice steady. "But if she's in danger, I'm in. Whatever it is, we'll figure it out together."

Sophia's eyes widened, disbelief mingling with fear. "You don't understand! These people... they don't play by the rules. They'll stop at nothing."

"Neither do we," I insisted, my resolve hardening. "If you're in danger, we need to know everything. We can't fight this blind."

She took a deep breath, the fight draining from her shoulders. "Okay. I'll tell you, but you have to promise me you'll stay safe. Promise me you won't get involved more than you have to."

"I can't promise that," Nathan interjected, his gaze unwavering. "If you're in this deep, we have to find a way to get you out."

Sophia stared at him, weighing her options, and then finally nodded. "Fine. But it won't be easy."

The tension hung in the air as she began to explain—details of her association with a group that had promised her the world but had instead plunged her into a nightmarish reality. Their insidious grasp had pulled her back into a world she had fought so hard to escape, filled with shadows and threats that loomed larger than life itself.

"And now they want something from me," she confessed, her voice trembling. "Something that puts you both in danger."

The realization settled over me like ice. "What do they want?"

"They want a list of names," she whispered, her gaze darting around as if she expected someone to jump out from the shadows.

"People who were involved in a deal gone wrong. I didn't think it would come to this."

Before I could respond, a black SUV rolled up to the curb, the engine purring like a predator stalking its prey. The driver's window slid down, revealing a familiar face, someone I had hoped to never see again. My heart sank as the weight of dread enveloped me. "Sophia, we need to go. Now."

The urgency in my voice was clear, but the moment hung suspended as the figure inside the vehicle grinned, an expression that sent chills down my spine. They beckoned, a gesture laden with menace, and I knew, deep down, that the storm wasn't over yet. As we turned to run, the world around us exploded into chaos, and I realized that the ashes we thought we had risen from were only the beginning.

Milton Keynes UK
Ingram Content Group UK Ltd.
UKHW041826131124
451149UK00001B/127